The Lords

of

Haff

Keith Gardner

Keith Gardner

Copyright

The Lords of Haff is a Science-Fiction novel.

And the first in what could be a series.

ISBN -13: 978-0-9575110-8-8

ISBN -10:0957511086

Contents:

Title Page:
Copyright:
Contents:
Acknowledgements/Dedications:

Chapter 1
Chapter 2
Chapter 3
Chapter 4
Chapter 5
Chapter 6
Chapter 7
Chapter 8
Chapter 9
Chapter 10
Chapter 11
Chapter 12
Chapter 13
Chapter 14
Chapter 15
Chapter 16
Chapter 17
Chapter 18
Chapter 19
Chapter 20

A Note From The Author
Other Books by the Author

Dedication:

To Sue L
Thanks for your support

Acknowledgements

To all my readers and fans for their offered feedback and reviews/comments on whatever retail site that any of my books have been bought by them

Thank You

And to those of you who are on my Twitter, Goodreads, and Facebook pages. For each book which has been written so far - and for any tweets and chats with me in those same places on how any of you view my different novels.

You can also look out for regular News or Book updates, and other new information on any of these pages too.

1

This letter is from some of the memoirs made by the former tyrant ruler of the Gelten System. Namely one Bork Gremplar of Briath; who is still currently under planetary arrest on Haff. This following work has been translated by Junus Silem Krot. Archivist Level 1 of the Haff Central Great Library. Translated from the Gelten language at the request of our own Prime Commander Raxx. Dated month six, day nine, of the year 3986 at the time of Luminescence.

There is *nothing* as terrifying as coming to a far too late understanding. Discovering that actually you yourself have made a complete error of personal judgement. I myself, Bork Gremplar, the former ruler and exalted familial leader of the planet Briath, and its four satellite worlds in the Gelten System. Have sadly now learned this very important fact to my own folly, and to the cost of my rule over them.

Plain and simple greed . . . *That* was my downfall!

Like most rulers in history - I who followed in my own fathers footsteps, just as he had followed in his. Like them, I thought that everything was there to be had. Waiting and ripe just for the taking of it like always. Oh, how wrong can you be . . .

Having somewhat unexpectedly found an unknown system, encompassing three suns with fifteen new found planets. It appeared as if they were just sitting there all ready for me to pluck. An error made by me here was one of these now far too late reminders to me. I should have known when my scout ship sent to check out one planet in particular failed to return. Then again from my fleet of heavily armed *Stell* class of Battle Cruiser, the one which I dispatched to its largest planet later. With its heavy weaponry and armour. Even this failed to test its defences or to land, or to conquer as had the others, and to then report their success and findings as the rest had . . .

Yet did I once even pause to reconsider my ideal? Even to think of what their disappearance might mean? Of course not! I was the enlightened imperial ruler of five entire planets. To me, I thought that some simple accident must have befallen each of them. That perhaps my spies had been caught at their initial task; even to thinking that the battle cruiser itself may simply have been outnumbered and destroyed, or met with an asteroid. As was I not the all mighty and powerful ruler who had entire worlds and civilizations at his command? So what did *I* have to fear from *anyone* with all of the ships and armies which I had at my command and disposal?

The reports received from the ships which I *had* sent out, and which *had* returned with my spies from fourteen of the planets in question in that far off system. One which I now knew was called the Barathon system. Filled me with hope of easy conquests. Their civilizations seemed as advanced as our own. If not more so in what they had to offer towards my own power, and also to what I could then do with them. But, as had been reported to me, there were no actual military structures or personnel to be seen anywhere upon any of them. And so, I wanted them all under my own rule and quickly now.

By the time my grandfather died, our family then had Briath and two planets, Goll and Chell who bowed to us. At the time when my own father passed we then had Nee, which made three. I myself then conquered the fourth and final free planet within our own system, Pelus.

The new ones I heard about at Barathon were certainly worlds of wild extremes, be they agriculture and horticulture. Mining of various precious metals - including some which in even miniscule amounts I knew were worth small or vast fortunes on their own. Vast bases of production in robotics and ship building. A strange animal planet of some kind. And there was also one which was a main producer of food from their waters.

Stories of their music and dance on one in particular were even offered to me. Although these latter items made no actual difference to my thoughts of taking them. As it was only a new dream for me to be able to add them *all* within my own growing collective power base.

And then, of course, there was *Haff* . . . that one single damnable planet. The largest of them all. The one which had *not* been able to be scouted by my spies. Or to know if any possible defences they may have had when attacked by my battle cruiser. All in readiness for my armies from the other fourteen planets to finally land there. *That* was the very beginning of my downfall. If only I had known about any of this in advance I may well have chosen what I did do very differently. More than likely I would have kept well clear of this system altogether! But now, in hindsight, without any spy reports returned to me from it. How was I to know what I had let myself in for in the coming days and weeks ahead.

Haff, as I now know it was called, and later found out all about it. Was also a planet which was at least five or more times the size of my own majestic Briath. And there within it, what unknown factors did it contain? How could I have possibly known in advance that it was a planet of at least eight billion humans. And that was not even counting all of those life-like androids they also had.

But far more importantly, and what I did not know. Was that it was a strictly regimented society. One that was completely based upon military ways. Their army, from those only in training, to those who were already fully trained and were as such highly skilled, was actually six billion strong.

That was my own Empires demise right there and then without my even knowing it. As how could my own, of what I had thought to be an unbeatable four million strong army. Perhaps even ten, if I called in another six million untrained workers from my domains as conscripts to join my army. It would never have mattered anyway, as how could I ever have hoped to compare with anything as immense as that!

Haff I then also later found out was also the protectorate *of* those same fourteen other planets within that same system of Barathon. We certainly did not know this at the time however. Nor did any of our scouts who landed to reconnoitre these various planets, ever once hear of this unexpected fact either. This was the sole reason why I took the conquest and subjugation of all of them as an easy accomplishment. To which I then gave my command to my generals with a limited number of my trained army to go out and take them for me.

Upon each of these planets wherever my ships landed, a forty thousand strong army was disgorged from them under the command of well experienced leaders. The rest of my troops I held here on Briath in reserve, and would only send them if General Shrum told me he needed more. Although the delay in these reaching him would be long.

Apparently they were not even required. As I was told by messages that there had been no defensive fighting or resistance on any of these planets after they had landed, at all . . . So not a single weapon of ours needed to be fired. Simply because no one on these planets actually had any weapons with which to shoot back at my troops. And *that* to me was the most strange and surprising fact of all.

The populace of each and every one of them had just watched and smiled, almost benignly at the leaders and men of my shock troops. As they freely began to march into each of their capital cities with their weapons ready to be used. My own imperial banners flying high. They easily took them over, with hardly a word being spoken much less a shot. And then the far too easy questioning of their own leaders was initiated by each of my generals. As to *why* they had not put up any resistance at all against us. Even if only so as to save their own planets from conquest.

Steadily enough, their responses to any questions being asked were completely honest. Even our truth detecting machines told my interrogators this. All information was openly forthcoming and being offered to them. After that, a constant stream of messages were being relayed and fed to me back on Briath. The only problem being the lengthy delay before any of their messages finally reached me.

To me personally, I had just undertaken a massive system conquest. At which I rubbed my hands together rather gleefully. As now almost an entire new planetary system was under my own personal control. So all of their wealth, products, technical skills and produce, lands. As well as their newly overpowered populations, were all mine to do with as I pleased towards ever furthering my greatness. I had not only achieved more, but also outdone any of my own descendants in that one quick surprise raid.

On one of their larger agricultural planets named Jitrus. Where they got their planet names from I have no idea, but they all sounded very odd to us!

An elderly man in appearance, dressed very neatly but with small tufts of greying hair and a slightly reddened face. A man who was called by the very unfamiliar name or title of *Mayor* Inas Rouf then approached my general. To us such a title was also very strange thing anyway. Yet he was found to be quite happy to answer everything that was asked of him by my highest ranking general, Akras Shrum.

Answers which as they were given so freely, sent a feeling of foreboding through my general. Just as the exact same thing was being replicated upon each of the other worlds. With their same kinds of named leaders, which we had also just taken over.

'My name is General Akras Shrum. Can you speak our language?' Shrum had asked of him.

'Yes . . . a variety of Gelten is it not?'

'It is - but how could *you* possibly even know this when none of us have never even been to your system before?'

'The scouts from Haff have been almost everywhere in many systems, General. And wherever they find an inhabited planet, they stay for a while so as to get to know that language well. After that they continue on their journey or return home again so as to pass this knowledge on.'

'That may be so. But surely you should be taught a language before you can understand it fully?'

'The androids who do all these searches for us can already speak many languages, General. If when they land they find it similar to one already known, then they will leave. Whereas if it is a completely new language, perhaps with even one or more dialects to it. Then the android will stay on that planet until it can learn as much as possible.

'Only when satisfied that it can learn no more will it then move on. As to how we can learn it . . . it is simply a means of using memory implants from them. In other words, those of us who may end up trading, making deals, or just talking to other races accept having these same implants so as to make communication easier.

'At this time, I know twelve languages. Which is good enough for me, although not as good as others who know a lot more. Some who trade much more than we do know up to fifty. Whereas the Prime Commander, last I heard, knows over two hundred!'

Not actually knowing what the old man was talking about in all reality. Shrum just nodded to him, happy that he could speak to someone on this planet.

'Why did you not even try to defend your planet against us, Inas Rouf?' asked my own battle hardened General Shrum of him.

'Because *we* simply have no need to do so,' the old so-called Mayor had replied to him. The general was confused by his outward calmness, and so had to ask him why.

'Our only defensive systems in place here, and on the other planets that you say you have now taken over are what are called listening posts; these were built by those from Haff. When we saw you landing, and then your many troops emerging from your ships. We only needed to have one of us press one of the buttons within that post.'

'Which does what?' asked my general.

'It sends a single high frequency boosted signal from our planet of Jitrus straight to Haff. Which advises them that we have either been invaded or that we are under attack. Each planet you have now invaded will have done the exact same thing as we have done, General.'

And then the old man had smiled what appeared to be a sad smile at him; and so my general then had to ask him why he had done such a strange thing.

'Because . . . by doing this, you really have no idea of what you have just brought upon yourselves from invading us. Haff does *not* rule any of us, it *protects* us from any such possibilities as this - and we in turn supply them with some of the things which we grow and produce here in return for this protection. As do all the planets in the Barathon system and elsewhere who live under their aid.'

'Our own leader, Bork Gremplar, can offer you the same aid and protection,' Shrum had stated.

'Would he also wish to rule us under *his* laws though?'

'Of course . . . that is what rulers do!'

'Well, Haff does not do it like that in a way that subjugates us. So we are free to do whatever it is we wish to do for our own planets freedom. While also still living under their protection. Which even means we have our own laws and leaders; these are also created by ourselves in which we then follow. Our elections are also democratic as well. The people here and on other planets are allowed to *choose* who they wish to have elected.

'Someone to be the main focal leader of a planet in order to represent us in anything. Haff does not even try to prevent us from doing this. If we have need of security, then Haff will provide. My advice to you, General, is to leave this and every other planet you have now went to and taken in great haste before they do arrive. As I'm afraid you have no idea at all of what *is* about to come.

'General . . . I will tell you honestly here and now that you may likely have never seen anything like these Haffian's in your life! What you may call an army here,' at which Rouf gestured around at Shrum's own troops. 'Are but an insignificant *group* when compared to the coming warriors of Haff. In fact, you may also be surprised at just how they are dressed too!'

My general had laughed uproariously at the old Mayor. When he had advised him that it would be better for he and all his men if they left their planet as quickly as they had came. As well as all of the others as rapidly as possible now. *Before* those from Haff came to set things straight . . .

My generals on each of these planets had also *all* laughed when they were told the very same thing by all these leaders. And when I was handed each of their incoming signal reports. I must confess that I also laughed heartily at their childish sounding wishes.

Little did I know that what advice of which they had freely given. Should then have been taken far more seriously and quickly followed . . . But, we were not to know this!

My generals did not leave as had been calmly expressed. So *they* came - and indeed they did come, and quickly! In ships that dwarfed any of our own by at least twenty or more times in size.

Upon each planet the exact same thing then took place. Immense ships which bristled with massive armaments. These strange ships also had a strange kind of glow around them which none of my men had ever set eyes on before. Only much later we would learn that these were called proactive bio-shields, whatever that meant. These massive machines now appeared in the sky to the cheers of each of these local populations, who due to this must have seen them at least once before.

In astonishing roars of power that made all ears ring, one by one they began to descend in order to land in whatever open space could take their immense size. My generals of course told those who remained upon our ships to fire at them before they could land. This was simply a wasted effort sadly. As either nothing penetrated whatever armour they each had - or it actually looked as if it just bounced off. Possibly this may have been from whatever caused that strange reflective light on them? Then one purple coloured shot from some weapon on theirs. Was returned at each of our own ships and which appeared to incapacitate them completely.

My generals were stunned at the simplicity of our own ships failure and inadequacy. And so they readied their own well trained ground troops for the ensuing fight that now seemed to be ahead of them. Shock . . . I fear that's what it was when the first of their great ships howled and whined as it reached the ground and shook it even as our men nervously watched. Doors large and small then opened up on the first ship to arrive even as it touched down on Jitrus.

Various kinds of vehicles sped out through the largest doors and began to encircle the city. These vehicles also seemed to glide over the ground without even the need to touch it, and so moved very quickly. Whilst from this and others, hordes of humans like those living upon the planets erupted from them like a tidal wave. At my generals count from his scanners, and only from that one ship alone, the newcomers quickly had a forty thousand army who were already on their way towards them. While yet more of them were still emerging from within it. He did not know then that some of these advance ships carried both vehicles and people for ground support. While others that were simply troop transports that could carry upto, and sometimes over a cargo of half a million strong. His own men were almost outnumbered already. And yet, as the general looked skywards, there were still another dozen or so of those huge ships that were yet to land. General Shrum new then that all was lost even before it had begun!

'I am sorry, but I did warn you, General,' said the as yet still smiling Inas Rouf. 'You never had any chance from the moment when you actually set foot upon our planet in such a belligerent manner. I would advise you right now to put your weapons down and surrender before you are all killed.'

'We can fight them and beat them!' stated my general.

'No, you cannot. If you fight - you will all die! I'm afraid its as simple as that. If you hold a weapon, you will be killed . . . Haff never takes prisoners if a battle begins. And they themselves would each die, or kill themselves before being allowed to become one.'

'What manner of people ever would ever wish to do that!' gasped Shrum.

Rouf gave a shrug of his slim shoulders. 'Haffian's are both bred and taught that way, General. They are purely and simply a warrior race, and that is *all* that they are. From birth to death, all are always classed as warriors. They always enjoy life to the full, knowing that only death awaits them you see. From a very long time ago in our own past, it has been said that they are raised in the same ways of which an ancient nation once was. Sparta, I think it was once called if my memory from reading about it long ago now serves me correctly. And it is said that the Haffian's are like those Spartans of old. *Life or Death* is their battle phrase, and one which they all shout when they go into battle . . .

'Well, it is more than enough to send shivers crawling up and down your spine so I am told. They fight to win, no matter the odds or the cost. And they also die bravely so as not to shame their own people or families. As I said, General, surrender now while you still can and *do* have this time available on your side. Because if you fight, you will surely all perish very soon!'

Shrum watched as rank by rank the newcomers formed up in an orderly fashion. As more ships landed, ever more ranks formed up alongside or behind those who had been the first to arrive and who were already on the move. 'It's too late now anyway,' decided Shrum.

'It's never too late to prevent it, until the fighting actually starts, General. Just be quick to decide what you wish it to be. Life or death! When all is ready, they will begin to march this way in their initial battle formations. So, you have until the first shot is fired by *you* in which to make a decision. They will not fire first - they never do. That is why you still have a choice. But . . . ' he warned, 'If even *one* of your men chooses to fire and it hits one of them. Then you will simply be wiped out to a man.'

Shrum raised his holo-glasses to study the enemy much closer. He was stunned at its growing size so quickly. 'Scanner?' he said to an aide nearby.

'The scanner shows that over two million of the enemy have formed up already, my General.' Then he glanced upwards into the sky himself. 'And there are *still* more than half of their ships yet to land! It seems that we are indeed both outnumbered and outclassed on this occasion, my General.'

Shrum shook his own head sadly and gave a deep sigh, *heavily* outclassed from what he could see already! And the newcomers had just began to march slowly towards the city now. 'Send the order out to our army immediately to stack their weapons and to stand well away from them!' he informed his nearby aides. 'And if you can get through to our other forces, tell them to do the same as well!'

'Sub-master Gelch states that his men are ready to fight at your command, Sir?' said a different communication aide.

This response came from one of the five commanders beneath him who had all positioned their men in readiness for the likely battle ahead.

Shrum shook his head again. 'Repeat the order that I have given. That on *no* condition is anyone to disobey my order and fire at any of these newcomers.'

'A *very* wise decision if I may say so,' offered Inas Rouf. 'By doing so, you have just spared all your lives.'

2

As the huge army marched as one into the capital city of Namak on the planet Jitrus. Even as more ships were landing and disgorging their own vehicles and troops. The army of recent interlopers could only stare at what soon confronted them. Legions of almost semi-naked, if not completely naked men and women who marched together in a cadenced step akin to that of an ancient watch ticking. A massed step that literally shook the ground beneath everyone.

Shrum himself was beyond being stunned at the sight of them. As yes, they all carried weapons of some type. Mostly those which looked like staffs. Although many were of quite strange designs. The most in evidence were like their own war clubs, but looked quite different. While others held very strange items in their hands or positioned over their shoulders. But why were they all semi-naked. Or, actually why were most of them so completely naked as they were, were his own main thoughts just then.

Neither he or his men had ever seen so many female breasts bouncing as they were now with each step they took. Nor had they ever seen so many male appendages all so open to view either. And then there were also those of the same mammary bouncing females again too. All which on their world were deemed as very private to their owners and barely ever seen at all by others.

The men were seemingly tall, all at least nearly six feet with less than an inch or so difference. Typically all of them were uniform in height, perhaps with only an inch or so between them. With only at most around three or four inches difference between the men and the women. Yes, it was true, as he could certainly see that women were in their ranks too! Who were again apparently all very closely matched in height themselves. He and his own men were shorter than even these women. Their own bodies were stocky and broader, with far heavier shoulders and much larger heads.

Their skin colours varied in differing tones too. As for hair colouring, unlike his own men who all showed short dark hair, theirs were not as utilitarian. Theirs was an array of colours, from the same black as all their own. To that of shades of red, brown, yellowy gold's and other hues also near to that. Some even had strange bright colours which Shrum could never have imagined being possible. The main difference being which he noted, were that few of them had hair as short as their own almost completely shaven headed military cut.

However, even if their body shapes differed slightly in build, each and every one of them all looked muscular with well formed, contoured and very distinct muscle signs. Many were adorned with various elaborate marks upon their bodies in various black or grey designs - while others wore far more colourful ones. The majority of them though had unblemished skin.

Then one even heavier muscled man with a thin almost hawk-like face who strode out ahead of them by just a few places. Looked much older than most of them did. Why this was Shrum did not know. All he could guess was, like himself, older age had brought wisdom, ability, and a high command role. Although how any of them could tell exactly who their particular leaders were within their own ranks and hierarchy; especially without some distinct means of identification as was worn upon their own clothing to show them as such troubled him. Unless those strange marks on his upper arms had something to do with it?

∞

The reverberations upon the ground increased the nearer they drew towards Shrum and his now unarmed men. His eyes watched keenly as the man who led them, raised an arm high and then dropped it suddenly. Shrum was unable to see all the other hands which had been raised in various places throughout their ranks by those below him in his command. But as one, as soon as the arm fell, the ranks behind came to a sudden halt. Leaving an ominous silence behind after all of their feet marching upon the ground. That same man then stepped forward so as to confront Shrum.

'All is well, Inas?' he enquired of the Mayor with his first words.

'All is well now, Low Commander Rist,' was the reply the Mayor offered in return by speaking in Gelten. This was so that Rist knew the man before him could understand his own words if spoken in the same dialect.

'I am glad to hear this from you. Your name?' he then asked the man standing beside him in the same language who was wearing some kind of dark body armour.

'General Akras Shrum, leader of the armies of Bork Gremplar of Briath.'

'My name is Octavus Rist, I am the Low Commander in command of the First Legion of Haff,' he offered in reply.

'You mean all of these are only from your First Legion?' asked Shrum in genuine awe.

Rist only smiled and then offered a low chuckle. 'This is only a part of the First Legion, General. Others under my own lower commanders were sent to the other planets by order of our much famed Prime Commander Raxx! The Prime Commander did not think that more than part of one legion would be required to alleviate this matter.

'Part?' he queried.

Rist gave a brief nod. 'Just one legion of Haff is of one hundred million troops, General. And we have many such. However, the Prime Commander chose to only send five million troops to each planet as a first stage. To see if more may be needed later, or not. It appears as if the Prime Commander was right, as is usual.'

Shrum's head was still shaking. If what was said was true, that if only one of their legions was one hundred million strong! It was an almost inconceivable figure to imagine of how many were still in readiness to be used.

Rist's voice broke into his thoughts at that moment. 'You were wise to lay down your arms, General. And because of this, you will all be treated fairly - if you answer any questions truthfully hereafter.'

Shrum nodded. 'If I may be so bold, can I ask a question of you?'

'Of course . . . ?'

Shrum took a deep breath. 'Can you tell me why it is that you all wear so little or if any, well, clothing?'

Rist gave a rare smile. 'To another military man, I thought the answer would be rather obvious!' Apparently not thought Rist as Shrum looked somewhat confused.

'Any likely injuries sustained in any battle will of course require medical aid, General. So, if there is nothing to hide the wounds, the medics can do their work far easier straight away. Yes?'

'Certainly.'

'And since we all have had to train from a very young age in all types of environments like this. From those of scorched deserts to frozen climates. Our bodies have, from that same very long training instilled into each one of us. Already become accustomed to any kind of climatic endurance as well. And so due to this, clothing of any kind worn on Haff itself is indeed a rarity, although we do allow it if wished. It is simply that we all see each other as brother and sister warriors there. We live together, train together, fight together - and lastly die together if need be!'

Shrum's head shook again. 'But does the sight of each other like that not bring about certain . . . thoughts and feelings shall I say?'

'Do you mean in some kind of attraction or sexual desire towards each other may take place?'

'Well, yes.'

'Of course that can happen. But until any young person reaches sixteen life cycles, nothing of that kind is allowed between anyone by law. Their own training comes first and foremost and they all know this. Training is our life!'

Rist then held a hand up to prevent Shrum from speaking to him. Holding a hand up to an ear, he then spoke aloud to no one in particular. 'Yes, Prime Commander?'

He listened for a short while it seemed, then gave a nod before answering whoever Shrum guessed he was talking to.

'Yes Prime Commander, Jitrus is safe and under our control again. No, there are no casualties to report at all here. How went the landings at the other planets . . . ? Oh, I see . . . Yes, it is a shame that not all of them had the same understanding that a certain General Shrum who landed here on Jitrus had, Prime Commander. Did we lose many troops on the planets Arcon and Spirit? Only two thousand dead or injured in total, but most will live after being treated? They did well, Prime Commander! Well, I thank you for your respect of my own abilities on this. But as you will know, it is only through your own tactical ability and that of our own long training regime which brings us such success!'

Shrum and his aides were listening to all of this one-sided talk as well. The newcomers from Haff had lost only two thousand troops in total on two of the planets. At which their own troops had apparently decided to fight. How many of their men had been lost they wondered. And then Shrum remembered Inas Roufe's earlier warning to himself.

'Yes Prime Commander, I am also pleased that so many on the other planets also followed the General's own choice in this way too. It is not pleasant for the inhabitants of these far more peaceful worlds to see what violent destruction and death such battles can bring. And what would you like doing with all the prisoners from here and as well as on the other eleven planets?'

He nodded again as if to himself. 'Very well Prime Commander, they will be escorted to Haff with us. As you say, those of our own who we cannot take on board will await empty ships; which you are already now despatching and are on route for them.'

Shrum waited until his conversation had appeared to come to an end before asking, 'Is it good news or bad, Low Commander Rist?'

For you, it was bad news - for us it was good! On the two planets of Arcon and Spirit which you also invaded. Your armies there decided to resist instead of surrendering as the rest of you did.'

'And?'

'I am sorry, but they fired the first shots.'

'Do you mean that they're all dead . . . all of them?'

'To a man I'm afraid. They should never have resisted.'

Shrum's shoulders slumped heavily. 'Eighty thousand of our men gone, just like that!'

'If fired upon we do not take any prisoners, General. We respond in the way in which we were trained. If attacked, we kill until there are none left to kill! As soon as one of our people are killed the battle cry is sounded.'

'But surely there must have been some wounded?'

Rist gave him a sad look. 'Any who managed to survive the battle were quickly dispatched.'

Shrum and his aides were aghast. 'Murdered But surely even your army does not also kill those who cannot fight back!'

'General . . . your men fired first! It does not matter to us about who in your armies on those two planets decided to give the order to fire or not. They simply did not listen! But, when you do fire at us so you must reap the aftermath. We do not take prisoners if we have been fired upon! So those of you who are alive right now can think yourselves lucky on this - and on all of the other planets where they have survived as well.

'Now, by order of our Prime Commander, those of you who have surrendered to us will be taken to Haff for the moment.'

'And then what?'

'That is not my decision to make, General,' said Rist as he then turned to face his own troops as he now called out, 'One unit of Section One will remain behind until another ship comes for you to embark upon it here shortly. As our Prime Commander wishes to have all the living captives taken to Haff as quickly as possible now.'

Rist then made a single gesture with his hands and the army before him in one movement turned in ranks like that of an well-oiled machine. Parting and taking ten steps to their rear. Which now left a large enough passageway for Rist, the General, and his own men to pass through.

'Follow me, General, with your men lined up and kept in an orderly fashion if you would, please.'

General Shrum passed his orders and did as he was asked. And as Rist began to walk through the offered passageway he beckoned to him to follow. At which he and his worried unarmed men did as ordered.

They marched back to the immense ships that now squatted on the ground like small mountains waiting to be reused. Leaving around fifty thousand troops behind them in the city at the moment until their own return transport arrived. Rist knew that they would be offered refreshments while they waited by those there, so he had no worries about that.

Shrum, upon reaching some of the craft resting beside those of his own army's transporters, was staggered by just how small their own ships were in comparison.

'The pilots in ours?' asked Shrum as he was walked past his own ships.

'Alive, and ready to fly yours to Haff under guard.'

'You didn't kill them for firing at you then?'

Rist gave a low chuckle. 'From what your ships fired at ours we sustained no damage or injuries. Which is also the only reason why they and *you* are all still alive! My own ships weapons incapacitated all of yours easily enough so they could not effect our ground troops emerging. As if they had been able to, then you may have all died for it!'

Of the fourteen other planets in the Barathon system. On twelve of them, both captives and troops were soon held within the great ships' hulls and were taking off to return to Haff. On two others, only those who were from the Haffian army boarded. No matter if they were dead, injured, or unharmed. Everyone of them were returned home if it was at all feasible.

To the usual inhabitants of Arcon and Spirit, the task of clearing up after the battle was theirs to do. No matter if they had never seen anything so repugnant, or as hideous a sight to their own eyes before. Haff had done their task and saved them, as was expected of them as protectors. And that basically, was all they were entitled to do. When they were asked what to do with all of the enemy bodies, the order which from their Prime Commander was passed to each of them. To inter their enemies within a single crystalline mausoleum and to then freeze them within it.

The citizens of Arcon and Spirit accepted the order that was given. And then with mostly looks of distaste and close to throwing up etched upon their own faces. Some began erecting the structure with which to hold them, while others who were slightly braver began to collect and stack the bodies ready for their later interment.

3

When the signals from each of the other planets in the system began to arrive on Haff within their own large communications building. Possible steps which could be taken were already in preparation.

Only as a warning to one unknown ship entering within their own planets defensive spatial area had come to nothing already. The same thing had occurred a short while ago with another much smaller one as well. Warnings had been broadcast to them a few times as the came nearer to the planet. Even to a final warning, stating that if no response was made; or the requested course deviation was not taken to move away, then they would be fired upon.

Those same two ships had continued on towards Haff without responding. And so warning shots came from the core-flux cannons on their nearest moon or asteroid based weapon platforms which were within range. They had sent precise energy bursts ahead and down the sides of them. All intentionally missing, just, as they had been initially ordered to. But this was only offered as more of a last warning to them if they persisted in their same direction more than anything else.

The first small ship had actually ignored any of these and had kept on coming closer to their planet. The later second much larger one, like that of a warship, even began returning their own fire right back towards the point of fire. Which was duly reported back to their command centre on Haff while they took almost inconsequential damage. The Prime Commander of Haff had heard enough.

'Destroy it!' were the only words uttered - and so it, just as the first one had been, was.

The remnants of both ships and crews had exploded and were left to drift in the eternal darkness of space. This was also the reason why neither Bork Gremplar or General Shrum had heard anything from either of them again.

∞

Haff itself was an immense planet with a radius of almost eighteen thousand miles. It was somewhat reminiscent of old Earth in a way. Except for its far different size. It had its various mountain ranges which were even higher here, some reaching in excess of over eighty thousand feet. Due to its actual size of course, and even where there were jungles, deserts, and ice-capped land masses - all were far larger than what there had been on Earth. Haff's normal, almost strangely regular temperature was of around 15c to 25c from night to day. The only differences being where it usually was typically cold or humid and was where its temperatures varied far more.

Or so the ancient archival records stated which had been studied in their library. From the time of the arrival of the *First Ones* at the beginning of the third millennia. Those who had fled a then steadily dying Earth to find a new home somewhere out in space. On Earth their had not only been continents but many separate countries. Many of these had vastly different temperatures to each other. Many being far colder or warmer than the other. Some they said had suffered from very cold winters, while others had droughts or floods . . . So different to Haff with its seemingly very steady circadian weather rhythms.

In the time before any such decision had to be taken, due to the ozone layer steadily thinning and dispersing too much in the 26th Century. Allowing more of the solar activity from their own Sun to cause far more potential problems on the planet. Basically, even when the levels of pollution rising into the air had been cut quite dramatically. However the unusual continuation of eruptions to so many volcanoes on the planet had an even more adverse effect upon it.

Each of these same eruptions always spewed out its toxic gases into the air. Such as carbon dioxide. Sulphur dioxide. Hydrogen sulphide. Hydrochloric acid as well as carbon monoxide. So really it was no wonder that the ozone layer above not only thinned even more - but also widened ever further. This allowed far higher levels of ultraviolet (UV) light to penetrate the Earth's former safety shield. With this now taking place, temperatures gradually rose as these rays got through, so the ice caps slowly melted and the waters levels of the seas rose.

There was just enough time for those countries with much lower lying land masses to have started to build protective sea walls to halt the invading water. The cost for such defences, as would be expected was exorbitant! And few could manage to afford to protect everything. In the end, low lying cities looked more like fortresses with huge walls.

This only added to the fear of the far too large population to their planets upcoming demise. And caused more thoughts of seeking a safer home somewhere out there.

Although, there had even been a suggestion by some scientists that their own sun would eventually come to an end as all suns did. All suns created light and heat, the only matter was how long they would continue to offer it. They all had their own lifespan. But in the end each of their cores would reach a certain point where a final change would occur.

Some would simply explode outwards, sending a singularly fierce and surprisingly fast solar burst emanating outwards. A burst which would scorch and burn any of these planets or moons it touched until its own blast radius ended. Then there were those suns that might implode and possibly become black holes. Or as with their thinking about their own sun, that it would gradually become larger as it burnt itself out leaving the Earth looking like a dry barren Venus before ending up turning into a huge Red Giant. When the outer layers eventually disappeared, it would then turn into a small white dwarf star.

These would offer little if no remnant light any longer, nor would they emit much heat. So any former civilizations upon any planets near to it, and which depended upon it, would end up in darkness. Without a sun, any system could not survive. Unless of course a planet was so advanced that an actual sun in their system may then not be needed. On Earth itself, the temperature would rise from the slowly dying sun. The ice at the poles would melt, just as all water on the planet would begin to evaporate, along with all life. The only thing that may survive all of this was bacteria.

Advances on Earth before this in many areas had been invented, created, studied, and finally reached. Space travel becoming one of the most important of all. Due in no small means to the state of what *could* well happen on Earth. Teleportation, even if it had been studied and pondered on for many centuries was still no nearer to finding any true answer to it as yet. The application of it from planning stage to a working model had been attempted many times already. But so far, sadly the hoped for possibilities of transmitting and reorganising the atoms of a human being or an animal back into their one true form had not yet been manageable. The scientists who worked at this would of course continue to do so. Until it either worked completely in the way that it should - or what knowledge and technology they had available to them right now still meant that for the moment it was not yet feasible to do.

The Magna-Pulse Drive was one of the more important and successful creations. Allowing time-drift wormholes to be formed to jump space in huge leaps. Automatically flown ships by robots was another. Within them were so much equipment that it had required a better power supply than even the latest Atomic would offer. On Earth, at first it was nearly always fossil fuels being used, be it coal, oil or gas. Then with the advent of Nuclear came the cry for much greener ways of harvesting the energy required to support life. And so from that came Solar power, Wind power, Wave power, Shale oil and gas. Yet even that wasn't enough to support an entire planet in which a population would never cease to grow.

So in their hundreds, huge self contained structures close to five hundred feet in height were being built, sometimes higher. These each held six water turbines to generate higher levels of power. Using its own core of continuous water supply. The water fell from the very top of the building down into each separate shaft of these turbines, which spun them from that flow. And that sent the energy being created into huge generators which could then feed many smaller generating buildings away from these. After causing the blades of the turbine to spin at high revolutions. The now used water would be pumped back up to the very top of the building to do it all over again.

As always though, no matter how much was being generated, ever more was always required. The Earth's population never ceased rising, and the demand for more food was also a constant. Until even that finally became impossible to sustain. Then, even after many new viruses appeared to strike unexpectedly and caused both panic and fear. The toll of death sometimes reached into the many millions. But still that never held the population back. The population was already nearing the four billion mark when scientists worked out just how long the ozone layer around the Earth would be able to keep them safe from the deadliest rays of the Sun.

The time-frame they offered had a large leeway, but the answer would surely be the same anyway! Yet, it gave time enough to work out what *could* be done. At which point underground cities began being planned and built. While others believed the only way to be safe was to head out into the stars to a new home. That, was when their Earth 2 Project came into being. Scientists from around the world then gathered together in various groups to discuss what they should look for - and as to what would be required to begin such a major step.

Robotics had moved on by leaps and bounds in the last four hundred years though. Just as spacecraft with enough power had been engineered to enable them to lift off from the ground themselves and to go up into orbit. Even to return and land again safely. But . . . launching and landing back in Earth's gravity was an already known factor. However, what lay out there which would be being searched for could differ by a far greater amount than this. Higher or lower gravity levels than Earth. Distance from ground level to reaching space could be another factor if the planet it reached was larger or smaller in size than their own.

Many programmers began to compute thousands of possibilities into their very latest super computing machines in order to devise a benchmark of what could be required. It took them over a year to create a possible formula. But they then also had a rough idea of what was needed. A better means of power generation was one. Their calculations showed that even the old Atomic power would not be enough to manage what it would have to do. Designers, engineers, and all matter of professionals in their chosen fields had to come together from around the world to work out what could be done in so many various ways and forms.

A further twenty long years of creating, designing; as well as testing these things over and over again. Until finally, it slowly but surely brought them the rewards they had since long sought.

Now they had a new ceramic superconductor in the offing. A two foot square block which incorporated so many elements within it, that just the one could power a city of ten million for over a thousand years. It had been tried, tested, and it worked . . . These were soon being made and replaced everything else power-wise on the planet. It was simply named as the SHC. In scientific circles though, it was of course known as the Smith-Hoch-Chu. From those who had not only invented, but had also designed and eventually built the first one. With these in place, the planets pollution output dropped to its lowest point ever recorded. But the ozone layer was just too far gone by now - and still the volcanoes would continue to erupt weakening it more.

The same advances also came through in other much needed areas too. New metals, fibres and polymers, new types of far tougher plastic and glass all towards the building of spacecraft. Even nano-technology was now being used for medicine as well as a variety of things. Hybrid agriculture for a new planet based colony if what was on it already wasn't edible. Or perhaps if there was nothing at all on them. Adapting possible animals from their own planet to that of a newer one. Such as various types of fish, for if there was a sea on one to populate it with known types. Everything that could be thought of to be able to exist in space, or after landing on what would be an unknown planet had to be either imagined or thought of well in advance at this time.

Atmosphere creators if it did not have a suitable enough one for human life. As well as the means of moving around if the planets own atmosphere would be hazardous or toxic to them at the very beginning. There were thousands of issues facing those who had to think about such things as these. Simply because none of them had any true idea of what could be expected out there. With these now able to be used, construction of them soon became fast-tracked.

The news around the world that ships to launch into space to find them a new home, or homes. Was soon being spoken about and travelled fast amongst them. Of how it could be done, in order to save as many of those who wanted to leave Earth and find a new home, somewhere out there!

The first ships launched were tiny in comparison to what would come later and which were already in construction for the general population. These first ones were drone ships, piloted by the latest androids. Human like in shape and form, but also with an awareness of what was required to be found and eventually reported on. Without having the need for any nutrients to stay alive. It was the only choice for the scientists to make for such a possible long journey. As even they had no idea how many months or years the search would take before any reports would return. All they could do, was to be ready for when they did.

For many more decades, they continued to build their ships, even to upgrading them sometimes as even newer developments emerged. And then all they could do was to wait. Some drone ships never even reported back again after a while. Perhaps they had met with unexpected forces out there in the vastness of space, such as black holes which led to this taking place. Or even other intelligent kinds of alien life who held them prisoner to learn what they knew. There may have also been those who when dropping into a planets atmosphere had been fired upon and destroyed. Or the ship itself may just not have even made it through its atmosphere. Those on Earth would never know what occurred with these, as there was simply no information from the lost ones for them to go off.

New generations were born while older ones died. But still the plans went ahead. Of course, later generations had a head start with many of their newest innovations, and quickly made them even better.

It was centuries before the remaining drone ships began to head back. And when they did, then it was back to sorting out all of the stored data from them. New charts were compiled of stars and suns which were of course so many light years away from Earth. None of which being so far away were as yet known about. Only as the returned droid ships came back would they know what these planets consisted of; or how large or small they were, and also of what they could offer.

Even to the people of Earth, many of whom had disputed the case for there actually being aliens out there for so many hundreds of years already. Were quite shocked by what had been brought back by some of their drones. There were not just one or two, as had been thought previously. As there had been literally hundreds of planets at which their drones scanners had found to have life forms or buildings on them in some way or another. Contact could have been made. Yet there may have been problems with doing such a thing as this, too. Any alien planet found could far outreach any of their own capabilities. And far from seeking friends, they may just find enemies on them instead. So all of these would be left well alone! What they *were* searching for, was a large planet, or group of them which they could make their own. Basically, somewhere safe for them to start to build their new lives again.

More decades passed while both theories and plans were discussed and used - or possibly even thrown out altogether. Until finally, a general consensus was reached of what was required. and only then were the final plans and objectives being made.

Only when all questions had been ratified and answered as best they could, was a time set for departure. From the options available, they had chosen a solar system where no life forms had shown up from its scanning. It was a system which comprised of three varying sized suns and fifteen planets which they hoped their joint heat and light would sustain them all.

But unlike Earth, where all types of industry were gathered on only the one. They decided to make their new worlds completely different to avoid any such similar problems again. They chose to make some only agricultural for food support. Others would be for manufacturing and building. One was even a ninety percent water planet for the breeding of fish stocks and other marine life. Yet another was given just to those who were thought of as creative. Those who could offer new concepts and ideas for the rest of them to use or to build. Along with these went the artists, singers and dancers - anything at all that would be considered as being of a creative outlook.

To support any of them if any kind of trouble occurred anywhere, the largest of them was to become a military planet. To not only train, but also to hold anything that was needed for any sudden requirement or deployment.

With all that having been decided at long last. Newer ships were soon launched with higher versions of android pilots and crews. These one would be setting the stage for human life to be able to exist on them. Inside these far larger ships were the machines with which to do this. Their latest atmosphere generators and terraforming machines. Which would start to alter these planets to what was required ready for their human incursion to them. Android builders would be waiting in the ships to begin to construct the required cities and buildings using their newest techniques and materials. Only when everything was close to being ready would those who were leaving finally abandon Earth and head there.

It was fifty more years before the one word message they had waited for was sent back and received. And all that it did say was - *Come!*

Within a month, everything was ready. Those who had feared leaving and so decided to stay behind; who also hoped to survive this way. Had already said their good-byes and farewells to those who were about to leave them.

And as it was also a new beginning for those leaving. Referendums and options were held as to naming the new planets for those who would soon be living on them. Surprisingly, there were no New Earths . . . nor were there any named after former countries either. It was just as if everyone wished to start afresh now. For thirteen of the planets, it was as if a set of children's blocks had been thrown upon the floor and then a name had been chosen from what showed on them.

For the actual system itself, they called it Barathon. While the names of Haff - Jitrus - Burle - Greener - Cerne - Dilos - Efas - Hende - Klimm - Marmm - Manay - Aqua - Spirit - Wance and lastly Yellos were given to the planets.

Only Spirit and Aqua had made any sense at all really. Perhaps Greener as well with it going to be agricultural. Possibly this was because Spirit would be the home to those with either creative or artistic abilities, so they had kept it far more normal and reserved. While the one given the name of Aqua was the water based planet.

Then, upon the announced day given, on the eighteenth of June of the year 2723, one huge ship after another began to lift off from the planet surface. All of their engines roaring loud enough to shake it as they each struggled to lift their massive combined weights upwards.

Those who were staying behind watched as each one of them climbed higher and higher into their own skies. From each starting off level with the ground, they slowly began tilting towards the heavens above. Where only as they all reached their most opportune inclination, maximum power was then given, and the other additional engines were seen to be lighting up so as to push them higher while also at a faster rate. And then, they were all gone . . .

What they were leaving behind them now, was a much reduced population. As well as sea levels which had already risen by six feet due to the planets global warming.

Those left below quickly rushed back underground again where it was much cooler. And could then only wonder if one day, or at some time in the future, maybe. That anyone would actually return to see if any of *them* had managed to survive on Earth.

4

Their return trip to Haff did not take as long as General Shrum had actually expected. Even for such gigantic ships as these. One moment they were leaving the ground of Jitrus. Yet whatever means of power they used seemed more than sufficient to be able to lift these machines from its surface quite easily. It was also a kind of power that far exceeded anything which they had.

And as they were both classed as the highest ranking officers from each others army. Rist sat beside his opposite number in one of the many long lines of seats when they entered the ship. In the same way that the general's men took up their positions wherever they were told to do so, to sit beside either a man or woman. The ship steadily rose upwards, gaining speed incrementally until it reached the height required to merge into the darkness of space. It was only then when a small and brief alarm sounded throughout its hull that Shrum's face showed worry.

'It's nothing to worry about, only a warning to those of us who are inside the ship, General. The pilots are simply alerting us that they are about to activate the Magna-pulse engines now.'

'Magna-pulse? I've never heard of that kind of power for travelling being used before. What is it? What makes it work?'

Rist sighed. 'General, I am a warrior, not an engineer! Tell me to fight, and I'll fight. Order me to take a planet and I will attempt to do so. Ask me to change any part on this ship large or small, and I will just look at you. As if to question why you would even ask me to do this. Give me a weapon and I'll use it. Give me a ship and I'll fly it. But if tell me to fix something, then I would be just as lost as you would be. That's why there *are* engineers to do this!

'Anyway, it's what we have used for a long time to allow us to jump through space. You will also soon feel a hum travel through your body, this is simply a type of holding shield - a means we use to prevent any of us from being thrown around. You will then feel a slight jerk, and then another one not that much later. It only means that we have left Jitrus's orbit. Although only when we are far enough away so we will also not leave any vortex behind which could effect the planet itself. The following one after this will be as we almost reach Haff. As then we will be coming out of our jump so as to slow down again; only then will the holding shield upon us disappear. For this very short distance between our two planets, the jump time is only about five minutes.'

Shrum had carefully studied the plans of the Barathon system back on Briath with Bork Gremplar before their own attack armada had left to conquer this entire system. For their own ships, which had taken a good twenty-six days to reach this far off one. They knew it would have taken at least a day or more for any of their own ships to reach any one of the other orbiting planets which were nearest to the next.

Their own ships certainly did not have this kind of advantage. Theirs could jump but not very far. Then they would have to recharge from solar activity to jump again. It was rather a timely affair and also quite a slow way. It was also why they still knew so very little about any other planets or systems which were outside that of their own.

This is why he had suggested to his leader that they attack each of the fourteen planets simultaneously. Mainly due to their own ships travel time between them. As any troops in their army not required after that could all head towards its largest planet to capture it last.

They had thought at the time, that it would be the same for those were already in this system too. Which meant as each attack went ahead at a certain set time parameter. That no other planet would be able to assist the other one out in their ensuing takeover attempt. So for at least a day or more if any attack on one or more did fail, they would still have time to plan again.

This was what they had expected anyway. Time enough to land upon each one and then to prevent any help coming from another. Haff of course, had been the only one of the fifteen which had not been attacked at once. Due to having received no response from their initial scout ship that went to it. Nor had any message been sent from the ship in their battle group that was to check if it had any defences. They did not know that Haff had quite a wide system in place to block such things, which of course they were also unaware of. A few simple mistakes or errors which had now since cost them so dearly!

It had not felt like five of their so-called minutes when the warning alarm sounded once again, and then the same slight jerk was felt. For Rist and the men and women in his ranks they were almost home and could move more freely again. As for General Shrum though, he had no idea at all what he and his men could expect for their attempt to take over planets held under their protectorate. Eighty thousand of his own troops were already lost he again remembered, and now close to half a million of those who had survived were being escorted to Haff; for whatever this Prime Commander of theirs wished to do with them soon.

'What will happen to us here?' asked Shrum, mainly voicing his own fears for his troops.

'That I simply cannot say, General. The Prime Commander alone will decide whatever your fate is to be. The only thing that I will tell you - is that if she does question you, *do not lie*. As the Prime Commander is also able to sense when someone is lying to her. Your outcome, as well as those of your troops may truly depend upon your own honesty.'

'Is he the leader of your planet?'

Rist emitted a small chuckle. '*She* is our military commander, General. On all things military, Prime Commander Raxx holds total power.'

'So who does rule your planet then?'

'The Garen Royal Family are *seen* as that, but only in a titular way, and beneath them are the Lord's and Ladies of Haff. But we all know that this is only in name. They are seen more as a token to our own far off old home planet for various things. Such as a look back into our own past of early history of the peoples who had hereditary status.

'Here on Haff, their duties now include handing out awards to families of fallen troops, opening any of our holiday celebrations or festivals. Leading parades and created events. Once upon a time, we do know that these people would have once ruled many parts of a planet. But here on Haff, and as ours is a military planet above all else, General. So it is the leader of our military who holds sway on almost everything to do that may concern it.'

The roar of the engine power mounted as they felt the ship now dropping vertically beneath them. Shrum had digested all of this information, in case it could be of use if they were set free later for his reports.

'May I ask how old your Prime Commander may be?'

'In the old terms which we still mainly use, she has just reached her three hundred and thirty-fourth year.'

Shrum was well and truly stunned. He knew of *no-one* who had ever lived as long as that before. Even in his own system of planets, sixty to seventy cycles was their usual limit.

He could then only ask hoping for an answer, 'Do you *all* live such long lives on this planet?'

Rist's chuckle was again prominent. 'Certainly not! Our maximum life cycle is upto one hundred, and that is only if we're that lucky.'

'So how *can* she be that old?'

'It is *because* she is the Prime Commander! Our genetic scientists a long time ago now were finally able to create clones. Only those whose talents are deemed as being unequalled, and so they are considered as a continued necessary requirement to Haff are done so. Even upon some of our protected planets too, some people of high regard or esteem were also considered for this. The Prime Commander was one of these here. On our own planet, there are around five thousand clones such as these held in continuation. Memories can be implanted into any of their new clones each time you see. Which also means that for many thousands of years, they can all retain those memories of what has happened and what was done back then right upto the present.

'Whenever the Prime Commander or others are incarnated into their next life. Their memories are taken from their old bodies and implanted in those which are new. Due to this, their new bodies hold memories that go back a long time - recalling events as well as people who are by now already long since dead.

'Our scientists, as well as those on Spirit never cease to create. Through their genetic coding, the next incarnations may be stronger and fitter, perhaps even living much longer also. Memories and brain functions can also be heightened too, offering them further abilities for yet more adaptability that may be needed for various functions. Those who are allowed this, ask our scientists to work on solutions towards their next incarnation so that they can be added to them.'

Shrum had never heard anything quite like this in his entire life before. Upgraded humans who can actually live for centuries each time . . . it was almost unthinkable! Were they trying to design a way of no death? Immortal beings even? Was it an attempt to make themselves become something similar to actual God's! Shrum was just going to ask him about that.

When any chance of further speech between them was now drowned out. The ship they were in must have went on to maximum thrust for landing. So it was quite deafening inside the ship. And he already knew what they had sounded like from without when they landed on Jitrus. Which could only be ten times worse to those below on the planet itself.

'You may look out of the nearest porthole if you are at all curious about our planet, General?' Rist literally then bellowed into one of his unusually low ears.

Shrum turned as best he could under the seat restraints they had also all worn prior to take-off. His head twisting to an acute angle as he peered almost one-eyed out of the nearest porthole window. It appeared as if the ship was actually landing between buildings! And what buildings they were . . .

Indeed what buildings they were he thought from those he could see. Immensely tall monoliths which all gave off a shimmering quality against their different coloured outer material structures. He nearly pulled an arm out from its socket as he tried to see even more of it.

'This is Haff Central, General, which is our capital. We have five others almost as large as this which the lords and ladies oversee. The rest of them by this standard are small and only occupy between five hundred million to one billion of our people.'

The figures which were now being quoted staggered him. And *still* the ship was dropping! Leaving the tops of the buildings surrounding them now high above their heads.

'How tall are these?' Shrum shouted back at him as he turned to face his smiling captor.

'Usually around a mile or two high as we call one of our heights here. A few are slightly higher than that. although it depends mainly upon what they are used for. While most of our buildings are often far less.'

Shrum was trying to take it all in, but it was almost impossible to conceive. Stretching his neck as far as he could. He was then actually able to see insect like people moving about below. While the lower they reached, the clearer they also soon became to him. Even some of their smaller buildings would dwarf Gremplar's own citadel!

Lower and lower as it continued to sink, its throbbing engines were still whining and straining due to its own immense bulk. So low that Shrum could soon begin to make out faces appearing, as well as other things. Like the same basic lack of clothing shown by those who had landed on Jitrus to take them prisoner. He noted just like the troops of his adversary, that those who did wear anything on their person was either so short, brief, daring, or even ephemeral. That they were so transparent that it was barely worth any of them wearing anyway, as they certainly hid nothing from his looking eye.

He could only shake his head at the thoughts assailing his brain. Just what kind of people *were* these Haffian's? Who took semi-nudity, or even complete nudity to such an extreme as this. He decided to ask Rist this.

'Our bodies are only the carrying shell of all our thoughts and dreams, General. We are what we are and who we are. Being without clothing is simply a freedom of movement to us all. In this way we are also in this way, offering a lack of jealous thoughts over who has what and can afford what.

'As a Low Commander, I am paid more than my own subordinates. But less than our Prime Commander and High Commanders. Just as they are paid more than theirs, and so on and so forth. Yet even with this, we all enjoy a good lifestyle and living standard here nonetheless. Our lack of clothing, or some as brief as you may see are simply a basic style of fashion. It simply tells those that see you that you are just like, as well as being one of them in all ways.'

The ship was still moving, until with a low juddering thump it appeared as if it had settled upon the ground. Shrum thought this only as the sounds of the engines were cut-off. The loud howl slowly died away until there was no further sound from it. He still gazed through the portal, only now much nearer to ground level. Now he was even further mystified when he saw a huge number of people from their city as they apparently gathered and sat on an immensely long row of stone benching, or whatever it was made from.

Though to him they looked like a series of simple blocks. He quickly thought his eyes were playing tricks on him though. When he saw a man who was stood facing one of these groups. And he was almost sure that he was urinating at a block by the stream he could see. Even while at the same time also gesturing with a free hand as if talking to those around him. He shook his head - these people were more savage and uncivilized than anyone he knew the more he saw of them.

'What's the matter now, General? asked Rist of him, even as the ship began to sink beneath the ground on its own lifting mechanism.

'I am sorry, but I could have sworn that I just saw a man urinating openly while standing and actually having a conversation with some others at some low blocks.'

'Of course, we have many public toilet utilities like these scattered all around the city.'

'A utility? But it was all being done in the open - I mean right in front of everyone. Why do you do this? Have you no shame?'

'Shame, General? Have I not told you that if clothing is unimportant to us. What do you think happens when our young boys and girls at the age of five begin their training? Just as our men and women also constantly do to keep themselves ready . . . Do you think they have time to leave their training areas to do so. Or return back to their homes simply to use some kind of an enclosed convenience? One that may be somewhere which could be many miles away from where they are busy at that time? Of course not - that would be impracticable for them. This is why we have these public amenities scattered wherever a large number of us may be, General. That way little time is lost to them whenever such a functional need may arise. This of course also means that they are soon back to their set task again.'

The lift finally ceased its motion as the ship settled underground. Above them, the roof closed over their ship to again offer a place for people to walk upon again, instead of having to bypass the enormous hole. Just as it had or was doing with all the others which were, or had also landed by now.

∞

As the various doors of the ship began to lower to allow those inside to disembark. Rist added a further word of warning to the General now standing beside him.

'Our planet may feel heavier to all of you, as it has a much denser gravity level than most. Roughly about three times to that of Jitrus and some of the others in our system. And as I don't know about your own planet, I do not know how your own body may react to this. Your own movements may feel slow and sluggish to you. You may even have trouble breathing properly for a short while, or longer even, until you acclimatise better. However, even with this, all of you will now be fully screened, General.'

'In what way?'

'The security portals that you will all walk through. Just as we always must do, will seek out any weapons which may still be hidden of which have been forgotten about. After that portal will come the medical screening. This is only to make sure that none of you may be carrying any kind of known virus or toxins back onto our own planet. Like your troops, this will mean you must also disrobe for it. While here, as far as I am aware and if none of your men cause any trouble. They will then be fed and a place for them to rest will be offered. It will still be under guard of course. As for you yourself, once you have been cleared through the screening processes. I will then take you to meet with our Prime Commander.'

'Very well, I hope I can use my own uniform again after it to meet her. Or failing that you have something for me to wear for it.'

'I'm afraid that while you are all here on our planet, General. Your own state will be the same as ours.'

He thought for a moment to follow that, and then flushed. 'You mean to say that not only my men, but even I *myself* must remain naked while we are held here?'

'You are on our world now, General. And I do not make the rules and regulations that must not only be observed, but adhered to. *Anyone* who comes to our planet faces the very same directive. Even if it may be any of the Mayors or citizens from any of the other fourteen planets within our system, or elsewhere. On their own planets, they may dress according to however they wish to do so and we have no complaints about that. As you will have already seen for yourself from those on Jitrus. Whereas when they are on ours, they must all follow and conform to what is our own codes and rules whenever they arrive!'

∞

After leaving the ship, Rist stood aside with General Shrum to look around for a short while as his men filed off it. Again, he had never seen, or could imagine anything so mind shattering. As he was now stood in what he now knew has an underground cavern of truly immense proportions. As far as his eyes could see, and in any which way that he now turned to look. There were far more ships like the one he had just arrived on squatting around ungainly. There were also a lot of smaller ones than those, yet even those would have dwarfed the largest of their own ships. Others that he saw there were very small by comparison, though he did not know that these were their fighters.

Then there were the heavy load bearing tall and rounded wide pillars which rose high to the roof here and there from various strategic positions. He supposed correctly, this time. That these were the sole means which supported the vast city above this place from it all possibly collapsing in upon itself.

He also not only felt that his own body weighed a great deal heavier than it used to. Only as the movements of both he and his men were now really sluggish. He then knew that none of them must never have been on such a heavy gravity world like this one before. And also just as Rist had said, simply trying to inhale enough air into the lungs in order to breathe was a very strange feeling. It was if it took many times the same normal effort just to manage only the one. Although that part of it was nothing. It was when he himself personally felt far more worried and unusually embarrassed after his nude screenings were finally done.

Not very long after all of this, he was then being led by a similarly naked Rist through what felt like mile upon mile of brightly lit corridors. Which meandered underground in a variety of directions as he was taken to his meeting with their military leader. Rist had even waited for him to have a meal himself before the journey had began. The food itself had been strange to his eyes, although very nourishing and oddly enjoyable to his taste buds.

He felt surprised that his also having to look at so many naked men and women on his journey had almost dulled his senses to it already. His only problem was, that he was just like them and so he could now be seen in the exact same way by all of them too.

Rist suddenly halted in the maze of corridors at one of many doorways as Shrum continued to walk on. Caught unexpectedly by his stop. He needed to come back to be able to stand beside him again.

'Just remember, General. Only speak when you are spoken to, and whatever you do, answer truthfully.'

Rist then waved his hand over a pad on the wall which opened the twin doors. They stepped inside, where Rist tapped the uppermost light on the panel. Shrum's newly filled stomach was then almost left behind. As the transport he was in rose upwards at what he could only imagine was a phenomenal speed.

It then felt as if his stomach rose up somewhere towards his upper chest as the rate slowed immeasurably before it finally stopped. There had not been any shaking during this, nor was there even any sound or juddering as it ceased to move so rapidly upwards either. It had been a silky smooth experience from beginning to end. Another type of movement technology which no planet within their own system had.

The doors opened again. Whereas this time it opened into an immense room. Far larger than anything he had seen before in his life. Even to any of those inside Bork Gremplar's enormous citadel on Briath. Or what he'd once imagined to have been enormous. Yet here on their planet, that same citadel would have been dwarfed beside many of their own.

Again, naked people were everywhere. Most were seated behind some type of information screen, although many were also just walking around from desk to desk for some reason.

One man walked towards them, with some kind of small information tablet held in one hand which constantly displayed various messages.

'Greetings Low Commander Rist. It is good to see that you have returned to us safely.'

'Thank you, Morg. Is the Prime commander ready for us?'

He nodded perfunctorily. 'The Prime Commander has been waiting quite a while for you now. But she also understood that the General here also required some sustenance since arriving. So just as she would do, she waited for that to be carried out first. Come, I will take you to her,' stated the man perfunctorily, after giving a complete once over casual glance upon the general.

He led them along the long room to where an immense pair of doors now began to open expectantly. Upon reaching the doors, he gestured for them to go through, while he turned and went back to his other duties.

∞

'Remember what I told you!' Rist hissed softly as the doors closed behind them in silence.

'Octavus . . . it is good to see you back again so soon!' said the voice in an old crackling way of speech.

Rist offered a perfect salute and bow in response. 'I am pleased that things went so well, Prime Commander. Luckily the General here listened to Mayor Rouf before it may have escalated.' Her head gave a nod, while she gestured for them to sit before her.

'Yes, indeed. It was only a pity that the others invading Arcon and Spirit did not have the same clear thoughts. In the end, they chose the wrong path to take . . . and so they paid dearly for it.'

Shrum was yet again quite amazed at the sight before him. The woman seated there did indeed actually look ancient. Probably just like the others who were completely naked of course too, he assumed. As due to her seated position he could only see the upper half of her torso. Yet even that was more than enough for his eyes. The hair was short, sparse even, and fully white. What once may have been a well muscled body, almost appeared wasted to him. The sagging and wrinkling of the flesh around her face, throat, arms and upper torso truly showed her age. Her face was odd to him though. It was not round, or square, long or even angular. It appeared a mixture of them all at the same time and offered her a quite striking countenance along with its bone structure.

Her arms looked so thin that he was surprised she could even lift them. Her elderly breasts were now not very prominent at all. Very close to being totally flat and not a good sight for his own eyes to behold at all. Apparently no matter what their age must be - personal nudity must not bother them one little bit as to how anyone else actually saw them. And yet, this one ancient woman sitting there before him held all of this planets enormous power and might at her own command.

'So, *you* are General Shrum then, are you? You are the leader of your tyrants army who was sent to invade our own planetary system?' Her small head shook slowly from side to side. As if afraid that doing so too quickly would injure her own thin and scrawny neck.

'I will now ask some questions which you will answer to the best of your own ability, General. There is only thing you must know. Which is please do not attempt to lie to me when you do so. As your own, as well as the lives of your men who were also brought here will depend upon your responses.'

She stood up then and came around her large desk and sat on its edge facing him. Appearing very much relaxed, and as if what she was now doing was of little consequence to how he might see her. This was still about ten feet away from the general, but he saw that her legs were now just as thin and spindly as her arms had been. And again, and especially more due to her age and remaining looks - not such a pleasant sight to be placed right there in front of him now either.

'Your title is General Akras Shrum?'

'Yes.'

'You serve who we shall now call, *The Tyrant of Briath*, Bork Gremplar. Yes?'

'Yes,' he said, even to adding a nod.

'Your system name is what?'

'Gelten.'

'How many living planets does this system contain?'

'*Living?*' he asked being somewhat confused by the terminology she used.

'In the way it is said, *living* means that a planet has populations of beings upon them. No matter if they are of the human type, or not. Only as long as they are capable of speech and a reasonable standard of rational thought, General.'

'Oh, then the answer would be five. That is all we have in our system, including Briath.'

'The distance from your system to ours?'

'Sixty-eight krens.'

'What is a *kren*?'

'A distance that we use to formulate travel.'

'That word is new to me - but we will come back to it at a later time. What time does the rotation of your planet Briath have?'

'*Time?*' he queried with an odd look again.

Raxx thought. 'On Briath, how long does one day take to make a circuit? That is from morning, to dark, to morning light again.'

'Ahhh. Then Briath has a period of sixteen point three zorems.'

Raxx now assumed that Briath had just over a sixteen hour rotation of night and day in time parameters. And that a zorem must be equivalent to what they still called hours.

'Are your planets all the same like this?'

'No. Goll only has a fourteen point eight zorem. Briath and two more have around sixteen. While Chell is a twenty-six zorem.'

'By what names are the other two known?'

'Nee and Pelus.'

'So are these four others all being subdued by the tyrant? And by that, I mean that they have no true say in anything at all. Even to how their own planets are being ruled or used? That the tyrant himself creates and makes any laws and rules which these all must obey?'

'Yes.'

'You are, as I have since been made aware and already know, the leader of your armed service? How many does your complete army consist of in total?'

'Before *today*, we had a four million army. Although we can conscript from any of the five planets within our system to take our army anywhere up to ten million if the need came up.'

'So, of these additional six million conscripts, are any trained like you have been? As in able to function like a regular military troop?'

He shook his head. 'They are basically only to bolster our strength if we have to.'

She nodded. 'Poor devils. Only to be used as fodder then to help your own main troops survive.'

She appeared to digest all of that to think for a few seconds at most. 'So, if your actual army is four million strong. Why did you not send them all at one time?'

He shrugged. 'From the earlier findings from our spy scouts, who had been sent to seek out possible new worlds for us to bring under our own control. The ones who came to this system reported that none of them had any defences or military personnel to be seen.

'Both Bork Gremplar and I then thought that forty thousand sent to each would be more than enough to both sustain, and also to accomplish the mission. The rest were on standby if needed, while a few thousand are based on other planets to also keep those on them subservient.'

Raxx nodded her head again. 'So you use the threat of force and violence to exercise your wishes upon them. Which means if they do not obey - then the troops who have been stationed there are used to make sure that they must comply by this force?'

'Of course, it must the same everywhere! Without troops there to be able to keep a tight rein upon a population under your control. Well, *anything* could happen!'

'Not so, General,' stated Raxx with what he thought was a smile. 'We station not one single military person from our own planet upon any of the other fourteen planets that are here within our own system. Nor elsewhere on any others that we protect either.'

Shrum shook his head. 'I do not know how that could work then, Prime Commander. Without a force at hand to keep an eye on them, a planets population could simply become lazy. What I mean to say is, that if they aren't pushed to work - then they likely wouldn't do any at all!'

'Basically in our system it is all about democracy, General.'

'Which is what? I do not know that word.'

'You have never heard of democracy, General?'

He shook his large head.

'Democracy is an old, if even an ancient term to us. Basically it means that a population has a choice to do what they wish to do. As in who is in charge at that time. What steps can be taken by this person. What should be done if ever a specific need arises, and so on. The people on these planets are those who are chosen to be their leaders for a set time period. And these people then make choices that bring about a group of people. Who then make the decisions needed during this term of office whilst they are placed in charge. Each one of them has a various task to perform in what we also call a government. Typically, their leadership is then all about for whatever may be best for the people of their planet. To whom they have been chosen to serve for a stated period of time.

'They can also change laws and rules while they lead. Even to altering some from those who were in charge previously if it may be more beneficial. Or perhaps only to make changes to those same laws or regulations for their relevant populations. Of course, some new laws, rules, regulations, or other changes may require doing if some certain, yet unexpected problems occur. But that is why they were chosen, or elected to do so by their people. For them to be able to decide to do things like this. A planet wide vote, or referendum, may also be held if something very major requires *all* of its people to decide . . .'

Shrum looked as if he was frowning. But with such a heavy facial countenance like all his race, it was difficult for her to tell. 'You wish to ask something?'

He nodded. 'But surely its much easier if only one person decides all that, Prime Commander, just as you do here? What I mean is, a group of people could have difficulty coming to any final solution if they have different thoughts on any of these things. Whereas one person, alone, who makes all the decisions can just say this or that. And then by their word alone it is then done and carried out!'

'I see your point, General. Yet that is why it is also called democracy. Simply because it takes an existing thought or plan to be voiced by one of them. And then between those who have been placed in charge, they must now talk to each other about it. Usually they will then end up having to vote on it. If it then receives more votes for it to be carried out than not. Then the topic which has been under discussion will be done, or not done if the vote goes the other way.'

To Shrum it was a very strange way indeed of doing things. Back home on Briath, Bork Gremplar simply gave a command. He gave his orders out and then waited for them to be initiated and complied with. Their way here seemed a far longer route to get what was likely needed each time. Although from what Rist had told him, this woman also ruled in a similar way to that of his own leader.

After a while of thought, he said in response, 'It *almost* sounds like it may be a good way to offer possibilities. But, it would also likely just take too long to make things happen. I still say that it's easier for only one person to make a effective decision and just say, *I want that done* - or, *do this*! As you also seem to do here too, Prime Commander!' he added, only hoping that he wasn't going too far.

'Yes, but that is the true difference, General. Which is that only one person is deciding what he or she may want to happen. Here on Haff you are quite correct. As for the question you made about myself. Yes, in a way I am in charge of Haff, but only of Haff . . . not any other planet. It is I myself who offer various suggestions and thoughts about a great variety of things which may affect our planet. However . . . ' she said then, 'if the majority of the people here on Haff were not happy about what I do for them. Then they do know that I would happily step down and let another take my place if they actually wished to do so. I am no tyrant you see - I only do *what* I do due to the will of the people.

'In a way, General, what I do I only do for my own love of Haff and those who live upon it. Simply as I myself am no tyrant who wishes to force her own will upon those here. I do what I do for the betterment of them all. It is likely the reason *why* I have kept being incarnated to do this for so many thousands of life cycles now. Because they wish me to continue doing what I do for them. As if they were *not* happy about how I have done these things for them. Then all they would do is to not awaken a new clone of myself as one died. Possibly even to shut down all those others of me who are growing. If that happened, then there would be no hope of another me returning.'

'That's preposterous! Unthinkable!' gasped a quite alarmed Rist at even her thinking such a thought.

Raxx just gave him a smile. 'As for your system, General. No matter if those who are being governed *do not* want or wish it to happen. It's coming from a law made by only one leader alone. A law which no other person or being can refuse. That is more like slavery to a mass population.'

'Possibly . . .'

'Tell me this then, General. Just how rich is your tyrant? I mean in regards to how rich, or how enjoyable a life the lowest beneath him has?'

'Our Tyr---- our leader is extraordinarily rich, Prime Commander.' said Shrum just catching himself, almost forgetting to use Gremplar's title. 'He can have what he wants whenever he wants. As to the lower classes you refer to, it will depend upon what they do and what they can make from it.'

'Indeed . . . so in your own words, General. Those who have trouble simply trying to stay alive and survive are left to do so? There are no other means available, or probably even offered which can help them? Whereas for I myself, I am only on a slightly higher payment then that of any High Commander below me. Wealth, power, and how you think of yourself before others, is not as good as doing whatever you can for them all.'

'Of course. It will be those who perform the most menial or degrading of tasks, who will be at the lower end. Of that I am sure, yes? It will be about what level of service they are able to offer, so their payments will be judged accordingly. They cannot be offered the same payments as those who are considered to be doing a far higher task. That would simply not be right.'

'Of course I understand that, General. Even in some way I can even also understand how these others may think about those who they feel are *so* low beneath them. Especially if they were earning so much from doing it.' Shrum began to nod, finally this ancient woman was gaining some insight in return.

'However,' she then said which quickly halted his nodding head. 'Hate and jealousy of those who are classed as being so high and mighty - and who are *so* well-off above them can also breed contempt. Contempt in itself can also cause other passions to rear their heads. What would your so-called higher paid populations do if all those who you see as being the lowest of the low simply ceased working? Would what they provide for you make any difference to your own richer lives? Would any of you who are considered as being higher than they are do it themselves if they had no choice but to do it in order to survive?'

Shrum began to think about that. He honestly could not see those in their far better positions lowering themselves to that menial level at all. Even to he himself. Serving others at home, or in places of rest and relaxation. The cleaners who tidied their walkways and areas of transportation, as well as inside the buildings or houses. The farmers who produced all of their food and who he knew were paid a pittance for their produce when sold. Their amenity cleaners. As he thought about it, the list became almost endless. So many of those who kept the cogs and wheels turning and those from higher levels happy. He knew in return received very little for all their efforts. Yet without any of these workers doing their work, all five of their planets would likely just grind to a complete stop.

'I have no response to that, Prime Commander. They do it because in effect it is all they are good for!'

'Just as I thought, General. It is those who are considered as almost being worthless who carry out the most important work if you wish to think about it. Where would you be without any of them actually *doing* it, is what you should be trying to imagine . . .'

'I just did, and even just the thought of it to me was worrisome! But I know that our leader would not stand for that happening either, so something would be done.'

Raxx nodded. 'I can almost imagine his response, General. Troops then being used to force them back to work against their own wishes. Riots and spontaneous attacks suddenly breaking out and happening against your troops. Your troops fighting back . . . Many of these people being killed because your troops have weapons while they do not. And *still* they refuse to obey your commands and return to work. All of this happening while none of your, what you call *menial* tasks are being done. The more that are being killed only seems to harden the resolve of the rest of them simply because of this.

'Tell me this though, General, by what majority in total do you consider your five planets to be worked by these menials? Ten, twenty, fifty percent perhaps? Maybe more I myself would assume. Only as the balance is almost always a few percent who are placed at the very top. Then usually there is another five or ten percent below them, and then lastly about the same again. While the rest who are under those three levels are seen as the lowest of the low by all of those who are at the uppermost levels. Tell me, General, if your leader decides that the only way to eradicate this growing problem is to kill all of them. What then? What will the twenty, possibly as many as thirty percent of you who are left then decide to do?

'Especially if you have just eradicated from sixty to perhaps eighty percent of your own populations to prevent further such problems occurring. Who among you would be able to lower themselves by so much in order to now do that work? Because, as you must be thinking, if no one will, then your system would be doomed. In fact, would any of them even know *how* to do any of these menial jobs? By this, I mean what those who are left may have called the simplest of tasks if no one was left alive who did know how to do any of them?'

'I am becoming confused now, Prime Commander,' said Shrum, and he indeed looked it to both her and to Rist.

'It is really quite simple to understand, General. That in your own way, you are ringing your own systems death-knell. Without your main force of workers doing what they do for you every day without fail; you simply would not be able to survive without them. Yet you treat them *so* badly that I am almost surprised that they have not done this already to object. Again, if you have, or you once *had* four million trained troops. Say a million or more are above your level. That means the rest are only seen as the lowest, yes? How many menial workers is that, General. Ten million, twenty, thirty, fifty, perhaps a few hundred million? It should make you think, does it not? As to how could the remaining four or more million of you ever be able to do all of their work if they *were* gone?'

She gave another of her smiles at him. 'I may have to allow you to travel around our own system with Octavus here. Just so that you can judge for yourself about how a thing like democracy and looking after all the people *can* work, General. It is likely the best way in which you can then understand how important it is that *everyone* who lives upon a planet feels included. No matter if they are thought of as being of a high or low status upon it. You may also be able to see the subtle difference in the standards of living which is allowed upon those in our system here. Compared to what you have said of your own.'

Shrum did not even want to think of the possibility of such an outcome if it ever happened. As his own system would indeed be almost dead at that time. Gremplar himself would have very few left to rule over if it ever happened that way and such problems appeared.

He emitted a deep sigh. 'Thankfully nothing like this has ever taken place yet, Prime Commander. And as far as I know and am still aware. Everyone upon them knows their own station in life and conforms to it. Anyway, there has never been any need to change how it has always been.'

Raxx just gave a small smile. 'Things can change when you least expect it, General. And I can see a big change coming to own your system soon.'

'How so?'

'Your leader took it upon himself to attack *our* system, General. So I think it would be only fair if we in response returned the same favour. Don't you think so?' Raxx's smile widened even further at him now.

He instinctively knew what she meant though, and from it his thoughts were heavy. Bork Gremplar, ruler of the Gelten system, and his own homeland of Briath would stand no chance against the true and full might of Haff.

There was just something about her though, thought Shrum. She had a kind of presence. The way she both looked straight at you and talked to you. In what he could only describe as a no nonsense way. There was something - but what was it? Charisma! His brain finally gave up its struggle and brought this to its surface. That was it. Old or not, she like so many he knew, who was charismatic. She was also both intelligent and decisive. No wonder she was followed so loyally by all those on this planet of theirs!

5

As per Raxx's orders, and after her information gathering had finally came to an end with him. Rist requisitioned a smaller ship placed in readiness by her. So that he and Shrum could set off on a tour of their system, only so as to show the general exactly what she had spoken to him of.

Instead of that of a general commanding an army this time. Shrum was more like that of a tourist seeing the ordinary sights. As well as being able to note the differences between the planets here, to those which were held under Gremplar's own personal rule.

For the next full three days, Rist led him from one of their system planets to the next so that he could observe everything for himself. He took him to their creature planet first, where Shrum had never seen their like before. Then to the mainly water planet where fishing or breeding of marine stock took place. From then on it became busier. As in how their agricultural systems worked, including harvesting and processing. Then to how their vast mining was done. The proportions of many of their working machines, both outside and inside their warehouses and factories left him speechless. Many so large that they were even bigger than the ships they had came to conquer these same planets with.

Yet no matter where he went, and at whatever else Rist showed to him. Including some of their housing structures. It all left him feeling that most of his own system lived in little more but inadequate hovels by comparison. Most of these were even better than the one he lived in with his own partner and family. And he himself was their highest general, not just an ordinary worker.

The one thing which Shrum did quickly note though. Was the actual general happiness of the people everywhere, even those who were busy with their work. Even to what Rist offered up to him as their lowest standard of living to workers, just as he himself would have called them.

These people were also dressed to a far higher standard than any of his own people. And even had far more to show for it, too. Everywhere they went, they looked well nourished, as well as also being clean, fit and healthy. On the five in his system, all those who lived below the good living standard of the higher few. Went around in a typically sullen and morose kind of way. There was little evidence of any happiness as was shown here.

On the tech planets themselves, he saw the immense structures which not only built, but also repaired their own machines; along with ships including those from Haff if required. There were also foundries, where he watched the incoming ore from the mining planets being altered from its once raw state into huge sections of what appeared to be a type of metal ready to use for building various things. And far smaller ingots of much rarer metals being smelted.

Some factories were making the various sized engines they all must require. Another was an armament factory, which produced both ship weapons as well as hand-held ones for them.

Although his greatest surprise of all, was to actually see those spoken about android units slowly coming off a production line one by one. All were of a standard size as they hung from a frame in a long slowly moving line. Yet they did cover both the male and female gender.

'But what are they all used for?' he asked of Rist.

'Many are used by us and others as medical staff on our planets. We ourselves use them for wherever there is training taking place, or at any battles. As we do get injuries quite often from our training, mainly due to its realism. Also because it is very high standard which we all need to achieve from it. Which is most of the time - even at night as well.

'Many of them also do various other tasks, if not multiple ones, which can save any of our people much time. While the other planets also use them as medical staff simply because they have a complete knowledge of this held in their brains.'

'Such as what?'

Rist shrugged his shoulders. 'Because they are biogenic androids, sleep and their needing to rest is not a true issue for them. Only when they need to recharge will they be missing for a short while. Or if plugged in to an energy source they can carry on regardless. Which means that any, or all of them can be programmed to do multiple tasks. So no position is ever left vacant. Another of them will simply take its place while it does this. Their brain by now has also become a reactive one - which means that they do also have quite some semblance of reasoning skills and so they can learn, too. This also aids communication between them, so as one is about to go offline to recharge. Another will know this and take its place if that is required.'

'Do you have them in your army as well, as fighters?' Shrum asked worriedly.

'No, as I said before, as medical staff is our own main priority. That is one thing which we have *never* used any of them for, fighting. However, sending some of them out in drone ships to search for and to survey other systems and galaxies and such like in order to map it for us. And to land

and evaluate these new planets and civilizations on them, then yes. But as for them being built for actual combat, then no.

'The first ones, much older models than these, were initially created long ago by our ancestors as non-combatants and used in service roles as well. So we have always kept it like that. Mainly for us as a military planet, they are used more as medics, so are used wherever we may be training and sustaining injuries, or perhaps even *upon* an actual battlefield.

'As to the reason *why* we use them for such duties. Is simply because they are without any actual knowledge of fear, they will always attempt to treat anyone who is wounded or injured - even if that means that they are actually under direct fire at the time.

'But basically elsewhere in our system they are only used as utility workers. Those on the other planets around us prefer to have human contact when interacting with doctors. While they may still use androids as nursing staff. We do not know, as we are tended to by our own here at home.

'You will see them serving in stores and markets. Driving transportation vehicles. As well as in the health and beauty trades. Such as spa's, salons, massage parlours and so on. You may have already seen some of them in the mines I showed you where it may just have been far too dangerous for any humans to work.

'Also on the agricultural planets, where crop picking may be just too repetitious and boring for ordinary people to stay focused. Perhaps even tiring for our own bodies to simply manage it hour after hour, and day after day and so on. Their motors and servos do not tire as our muscles and joints would do. Yes, in time some of these may wear so much that they may need repairs, which is also why their parts are easily interchangeable. They are even able to do this for themselves, if their own internal status systems tell them that something is not working to its full capacity or potential.

'Again, it could mean working close to the harvesting machines where it could also be too dangerous a place for a human to be. It doesn't happen often so I have heard . . . But if one somehow loses an arm or a leg, or there is any accident such as that. Which the android cannot repair themselves, then it would simply be returned to the factory and have any such parts replaced. It is only if one of them is actually deemed totally unserviceable after such an event would its own parts then be used to repair others. This is also why they are all of a standard model type. So that in the event any parts are required, with only two sizes for the male and female models. It means easy duplication or renewal.'

By the time his tour was over and they were returning back to Haff again. Shrum had already seen in his own mind of what he would call the future. Possibly even a newer and brighter future for his own planet and its system. If their Prime Commander did in fact decide to take action against Gremplar.

∞

Unbeknown to Shrum, she had been doing many things since they had left on their three day sojourn. As not only had she had some of his own officers brought up to see her since then, but she even had some of their ordinary troops brought in to question quite closely too. Raxx had learned much more from all of them, especially from the troops themselves. At which point she finally decided that the Gelten system needed change.

Hopefully, after they had rid them of their tyrant, their own system after a short struggle could function just as well as their own did. And without there being a one person power structure above them. With some luck, they would be able to revert to a similar kind of planetary rule over themselves. Of course, she had smiled, their own system would of course naturally offer their help to allow them to do this if asked. And after Shrum's visiting trip, she was sure he would tell them what would be for the best for them all. She was always planning ahead.

Raxx had also decided that she would lead the oncoming fight personally. Only because at the age she was now at. She would attribute it to herself as her own final swansong. Her own health was starting to fail, just as her body had lost most of its former strength and agility. So she would lead the fight herself on Briath, in the knowledge that if their tyrant himself resisted surrender - then her own end would thankfully come in battle. She hesitated to think how many of her own people could die in the ensuing carnage to come when she fell. As she knew that the shouted words of *Life or Death* would echo around the troops who were there with her. And then there would only be one final and terrible end to it all.

Her memories would be quickly saved by one of the medics. Which would then be sent to Haff to place into her own best aged clone. Yet another one who would be brought out of her cryo-sleep to take up her place again within the halls of Haff. Once more, she would be young and beautiful again to all their eyes. Where yet again she would be needed to command their entire planet of men and women who had always followed her in an almost religious way. For to them, she had always been seen as the epitome of their planets military leadership. Since memories of far distant times were held within her. The simple reason behind her cloning being - to them, was that she was indispensable, the one person who they all felt their planet could never be without!

∞

Raxx left her comfortably padded and soft durcot seat to walk out upon the two mile high balcony of her office. No matter that she was so high up right now. The breeze was only nominal what with being on the sheltered side from it at the moment. The command centre, at its base level was already quite a large structure. Yet this only rose upwards like this for almost half a mile. Above that was the circular command tower which itself rose in height three times as much. All the way up to the top. This tower slowly rotated to offer both sun and coolness to those within it. As well as the changeable views out of its large armoured windows.

Raxx's office sat at the very top just below all of the transmitters and signal antennae's perched on its roof. She could control her own levels rotation, and this was already set more towards wind deflection. This was why whenever she stepped out upon the balcony, it was always more sheltered.

As the darkness of night had already begun to fall over the capital. The light sources from their three small suns began to shine together upon other areas of the planet instead. She stared upwards into the night sky, the loose skin of her neck tightening from such a movement. Light flickered everywhere from all the stars, suns. and distant galaxies up there. Just as she could also see three of Haff's many moons glowing slightly. The few orbiting asteroids held within Haff's own gravitational pull were far smaller than any of their moons, and so were unable to be seen with the naked eye. Sometimes though, and only if you were very lucky indeed, one might just happen to pass a moon so that its passage could be spotted momentarily. But such sights as those were very rare indeed.

She thought of the many thousands of her people who were up there on them in charge of their outer defences. As well as those who orbited their planet in their defence fleet. Who were always very focused while on their monthly guard rotation duty of their planet. They remained focused because their parents, siblings, friends, and everyone else below on the planet. Forever counted on them to be aware of any possible attack upon their home world.

Raxx emitted a soft sigh. Very soon she would not be able to look up and see this any longer. Her own time would be over here, just as a new and much younger pair of eyes would take in what she was now looking at. It did not fill her with the sadness many others may have had. Only because she had done this nearly every night for centuries. She had been "born" as they say at the age of twenty-two. So for what had now been a long three hundred and fourteen years, she had worked, planned, instructed, taught, and also ordered for the good of Haff for that amount of time.

Outliving various generations of Royal families, lords and ladies, and probably many billions of her own people who had succumbed to their own old age. She had helped to progress her planet as well as her people as far as she possibly could, she thought. That was and always had been her duty. To see to the safety and security of her world - along with the other fourteen in their system who they watched over constantly. They were also the protectors of another two systems and separate planets as well. Though this only amounted to another seventeen so far. With another four in discussion at the moment with envoys.

'I will miss seeing all of you every night!' she remarked sadly yet quietly to the twinkling sky above, before finally lowering her head. Then her eyes gazed slowly over the immense sprawl of their capital city below her. 'I will miss *you* too!' she said with another sigh. She would miss just walking around the city and stopping to speak to someone every now and then. She was one of them, just as they had all been such a huge part of her life for so long.

46

The dim glow which emanated from many of the buildings showed that their work day had ended. Whereas where the lights were brightest, was where many of their people were busy relaxing or working right now. In nearby offices or immensely tall housing structures.

But what *was* life without death . . . Those who were below in the city, and elsewhere on the planet had a natural rhythm to *their* lives unlike that of her own. Perhaps one hundred years possibly a few more if both luck and fate went their way and no illness or accident befell them. Accidents were always possible during their training. If it was too easy, then they would never be prepared. This was why it was made to be difficult - extremely difficult! That was also why all who survived it were very tough, simply as there *were* no weaklings among them.

Alertness and understanding was a way of life. Especially if you wished to get through it. Some though were sadly unfortunate. As of course, there were always some children or early teens who thought they knew it all already - so didn't fully listen to their trainers. Or they simply just didn't listen well enough to learn what they should be doing when they were. These were the ones who were most likely to fail. And during their training, failure usually ended up by them being in some type of accident. Those who were trained and ready to succeed may only break the occasional arm or leg at most. Cuts, burns, bruises, and dripping blood were almost a daily staple of any training. It was when you learned that what you were *being* taught was to not get it wrong! It was the abject failures which were the worrying ones. The trainers of course hoping that their mistakes would not get any of the better students injured or killed.

∞

With her day finally over for now, but with her head as always being filled with so many possibilities; both on her own planet and that of the recent invading force. Raxx made her way from her office to the lift. She said her good nights to the men and women outside it who had only just come on duty and were now on watch. Taking over from those who had left previously. She stepped into the lift which would as usual take her downwards two miles to just below ground level. Where her own personal bubble-pod would be waiting, as always, to take her home.

As happened on most nights when the final heat of each of their suns disappeared from the capital city's side on Haff. The air outside would begin to chill considerably. Unlike those who were probably out on the streets even now. Eating, shopping, or perhaps even just talking to various people they met or knew. Raxx's own aged body could now feel that very same chill as it came. Whereas in her younger days just like all the rest of them, her training in varied climates on the planet had made her almost immune to heat and cold. She knew that others would be out there right now enjoying the cooler night air after the hot day. Even if they were wearing little or nothing. While she, even just walking in the underground cavern towards her nearby transport could not contain a shiver.

She could have walked or ran home just as easily many years ago. But the trials of age had been creeping up on her steadily. The two hour walk, or forty-five minute run home which she had regularly enjoyed for many decades. By this time were just far too tiring upon her old and withering frame. Apart from that, tiredness had become an ever present factor in her everyday life for a long time now. Being true to herself, she couldn't wait to bring an end to what had sadly now become her much too old to bear life cycle.

Youth . . . Oh how she missed those earlier happy times when she could walk, run, jump, as well as train alongside the best of them. Yet not now. Her bones and limbs had become far too fragile over the past fifty years or so to even allow her to enjoy such pleasures. Right now, apart from sitting at a desk to carry out her never ending tasks regarding Haff and its people. The walk to the lift, and then out of the descended lift to her personal transport. Then stepping out of that to walk a few feet into her home was about all she could manage these days. Yes, she thought, it really did need to end, and soon . . .

It was not as if she was in any way ever ill or infirm. It was simply the case that her age had eventually caught up with her. Upto a hundred years life cycle might seem a very long time to some Haffian's - but maybe they should try being three hundred and thirty-six some time! Her own life pleasures by now had become nonexistent! In fact, if she could just manage to plan everything quickly enough now. Her own cycle would reach a wonderful end in a battle, and her much younger incarnation would take over it all . . . just as they always did - and just as she had.

As the doors opened into the city's underground system, where literally almost everything to do with its hidden functions. Such as their more normal modes of transportation, various machinery, relays and power cables which served them all. Hummed, thrummed, or steadily beat like that of a clock or heart. Even here work was always ongoing. Repairs to their space ships, utility vehicles, perhaps even to any buildings, beautiful parks, or the various parts and items which when integrated made Haff a well ran city.

She didn't have far to walk to reach her own gold coloured pod with its additional black crescent detailing, and for that she was thankful. As her far slower walking speed these days, showed everyone who saw her just how hard her body was fighting to cope with its constant demands of ageing. None of who had even been born, neither had their parents and possibly most of their grandparents when her last incarnation had taken place so many centuries ago.

Even to her it always felt strange that her own children and grandchildren were also long gone already too. Her own husband Marrse had also been dead for a good two hundred and sixty years. Their own children's offspring were already into their fifth breeding cycle. She'd married him aged forty, and he'd survived only until he reached seventy-six. A relatively young and unexpected age to die here on Haff if not in any battle - but at least they'd had just over forty years to spend together, with thirty-six of those being married.

Since his death from unexpected ill health, all she'd had were her family members visiting her. And then as always happened as their generations continued onwards. Their thoughts of the ancient woman who was still alive, and who had helped to actually begin all of their lives, slowly began to fade over the coming decades. It had went from mother, to grandmother, and then on to great grandmother and great-great grandmother. To those of her line who were alive right now - so much time had actually passed that she was to them like everyone else. Simply known as being that of *The Prime Commander* to whom their loyalty was paramount. The thoughts of any familial bonds to her had long since diminished into being more of a story that each of their own parents had recited.

She had been alone for so long now, that a life of utter loneliness could well have been a major issue in her life. That is, if not for her four ageless maids at home who had never and would never alter. Mi, Leenis, Dorro & Parri. They literally did everything for her. They cooked, they cleaned, they bathed, they dried, they massaged, they brushed. On the rare occasions when she had to attend some type of special event, they even saw to her rare times of make-up. Their own inner core of programming contained hundreds of possibilities and outcomes generated in sy-seconds. They could and would not hurt any human, but they would protect one with their own life or body if the need for such ever arose. This was why in their army they were all typically used as medics and doctors. Not to take any life - but to try and save them at all costs.

To say that they were also only maids was to put it mildly. They were all human-like androids and as such they were very well attuned to her own wants and needs completely. The reason for this was only because they had served her various incarnations for many thousands of years already. Over such a length of time, they also knew exactly what made her happy or sad. Along with what both pleased and contented her. Including her likes and dislikes. As each incarnation took place - they already knew *everything* that was required to be done even before the newly incarnated young Prime Commander had any idea of what she may have wanted herself. Even they had been upgraded many times in order to make them better in some way. Only as with them looking after the Prime Commander herself, they usually received any new upgrades first.

As she approached, she as usual saw that when her transport sensed her nearness to it, it opened up one side of itself. It was of a teardrop shape; and of approximately four metres in length and two metres in width. Able to carry six comfortably - but as was usual, there was only herself. Her maids and other possible passengers only went with her to special occasions.

Raxx gratefully slid herself into the almost fully recumbent seat position and offered a low sigh. Even as she lay there with her eyes already closed. She could hear the different sounds as it began to check itself over for any problems before asking its usual question. A small beep said that all of its systems were green.

A gentle female voice asked, 'Destination?'

'Home please - and please alert the house that I'm on my way.'

'They have been alerted as per your request - Please make yourself comfortable while I begin your journey.'

'I am ready, thank you.'

'The I.I.S.S. (Integral Inertia Stasis System) has now been activated.'

She always felt it as soon as the transport lifted itself gently from off the ground on its suspensors. So even with her eyes closed, she knew it was making its way across one of the hangars towards a transport tunnel. The last remark made was simply a reminder that the pod she was in was now also in its survival mode. So no matter if anything untoward may ever happen upon her journey home, and very rarely some malfunction could indeed happen in them in the air or inside the tunnels. Her own safety within it while travelling was also its main function. As of course the pod was also more than capable of flight to a certain height. But unless she herself requested flight mode, then the pod would use the usual transport tunnel options.

The I.I.S.S. system basically caused a new higher power fluctuation to begin which encompassed the entire interior of the vehicle no matter how many passengers it carried. From the much smaller twin seater pods right up to the far larger transportation pods for typical usage. In far simpler terms, she could not move a muscle even if she wanted to now.

The system itself restrained her in place almost forcibly. In a similar way to that of how the larger space ships used them for massive cargoes. Whereas her own pod used a miniature version of it. The air molecules within had been thickened considerably to prevent any movement whatsoever. A few times travelling within it she had felt the need to scratch her nose, or another part of her body - but that was actually impossible to do; as she could not even raise a finger now let alone an arm against the inside pressure. Her eyes could move, but that was about all.

The idea behind this was mainly in the event of any sudden accident and the deceleration caused from it. She, while sitting or reclining there within her interior cocoon would feel nothing until it was all over. The pod itself could literally become destroyed from whatever may happen. Whereas she, held by something almost like that of an all round powerful force field. Was protected within its strengthened inner cocoon so completely as to be almost immune from any harm.

She slightly opened an eye for just a second, seeing that the pod was now entering within one of the travel tunnels so closed it again. The pod quickly gathered speed, its own systems waiting for a gap to slip into. As one appeared, it slid across into the main flow and then it was just as if an ancient accelerator pedal had been floored! It had already sensed the speed of the pods both ahead and behind it, so when it matched theirs, its own lateral movement and merge was made without any trouble at all. It was quickly barrelling along at the speed of the one in front of it, which was going at three hundred and seventy miles per hour.

'Time to tunnel exit, six minutes and thirty two seconds at this speed, Prime Commander. Time to reach home, eleven minutes and thirty-eight seconds.'

Raxx heard it, but as she couldn't even nod, she didn't even bother to answer. The journey time either way rarely differed by more than a minute or so every time anyway. So there was really little to make a comment about. She herself was simply enjoying the relaxing position her body was in after sitting upright at her desk for so long again. By now she was also really looking forward to reaching her home. To relax in a hot foaming bath with its circulating systems; being bathed while she lay there while almost falling asleep in it. Even if she did fall asleep they would carry her out from it after a certain set time period only so as to dry her.

Then a quite wonderful massage would take place, and then a small meal would also be waiting for her. Seeing as all of them were equivalent to being top chefs and able to provide many other personal tasks too. She was sad that her lack of appetite now no longer allowed her to enjoy so many of their former skilfully prepared meals.

After her meal they would quickly clean anything which had been used up and then join her in the large resting room for a while. Previous clones of herself had steadily upped their intellect. Only so that she could talk to them about anything at all, and so enjoy a varied conversation with them. Other than that, there was always the strategically multi-player game of Ringee which could be chosen. In truth, outside of work that is, these four female androids were really her only friends if such a word could be used for it.

Her four maids also had a home rota of course. And as she retired to bed to rest for the day ahead. So the one who was at the lowest charge would go to recharge. While the other three were online not only for her protection, but also if she required anything at any time. Or if an urgent call came in for her and she needed to be woken for it. Then as one was recharged, another would then take that place.

Upon reaching her home, and only ten seconds later than was expected. Raxx thanked her pod and told it to garage and to re-power itself. The pod turned so as to reverse in as the garage door rose by its own command. It backed in until it sensed that it was in the correct position above the charging module set into the floor, and then powered itself down. With the suspensors off, it settled in exactly the right place and the display screen faded until it was dark. A barely discernible hum then began to emanate as it now began to charge up ready for its next journey with her.

∞

Her bathing soon done, the massage restoring her limbs to a more relaxed state. The small meal of Coufre soup served as always by them was exactly what she had needed to replete her own body's now minimal needs fully.

And now they were all together in the relaxation room. It was certainly high-tech. Colours, as like anywhere in the house could be altered to match her mood at any time. Music could also be played throughout it, at whatever level was necessary. Either as something to listen to, and possibly even to sing, dance, or workout to. Except there had been chance of her doing any workout exercises for a very long time now. Or the music could be set low as a barely audible background to aid relaxation more. There were also many other options available to them, as the producers and directors on Spirit were always bringing new films out for others to enjoy.

She gazed directly at the four of them seated across from her. Mi looked Asian in her conformation, while Parri appeared Oriental in hers. Leenis was white skinned with long flowing blonde locks. And Dorro was dark skinned with ebony hair which hung to her waist. They were typically all the same in length of hair, as that was what was initially chosen for them to have by one of her own predecessors. They had never been altered since that time, as all new clones after their memory integration took place would remember them straight away. So they had never been changed ever since they had first been requested and brought to life. If such it could be called . . . as in all truth, being *activated* was more nearer the mark!

To Raxx herself though, they felt more like daughters to her after being with them for such a long time now - although daughters who she knew would *never* age as she always did. It was also the reason that unlike so many, they had been allowed to use her first name when talking to her. They were sitting there patiently waiting for her to speak first, as was normal. She emitted a loud sigh before she began though.

'I am going to miss each one of you, my girls!' was what came from her mouth unexpectedly to them.

'You are leaving us, Derus?' asked Mi.

She gave them a slow nod. 'Sadly I am feeling just far too old now, girls. When we leave for battle shortly, I will, if I am lucky, not be returning. So, you will need to prepare for my newest incarnation to take my place after it.'

'We understand, Derus. And as always, we will make it as easy as we can for your new self to begin. Just as we did when we aided you to understand everything about yourself.'

'I know that you all will, Mi, and for that I am grateful. And I will also thank you for your help in advance of it too. As I know that when I came out of the chamber I actually knew nothing much about anything at all - well, not until all of these older memories were placed into me.'

'Will there be any changes taking place in your new incarnation that we may need to know about in advance, Derus?' asked Dorro of her.

'Not as far as I know. My likes and dislikes of all things already known should not change. As to anything else the scientists may add to my upcoming incarnations, as in body performance wise, I really cannot say. Although as you all know, I have always asked for higher brain functions and to be both stronger and fitter each time I return - so perhaps they may have added to that at a cellular level for me. I guess you will just have to wait and see about that. But as always, in my incarnation yet to come, it will likely be the one deemed most ready between twenty and thirty life cycles. From my own memories, I know that only once did I begin with a body below twenty, and again once above thirty. For all the rest, they have typically been between those two ranges.'

'We will miss you very much too, Derus,' stated Parri. 'As we have served you for a very long time now.'

Raxx nodded. 'And I have enjoyed all of your company over these many centuries too, my girls. In fact there are many things that I *will* miss soon. But I cannot be so selfish and wish to continue forever, can I?

'As we each do, if allowed . . . can always feel when our time has been enough. And right now, I have been here for a long time. In fact I also know that I am the longest serving clone of myself to date.

'However, as a clone from the original Derus Raxx. I also feel the sadness for all the others who have awaited their chance to be used, but who have never enjoyed such. Unlike you girls. the waiting clones, as I once was one, only have a certain timeline. As a certain age is reached within the growing tubes which hold so many of us in readiness. We are then judged too old to be used; and as such our functions are turned off. With that, a tube is freed and another child clone is begun.'

The four of them almost nodded together as one unit. 'It is a shame that such a thing must be done to any of you in that building, Derus. It is also sad that they cannot be allowed to be born to simply *be* alive and lead a more normal life,' said Mi.

'I asked them about that as you may remember? If they could, they would, Mi. However, having more than one Derus Raxx all walking around at the same time. Even at so many different ages would likely only lead to various difficulties as to which one was the true one and who held command. No doubt that was what was thought at the very start of the cloning programme.

'Then again, while you are held within a growing tube you are neither alive or dead. You are simply just, a thing . . . It is like being asleep and awaiting to be awoken. For many of us, we will sleep and never awaken. Only those who have been as lucky as I have been, will be allowed to awaken fully and take up their new role in life. Which is never an easy one for any of us I can tell you! To be awakened only to learn that you are something of a planetary overseer. The one who will make literally *every* decision that concerns both the safety and welfare of a planet containing as many as eight billion here. And the safety of billions more on all of our protected planets is not in itself an easy task to comprehend when you first take over. But, just as those before me have had to do it, and I have had to do it myself. So will others in the generations which follow I am sure are likely to do also.'

6

While Raxx was in her office the following morning. She had thought it strange at first that she had slept so well in such a long time. But then she had quickly understood the underlying reason which lay behind it. Peace. That was it really. She had already began planning what would hopefully be her own end. And with her now knowing that it would soon be approaching. All of her earlier tiring worries and previous stresses of needing to do her very best each and every day for her planet would then cease. The burden from her own shoulders would be lifted and placed upon what would soon be her new self.

While she was busy working out her plans for the upcoming relief of the Gelten System, as she called it. From beneath its tyrant ruler Bork Gremplar's yoke. Rist by this time at her own instigation, was now busy showing Shrum and some of his upper level staff around various parts of Haff. Much by walking, and some further away by using a typical six-seater bubble-pod transport.

Even the sheer speed of their most ordinary transportation system had awed them. Then they had also been just as shocked as Shrum himself had initially been. By the open toilet displays on view almost everywhere. The added shock which even Shrum had not witnessed before when with him, were of couples actually not only copulating freely, but openly!

'You even allow things like *that* to be seen by anyone!' gasped one of the men.

'You mean sex?' asked Rist of him. 'From the way you said it, I suppose you do not?'

'Of course not . . . I mean - Well, it's not something that should be seen by others as openly as that! It's more of a private and personal issue surely!'

'Why not? Sex is simply an urge that either a male or female body has at various times. Anyway, as I have already told your General previously. Only those of a certain age are allowed to do so without any rebuke. Pregnancy itself is not allowed until a female has reached at least thirty cycles of age. After that it is entirely her choice if she wishes to have children or not. Some do, some don't. So the sex which you may see is simply an availability to respond to the needs of pleasure between two people, if such is wished. One can simply ask another person, who then may accept or refuse. Or their chosen partner in life if they already have one. If they refuse, then that person will just ask someone else until they do find a willing volunteer who will aid them . . .'

'Why must they wait until they are thirty?' asked Shrum, from a point Rist had made earlier about pregnancy.

Rist glanced at him as they walked. 'When they have reached thirty cycles, it means that they have spent twenty-five of those in military service to Haff. It is only then that they are allowed to decide if they wish to have children. Of course they *can* marry as young as sixteen cycles if they so wish. That itself is allowed. But to have children must always wait until they reach the full thirty cycles, so that it does not interfere with their service duties to Haff. Even our own Prime Commander had to wait this way also.'

'Again, I am sorry to question you on this, but I have to ask why they must reach thirty cycles?' said Shrum again.

'It's quite simple really, General. Our own standard training takes fifteen cycles to complete fully. For the next ten cycles after that they are all then our front line battle troops. Those women who choose to have children after that are still trained troops, only now they would be considered as reserves if needed. Even as mothers of children they can still train others, serve as guards, or aid us in other ways which have less demanding roles made upon them. Whereas those females who do not wish to have children, can rise in the ranks and attain even greater heights of command just as with the men. As we certainly do not differentiate between our men and women when it comes to leadership. They have all been trained in the exact same way over such a long time, so they would all be capable enough to do so.'

'So how are they chosen to gain higher rank?

Rist gave a smile. 'The Prime Commander herself decides which of us will rise to a higher rank, naturally! She knows everyone's capabilities better than anyone else on Haff. And if she promotes someone, we all know that this person can carry out the role being both awarded and given to them.'

'And you have how many in training, or who are already trained at any one time?' asked Shrum.

'Those who are between five and twenty cycles and are still in training cannot of course rise in rank. Simply as they are not yet classed as being fully trained so as to merit such a thing as a promotion. Fully trained troops who are of battle age? There are around four billion right now I'd say. Another two to three billion are as we call them reserves. These reserves are the women who are having families, or those who have retired with honour after serving Haff for a long time already. Yet all can easily be called upon if ever the need of Haff arose. The rest of our population are our youngest children in training and those under five cycles.'

There were many murmurs among them when he had finished. This was mainly at the sheer size of their actual army which could be called upon or used.

After their city tour, and having returned for a quick meal. Rist had then requisitioned an actual ship to carry the five of them again as well as a few more who were interested. A ship which was also just slightly bigger than the previous one for when the two of them went planet hopping. He did not include a guard to watch over them. The reason for this being, that their own ships were far more technical than any they had seen belonging to Shrum's army. So it was deduced that they would have no clue as to how to make any of them work to their own advantage anyway, or be able to escape. In fact, even if they did manage to take a ship, they would be very lucky to get past any of the orbital defence systems without the needed input code.

As told to do by Raxx, he escorted them around many of their various training sites. Either in their vastly differing climates, or where they were taking part in different levels of training. While at three of them - at one they felt almost frozen due to the snow and ice. While at the desert they felt close to being boiled alive by the intense heat. And lastly was the jungle training camps, where the actual humidity to them was intolerable and their perspiration was heavy!

Very happy to leave those, they were then taken to huge camps. Where the five or six-year-old boys and girls were only just starting out to learn the basics of their long taught martial history; and some of its training. To then being shown around another for those who were just under their teens.

The difference in just that short five or six year age gap between them, was more than evident. As here they saw various skills being taught by older trainers to many different groups. Some were learning or practising fierce hand-to-hand combat, and from what they could see, already looked quite proficient to their eyes. Their actual sex did not appear to matter that much either. As there were same sex couples struggling against each other, just as there were also boys and girls doing the very same thing.

Apparently gender roles did not really seem to play that important of a role to these people, as long as you were able to fight someone and put them to the ground was all that seemed to count. Just so long as their actual training regimen worked. They not only saw, but also heard as both punches and kicks being thrown - and were landing as well. Along with various hand, arm, leg, or body grabbing. Yet the end was always the same, as they watched bodies here and there being thrown to the ground. Then they would get up and do it all over again. Blackened eyes, bloodied faces, and well bruised bodies showed them just how tough their training was even for the smallest children.

Others who were seemingly in unarmed units, looked as if they were learning how to move as one single unit or formation. While yet more utilised something which looked like various types and sizes of occasionally shimmering clear-view shields.

Be it either in various forms and strategies of attack, or in defence. While also near to them, another large group of young people were wielding strange looking rod-like weapons in a very strange kind of ferocity at each other. Weapons which appeared to spark brightly whenever they touched. Even Shrum and his men could clearly see quite a few burn marks which had been left upon the bodies of many of these slightly older children as they were walking around - likely from some slight mistake taking place.

'Why do you allow such young children to become injured during all of this training, Low Commander?' asked one of Shrum's men to Rist.

Rist looked at him. 'Without such risk, you do not know, or will ever understand the dangers you may face in real-life combat. This is why they must learn to fight so young. As what they may think is just a game at first, in no true sense is there such a thing. It is all about training to survive, to fight, and to die for each other if need be . . .

'As you saw earlier, even without weapons you must know how to defeat an enemy. So what you begin to learn with is only where your fists and feet may be used. After that, you start to learn the techniques of unarmed combat. Then the shield for various defensive protection - and lastly the attack skills.'

'Isn't it a bit brutal though?' queried Shrum. 'I mean for even children of this age to learn such things?' He wanted to know this himself, as on his own planet you actually had to be a young adult male before you could join their army; one much older than the girl they were now watching was, and only from then on would you start to learn.

'Mersh!' he called out.

At which point a naked young girl backed away slightly from her young male opponent. Saluted him with her charged weapon before switching it off, and then walked over to their group.

She stood at full attention, saluted Rist with her free hand while making a fist and then placed it against her chest. Then she gave a small bow of her head. 'Yes Low Commander?'

As the girl had approached, Shrum and his group only saw what looked to them to be more like that of an thin scrawny child's body. Although when she came to stand in front of Rist their thinking was soon altered. While most of the young girls on their own planets looked plumper, or chubbier even from doing far less energetic things. This young girl before them was already honed down by her few years of training.

Training which was offering stringy and resilient muscles to her build. There did not appear to be an ounce of fat upon her anywhere at all. In fact the showing lined muscle tone to her abdomen itself was probably better than any of their own were right now. While the remnants of old cuts, burns and scars upon a few parts of her bare young body could be plainly seen. Whereas bruises both new and old, and of differing hued shades of purple, black, blue and yellow. Showed them just how hard the training for her still was, even now. Or that it was growing even higher in intensity as she got older. These marks were situated on many other places upon her in a similar way.

'Mersh . . . what is the point of all of this which you do here?' he asked her.

Mersh thought he was testing her so she now recited from what she had herself been told, 'We train to live - just as we train to die, Low Commander . . . what more is there to our life for us to know. If our leaders say that we will fight and live, or die, then that is the way that it must be. We are Haffian, and so this is who we are and what we are. If told to attack we will attack, no matter what odds may be against us. If told to retreat then it means the same, except to live to fight for Haff once again. Only *surrender* is not allowed!' she stated.

'And for the Prime Commander?' he asked her.

They saw her small and barely breasted chest puff out almost proudly. Sure that something close to tears were now showing in her eyes filled with adulation. 'Ohhh, for our beloved, Prime Commander ... simply to serve her is everything - and my own death for her would be an honour!'

'When?' Shrum almost gasped.

'Right now if that was her wish, Sir! Even though I am not even half-way through my training right now. We here, and those at the other training camps all know that to die for our Prime Commander is all that we could ever want or wish to attain in life - A warriors death!'

Rist himself gave a small smile, as he knew what would happen to what he next said.

'Life or Death, Mersh, eh?'

He was expecting what came next, while neither Shrum or any man there in his group did. As the young girls head tilted back on her neck.

'Life or Death!' Mersh literally screamed as loud as she could in her own high pitched voice.

On the training field, no matter what they were all doing. All of them now stood there and screamed back, *'LIFE OR DEATH!'* at her own initial call. Over eighty thousand voices at this one training ground alone had roared these three base words out. Shrum and his men were almost deafened by it. And the chill which it gave to them sent shivers that ran up and down their spines like an electrical charge. It was also quite a new thing to them to hear such a thing. Yet those here were merely just youngsters, apart from their older trainers. Where even *they* appeared to hold such a high basic devotion to their leader already.

So what the adult fighters would be like after their even longer, possibly even more brutal training regime, were likely to be ten times worse. Amazingly enough, even further away from where their call had originated. More similar shouts could be heard from camps further away from them. To those who had heard their battle cry and were able to respond to it in the same way.

'Brainwashed . . . they're all brainwashed!' stated one of his men, who was still stunned by the almost sheer animal ferocity of their shouts.

'And what is *your* own answer to that, young Mersh? Are you all brainwashed as this man said?'

'We are Haff and Haff is us, Low Commander. No matter where we may be, we are *Haff*!'

'But what does that actually *mean*?' asked Shrum, now feeling quite lost.

'Haff is our world. We live, and we die for Haff. Our life cycles flow with Haff. So Haff must always survive!' she told him openly and quite frankly.

'I *still* don't understand, Octavus,' said Shrum, but then neither did any of his group.

Rist just smiled down at her. 'Mersh . . . if you were in a battle at any time, and let us say that only a hundred of your own unit were left alive. And then any low commander like myself or of a lower rank than I am. Then called out to you and said for you all to attack this or that group of thousands of enemies. What would you then do?'

'Why, we would attack of course. And we would try our very hardest to kill as many of them as we could before we died ourselves, Low Commander. A given order *must* be obeyed from *any* Commander no matter what may happen to any of us.'

'A suicide attack?'

'If that is what is needed then we of course would obey such a command. But, none of us can ever really know what the full plans of any battle that our Prime Commander may have designed are. Our attack may even be only a feint to place others of our army into a better position at the same time. So as we all fight, *and die*. Another unit or section may then be sent to exactly the right place in order to attack the enemy from yet another direction.

'With the Prime Commander handling our battle tactics, some battles can be all about misdirecting an enemy at the most opportune time. So if our few lives are to be sacrificed so that our beloved Haff will win a major battle; and in turn maybe save many more of our own people. Then that is what our training is all about, Sir. We live to fight together, just as we live to die together too.'

Rist now hid a smile as he asked of Shrum's own group. 'Would one of you perhaps like to care to test yourself against young Mersh here?'

The young girl herself even gasped.

'What?' he asked of her.

'But surely none of them have had any training in using the *Grem*, Low Commander . . . it could be much too dangerous for them to attempt it.'

'What's a Grem?' asked Shrum.

''What young Mersh here holds in her hand, General. It is one of our basic weapons with a dual purpose use. Both as an attack lance, and also as a defensive shield.'

'I'll try,' said one of Shrum's own stocky battle commanders. 'I only hope I won't injure this young girl during it though.'

'What do you say to that, young Mersh?'

'If he is willing, then by your order I will offer myself as a fighting partner, Low Commander. But pain is survival, and survival is life.' she stated curiously. Which of course only caused Shrum to seek an explanation from Rist.

Rist smiled. 'To our people, training is learning, General. Without any chance of an injury taking place you cannot learn fully. How can you ever conquer the feeling of fear over something which cannot harm you? So our training allows for this.'

'What setting should we use, Low Commander?' she asked.

'As . . . ' he looked at the man questioningly.

'Borth, Remplar of General Shrum's army.'

Neither Rist or Mersh had any idea as to what a Remplar was. But each deduced that it could only be a position he held beneath Shrum.

Rist gave a nod. 'As Borth here has never used a Grem before, we will only use the lowest setting possible on them, Mersh.'

He then called to the young boy who she had been training with to come over. 'Tryn, we need to borrow your Grem for a moment for young Mersh's opponent.'

The young boy walked over, saluted and bowed. 'Is it a death fight, Low Commander? As even I would hesitate to go up against Mersh in a death fight!' he announced openly.

'No Tryn. I am just trying to show the General here how well you have already been trained so far. So it will only be a practise fight at the Grem's lowest level setting.'

The young boy handed it over to Rist, who then passed it over to Borth. Who was then indeed very surprised at its actual weight due to the way all the youngsters had been using them. In Haff terms, just as in old Earth terms. It carried the weight of almost ten pounds.

Rist passed it to him and showed him its controls. 'Try and keep it in one hand only, your best hand. This button here when pressed will activate the Grem at level one. Hold that press until you hear a beep which means that this setting is locked in. This other button activates the shielding option. Now this you must understand, you cannot use both of the weapons options at the same time. It is either a shield for defence, or an attack weapon.

'This button here takes the charge from the Grem and alters it into a shield. If you press that same button again, then the shield disappears and it is ready to be used in attack mode right away. Try them out.'

Borth pressed and held the button stated until it beeped. Yet although he couldn't actually see anything happening around the weapon itself to show that it was working. By the tingling sensation running up through his arm he now assumed that it was.

'Show Borth the first phase training wield of a Grem if you would please, Mersh. From attack, to defence, then back to attack again.''

Borth now watched her keenly, to observe how this young girl handled this weapon. He saw her finger depress a button and then the same beep. He barely saw what took place over the next minute or so, as Mersh moved so fast.

Her one hand twirled and spun the weapon, in various positions until it slapped into her other hand as well. That was where a buzz took place and a small energy field radiated around the actual weapon. Yet it was still being twirled and spun though, but not only in front of her. As she also had it spinning at her sides and behind her as well. And then finally, and with almost a flourish, the shield disappeared and with a few more spins in front of her. It came to a sudden stop as she stood one of its ends on the ground before her. Borth then noted that her chest barely moved at all. That after all of that, she was not even breathing hard.

'You can try to do some of the actions that she just used there before actually switching it on if you wish, Borth. It will also be safer for you while its off, too.' He was informed by Rist.

Borth did so . . . well, at least he tried to do that.

'What's it like Borth?' queried Shrum.

'They are a little heavier than our Gan war clubs are, General.'

'Your have war clubs which are similar weapons of attack and defence like ours are, too?' asked Rist.

'No,' said Borth as he then attempted to do some two-handed moves with it. 'Our clubs are thinner, lighter, made of metal and with a point at one end, that's all. They have no inner power source as this weapon does.'

With his movements finished, he looked at Rist. 'What now?'

'Now you can have a low level practise fight with Mersh if you feel comfortable enough with it.'

'It feels similar to our war clubs. But our own do not have all these buttons, or the heavier weight of these.'

'Low Commander . . . '

'Yes, Mersh?'

'What if even our lowest setting could be fatal to Borth? Do we know his physiology well enough to be sure, as I would not wish to injure him unknowingly.'

'Why,' asked her opponent, 'what settings do you use now?'

'Most of us who train here are now at the level five setting.'

'So what's setting one?'

'Setting one is what we first use when we are much younger children after being shown the rudiments of Grem handling by a trainer.'

'Well how bad could setting one be?'

Mersh charged her own weapon up again. When it gave a beep, she then tapped it against her shoulder. As it bounced back from her. Shrum and his officers saw that even at that lowest setting on it, it had left a red weal on her skin.

'And that did not hurt you?'

Mersh smiled. 'When I was only five cycles of age it was very painful - at first. After a while my body became used to its charge far better. It did the same as we all progressed from level one upto where we are now - which is level five.'

'And level five is what?' he asked with some caution.

Mersh pointed at the ribs on her left side. 'This was where Tryn caught me with one of his attacks three days ago.' she told him. While all he could see was a quite large area of raw and discoloured skin, although by now it was only a fading red mass turning to yellow with some black patches.

Borth selected level one as she had done on his own weapon, and then tapped it against his own shoulder. He grimaced and emitted a loud gasp at the actual pain which it inflicted on him. He again looked down at the small girl before him with new eyes and higher esteem. As she had not even noticed her burn or the pain which it had inflicted.

'And the five that she is on now?'

'I would not advise it, Borth,' stated Rist quickly. 'Mersh and the others have been trained to accept the pain which comes with each of the rising levels. Whereas you have not.'

'I'd still like to try, just to see what the difference is between one and five.'

'Very well then, but you cannot hold us accountable for what may happen from it.' He looked at Shrum for assurance of this.

Who nodded his head before speaking. 'If Borth wishes to test himself against that higher setting - then no blame will be placed upon any of you. Agreed, Borth?'

'Of course, General.'

Rist nodded at him. 'Very well then, but you cannot do it the same way to yourself on that setting - as it could be too dangerous for you.'

'In what way?'

'You will soon see *why* if you wish to carry on?'

Borth did, so Rist asked him for the weapon. Borth handed it to him, and watched as his finger went to another button further up the row. Where even as Rist activated it, the sound which came from the weapon was far louder to hear, almost menacing really.

Rist gave a low sigh. 'Are you prepared? And are you still sure that you wish to do this?'

Borth gave a quick nod and tensed his body for whatever was coming.

'Do not tense yourself, as it will hurt you far less if you stay loose and relaxed. That is how we teach them.'

At such words as these, Borth's former tenseness turned into more of a worried anxiety instead. He saw Rist's arm as it moved slowly towards him. Just as he saw the weapon held in his hand being aimed carefully at his heavily muscled shoulder.

There was a highly charged flash as it touched his bare skin.

'By the Gods of Aldur!' exclaimed Shrum loudly in shock. As he watched the heavy body of Borth being thrown back a good ten feet through the air to lie inert on the ground. 'Did you change the setting to an even higher one, Octavus?' he queried of him suspiciously.

'No, it's still only at five as I said.'

'But that's . . . I cannot even find the words!'

'Violent?'

'Yes! Yes! That is just what I was thinking!!'

'Which is why I warned him beforehand. Five is halfway to its maximum, so is already dangerous.'

'And you, Octavus? Does it also affect *you* like this?' he asked, as he made a gesture to Borth where he lay stunned upon the ground. Where he was also now being attended to by two of his men.

'Only at the beginning of training at that level. As Mersh told you, your body learns to accept it over time until a kind of resistance is formed.'

'You mean you do not feel the pain from it?'

'Of course we do. You *learn* though pain! What we do not do after a while is become unconscious from it. The children here will at the start, and they can be thrown a good twenty feet. But until their mind and body have had enough hits at this level. They cannot as such achieve a point of resistance to it. Yes, they will still be thrown from it for a while, but no longer will they be left unable to fight.'

'And you can manage this five yourself?' asked a member of Shrum's group.

Rist showed his teeth. 'As a *fully* trained warrior of Haff, I have reached the death levels.'

'What?'

'Death levels are from eight to ten. But you must overcome and survive level ten to become a warrior of Haff.'

'What do you mean by death levels, exactly?'

'The name tells you what it is really. If set from eight to ten against an enemy - it will simply make their heart stop and kill them instantly. Their bodies have not been trained over the same ten or fifteen year period as we have to be able to survive such an event as that, you see. Listen ... '

Shrum and the others did so as Rist then notched it all the way upto ten. And if level five had sounded bad; level ten with an attributed deep ear bothering buzz sounded not only intense but wicked.

They all then watched open mouthed as Rist performed a routine somewhat similar to the young girls earlier. Only now it was more of a blur as it whipped all around his body. Only ceasing in movement whenever it became a shield. Changing from a weapon of frightening attack, to that of a shield again and again. Only now though, as with the charge set so high. The shield it emitted was far larger than before. It had became slightly taller in height than Rist himself. While also widening into a concave shape which surrounded all of his frontal body area. Only at his back did there still remain an opening.

Even Mersh and Tryn were just as enthralled at Rist's lengthy yet superlative display, as were Shrum and his men. This was because Rist was also a Master of the Grem, and it showed. With a final dazzling whirl, the end of the Grem thudded into the ground and the insane sounding buzzing from it now died away. He then reset it back to five level and tapped it again his own shoulder. He gave a low grunt as it flashed upon touching his own bare skin. But he did not move a muscle, nor was he thrown by its power. This was only since his own training had previously surpassed it by a further five settings. It's powerful charge had of course left its heavy mark upon him. Yet this appeared to be borne without worry or any further thought.

'I heard you earlier mention an Aldur, General. Is that one of your deities where you are from?'

'One of many,' he offered with a chuckle. 'We have many God's of which our people pray too for various things. And your people?'

'A very long time ago in our past. Even before we all came here to this system, so it has been said. But in our case, the various God's and religions that were followed sometimes brought about chaos and wars. I think that there finally came a time in our own past when it was decreed that for us, as a people. These things were causing far more trouble to us than benefitting us. And so eventually it managed to change into a non-religious planet. Instead of us having all of the different religious elements and sects who were worshipped. It became only about the people living on the planet itself. Where without all of the hatred and feuds between them, the end of all religion allowed us to finally become that of one people all working together. It was also how we achieved so much prior to our coming here to settle upon these new worlds. What I mean to say is, that now, its more about the people we *are* than of any God's or such.'

Upon finally managing to get back to his feet, Borth shook his dazed head back and forth. After a few minutes, he walked back towards their large group.

'Are you all right now? How are you feeling?' asked Rist.

'Still a little shaken. I just did not expect the weapon to have such a kick to it!'

Shrum gave a laugh. 'While you were lying over there having a rest, Borth. You should have seen what level ten on it looked like! You can only thank Aldur that you did not ask Octavus to try that one upon you while it was set at *that* level!'

Borth returned a small grin at Shrum's laugh. 'I have no wish to test it again, even at level five, General!'

Shrum laughed again at his officers reply. Then asked, 'Do you still wish to continue against this young girl, Borth? Or has it changed your mind now?'

His smile was still in place as he answered, 'Well, at level one I did not mind *too* much, General. Even if the unexpected touch from it did sting a little. But, since it is nowhere as near as bad as that of level five I am still willing to try it.'

Shrum nodded, 'Then may the Great Aldur protect you!'

'Are you ready?' Borth asked of the young girl in front of him.

'I do not know, Sir.' She looked to Rist for more information. 'What is your order, Low Commander? Am I to defend, attack, or both?'

Rist then looked to Borth. 'What say you, Borth? In which way would you prefer young Mersh here to act?'

Borth's own heavy shoulders gave a shrug. 'To fight fairly against any opponent I would say that all things must be used equally surely? It would not be fair if one is only attacking and one defending.'

'Both ways it is then, Mersh.'

'Very well, Low Commander. And for how long should this last?'

'I would say until Borth himself tells us that he's seen enough. Is that satisfactory to you both?' He looked at each as they both gave him a nod of consent.

'In which case, you may charge your weapons ready at level one again.'

Mersh still had one thought though, so quickly asked as she activated her own weapon. 'Am I also allowed to hit him with my Grem, Low Commander? Or not?'

To which Borth answered even before Rist could. 'Well, I'll be trying to hit *you* little one. So you must also try and hit me as well, too!'

Mersh gave a nod just as Rist said, 'Prepare!' Mersh then gave him one of her salutes, while Borth bowed his head to her in a nod.

'Battle!' Rist called out.

∞

Borth was quickly lost. As before him the young girl was quickly spinning her own Grem like a flail in front of her. To the left, to the right, again and again. And then he felt the sudden impact of it on a bicep along with its sharp burn.

'By the---- . . .' was about all he managed to say before it happened again on yet another part of his body, his ribcage. And still the tiny young girl was spinning her weapon in front of her as if born to it. Even now he could never wield his own gan club in such a way as she was doing it with this one, he thought. As yet another burn appeared upon his opposite bicep.

Unhappy with his failure so far, he swung his Grem like a normal club at her. Mersh had already seen the attack coming and her spinning ceased instantly at Borth's attack to only be met by a raised shield. At which point as his Grem rebounded from it, and he took a further burn upon one of his thick thighs as she changed her weapon over instantly.

'Wait!' he called out to her.

Mersh stepped back, although still in a ready pose.

'Is there a problem, Borth?' asked Rist hiding a smile.

'Indeed there is . . . How can she stop spinning it so quickly *and* find its shield button for when I made my attack on her?'

Rist emitted one of his chuckles while looking upwards. As it had just began to rain steadily now. 'Have I not already told you that we start our early training regime at only five cycles of age? This is what our long cycles of training *are* there for, Borth. We have to become at one with any of our weapons. In darkness or light, we must know where everything is upon them. At this stage in her life, and area of her training, Mersh has already been taught the cyclone. Which is the named movement by spinning the Grem around you - as you saw her do. A tactic which we use to disorient any enemy so they do not know what will occur next. Due to this, it also means that she is also now at one with her weapon. She can alter from attack to defence within an instant now.'

Borth's shook his head. 'I cannot really win, can I?'

'You could have used your own shield to prevent her from hitting you each time.'

'I would have done that. But then I'd have had to take my eyes off her to find where the shield butt---- Ahhhh . . .' he murmured as he finally saw the logic.

Rist gave him a nod. 'Now you are understanding why they have to train *so much* perhaps?'

'Yes. Indeed I can now! While I am lost seeking the right button. Even if it was a weapon which had been captured upon a battleground. She already knows where it is from long use and training.'

'Exactly so. I think even against one of our seven cycle children you would have struggled in the same way. As by that time, they are also becoming at one with the Grem.'

Borth sighed and nodded, even as the rivulets of falling rain began to run off all their bodies. He looked down at the young girl and bowed low from the waist to her. 'I concede to your skill with this weapon, little one. You have surely bested me with it far too easily! I can see you becoming a much feared warrior indeed!'

'Thank you, Sir,' Mersh responded by offering him a salute of her own in return as she disabled her weapon. Borth handed his over to Rist, who switched that one off as well before handing it back over to Tryn.

'Thank you for your time, Mersh, and you Tryn. You may both now carry on with your own training schedule once again.' The young girl and boy both saluted and bowed to him once more before returning to where they had been standing originally to continue with their practise.

As Rist led them away towards the waiting ship. An enormous crash of lightning, followed only moments later by the bass rumble of thunder took place. At which point, the falling rain became a sudden torrent which pelted heavily upon all their bare skins. Some of them turned around, and all they saw was that the training continued; even in that heavier downpour from above. As they all began to walk again, Rist could hear the commotion begin from behind him as they talked between themselves. Basically amazed at what they had just heard and seen here. And of course, of just what kind of army those from this planet could wield in force - especially if even their young children were already like this. All who were seemingly ready to offer their own lives if asked already.

Rist shook his head. How could the Prime Commander have possibly known what would take place here? He could only shake his head again. No doubt that was why she *was* their one and only Prime Commander, and all others like he himself were not he finally decided. Then offered a nod to himself as if to confirm those same thoughts.

∞

Within the large office of Derus Raxx, her desk was littered with files and maps. More would then come via her aides, just as she would then speak to them, maybe even hand some of the earlier ones back.

Her major-domo Morg then entered. 'Are sure you want to see a list of *every* section, Prime Commander?'

Standing behind her desk moving papers around, Raxx simply looked up at him.

'Yes. I need to know the exact status of all sections in our legions at the moment. I need to know which of them are at full strength. Even to how many may be missing in each through illness or injury. You should already know this, Morg. That when I begin to plan I need every fact and figure possible at my disposal.'

'It will be as you wish,' he responded, then left. As now he would have to get all of those outside of her office making sure that every single piece of information about to be brought in was indeed complete and error free.

Raxx continued to shuffle the papers around which were there on her desk. Some of which only had small notations, while others were far more detailed about the planets in the Gelten system. Others were almost like small hand drawn maps of what was placed where. All this had been done by the troops who she'd had brought up to question. She'd questioned quite a lot of them in fact. In an attempt to reach an accurate assessment of what would be required for a full scale invasion of their system to take place.

∞

When Shrum and his staff were safely back inside the building which housed all of them. Rist returned back to Raxx once more as per her own instructions to him.

'Well, Octavus, how did it go?' she asked of him.

'Just as you said it would, Prime Commander. Even to one of them being willing to take on one of the children with a Grem. Mersh it was. Although on the way through the city I must tell you that they were all shocked to see some of our people who were having sex.'

Raxx's head nodded. I've heard good things about her for a while, Octavus. In time, she may reach a very high position - if she can keep it up that long!' she replied to him. Then her mind returned to his earlier point. 'Shocked . . . but why?'

'Apparently in their way of thinking, sex is something which *their* people do in comparative seclusion with each other. To me, it felt as if they were simply scared or worried about something taking place as openly as that on their world.'

'How strange . . . ' Raxx murmured. 'Do you think that their populations must then be a far more introverted one than we originally thought?'

'That's what it sounded like to me, Prime Commander. In fact, even his seeing some of our people seeing to their toilet needs outside were just as surprising to me too.'

'What a strange world they must come from, Octavus,' Raxx added. 'Where the sight of a naked body, as well as the ordinary needs of people are so frightening to them.'

'Well to be fair, Prime Commander only a few of our own systems planets use the same methods as we do. Although none are the same when it comes to our own lack of clothing or sex at any time you feel an urge. While many others still *do* use places or buildings with their required toileting facilities hidden away from one another's actual view.'

She nodded. 'Indeed. But I have also felt that they are simply not as enlightened to the sight of unclothed bodies. Well, at least not in the way in which we have become accustomed to. In the privacy of ones home we deem such a thing as using a hidden toilet as being quite acceptable, Octavus. However, when you could be quite a long way from your home, then the options are far more limited I would think. Just imagine if you start to feel the need to use one of those places - yet the nearest one to you is quite a good way off. What on earth do they do then, I can but wonder?'

'I simply have no idea. I have always just been pleased that if *I* ever felt the urge or need to go. That there has never been a shortage of places where we can go to do so! Especially more so now due to my age since it is also harder to control.' he remarked with a grin.

'As I said. Strange!' Raxx commented.

She looked up at him for a brief moment. 'For how long have we now known each other, Octavus?'

He had to think about that. 'I first knew *of you* when I was but five cycles of age, Prime Commander. Which was when I was sent off to train as a child. But I wouldn't say that I'd actually *known* you until I came to see you. And that was only when you first promoted me many years later. So, perhaps for about forty cycles now all told?' he answered in a querying tone.

Raxx gave a nod. 'Quite long enough then, Octavus. As you likely already know, I have now reached three hundred and thirty-six cycles of life.'

'And long may you continue to do so!'

Raxx gave a smile at him. 'The loyalty of which you all show me never fails to move me, Octavus. However, there always comes a time to those like myself when we know we are reaching a certain age. An age when we each know that it is time to allow new flesh to take over from the old.'

'No - Please!'

'No? Octavus . . . I am ancient now. And also feeling far too old to carry out the burden of all of these duties for very much longer. So, and this is for your ears alone. At the coming invasion ahead my own life will finally cease!'

'But . . . ' was all he managed to exclaim, before she carried on.

'Due to this, and because of how long I have know you for, Octavus. You may call me Derus when we are alone and talking like this.'

His head hung low. Unhappy at the thought of not only being told this - but also that he now knew when it was going to happen.

'You do not seem pleased about my decision, Octavus?' she asked him.

'Why must you do this, Prime Commander? When you know we all need you so much.'

'Derus.'

'Derus . . .' he said finally, at which she again smiled at him.

'Simply because I am almost three hundred cycles older than you, Octavus. If you yourself are ever feeling old, tired, or perhaps even worn out. How do you think my mind and body feel to me right now?

'I not only knew your father and your grandfather, but also your great, and great-great grandfather in my time. I am just tired, Octavus. Tired and worn out by all the constant demands which have been placed upon me ever since the first day I came out of the cryo-cell.

'My body needs to rest. My mind needs to finally be allowed to switch-off! And so - I will die. In battle I hope as we all do. As you already know, the nearest medic to me will save my consciousness for my successor anyway. Any of my final thoughts right up until my last breath - or when my mind has ceased to function as a whole.

'These memories will be brought home and placed into my new self. Who as we know, will be a young version of me yet again. Just as my last thoughts once induced will help her to become aware of how my own death took place. And of all of her own tasks that will lie ahead. Everything that I already know, and knew. Along with those who went before me in the same way will be placed within her for her to use if ever she needs to and if she sees fit. But I have to leave, Octavus. I cannot continue to do this much longer anyway. As my body, even with its genetic engineering still only has a certain lifespan. And I'd rather go out in my own way than become a sad and old looking shambling invalid.'

Even with his lowered head, she could see the tears which were leaking from his eyes at what he was hearing.

'Do not cry for me, Octavus, nor should any of my loyal and brave warriors need to mourn me either. In my own lifetime, even though I thought I would not. I myself have shed untold countless tears upon those who became very close to me also. But who also eventually died of old age, or otherwise. So please, try and remember me as I was when you first saw me, if you can do so. As I certainly looked a hell of a lot better then than I do now, didn't I?'

At which point she laughed openly. 'Which wouldn't be hard would it . . . ? Look at me, Octavus . . . look, and see me - for *me* as I really am right now!'

As he looked at her, she added, 'I am slowly wearing away now, both without and within. I barely have any appetite at all now these days. Which is likely why I have become so thin. So do not cry for me, my dear old friend. I have already lived a long and blessed life. One which has been far longer than most peoples we know can enjoy. Which is why I know that my time has arrived.

'Your new Prime Commander to come will have all the benefits of youth which I once had, and thought so little of at the time. The oh so wonderful images of being a good looking young woman again. Having the stamina and agility of youth. Being able to test her skills against some of our finest warriors, as I also once used to enjoy. To tuck into some of the wonderfully sublime meals which my maids can make for her, without having to say no as I must do now.

'Oh, and to be able to walk quickly or to run again! Octavus. You have no idea how much my being unable to do just those two small things has angered me for so many decades. So, as I say, do not mourn me when I do go. Simply appreciate the new me that will emerge from the cryo-cell and begin her work anew for those of you upon our dearest Haff.'

Rist wiped his eyes on his bare arm. Consoling himself that what she was telling him, was her being completely honest with him. Yes, even he had felt as if his older years were catching up with him and slowing him down now. As even for him, his own time for retirement was already beckoning even faster.

But for her . . . he only just managed to hold back the beginning of new tears starting. When he thought of everything which she had had to go through for them all for so long. Derus . . . he was both proud and honoured that she had even allowed him such a gift as being able to call her by name. Even if it may not be for very long. With his emotions now held in check, she began to discuss with him the far more important events which would soon come to pass.

∞

Shrum and his men were by now gathered around one of the long uniform metallic tables which had been placed inside the building for them all. Still talking while they ate a meal after their long trip around the planet with Rist.

'What do *you* think, General?' asked one of his subordinates.

He looked up to see all of their heads were now raised, all waiting to hear his own thoughts.

He gave a shrug firstly. 'I don't really know whether to say that our system is doomed. Or whether it's going to be a very lucky one soon,' he answered.

'In what way?' asked one of his commanders.

'Well, we have all now seen the far higher technology they have to use over our own. Those bubble-pod things for either ground or low flight travelling. The actual cleanliness of everything. And as for their ships . . . !' he shook his head. 'Our own are like children's toys compared to theirs! Perhaps when it is over, even the remnants of our own army will be allowed to train or work along with theirs?'

Their heads were nodding in agreement.

'But I have also seen far more than any of you have. When Rist took me to some of their planets to look for myself after we were captured. Their agriculture is staggering to see, as are the machines which they use to both cultivate and harvest with. It was just the same with their planets for manufacturing and for mining. Not to mention that they can make what they call androids. Those life-like looking beings which are no more than electronics and servo's, machinery and circuits . . . although very highly developed ones!'

'It is their army which bothered me the most.'

'And so it should! As they are far more than just an army, Telleg - they are a force!' Shrum stated quietly. 'We all saw how well-trained even their young children were. Something that even Borth here can now attest to! As well as seeing the display which Octavus himself gave us. So even I cannot imagine what the older adults would be like when it came to fighting them.'

'Well, they must be tough from what you said about those two planets where our commanders chose to fight. I mean from our own losses on them compared to theirs.'

Shrum gave a slow nod. He paused for a moment while looking around at his men, before saying, 'I was just thinking there about what these *children* of theirs would be like to fight - never mind their parents! No fear of death, in fact ready to die by someone's order instantly if necessary. And even you now know just how good *they* are now, Borth.'

The man mentioned nodded back. 'Truly even at her age she is definitely a warrior child, General. The weapon I used surprised me also.

It was a lot heavier than I imagined it would be from our watching both the boy child and she practising with each other. So now I also know where they would get a lot of their actual fitness and strength from too!'

7

In an enormous large vaulted room in a small palace set in one of the large Haffian cities known as Erin. The five Lords of Haff were sat around a large smoothly polished table of Bluemarium stone in a rare kind of secrecy together. Their host, who was pouring out more wine from a container into their glasses was Lord Dacras of Erin. The other noted attendees there were Lord Arne of Bollus, Lord Budle of Ceday, Lord Flent of Golgos and Lord Wynoc of Humme. There were no servants as always in place to see to any of their needs. Only as this was another of their secret meetings, and they wished it to remain so.

Those who had never been present, or asked to be at any of their meetings were the Lady Mell of Nerv, Lady Winsher of Sereth, and Lady Yu of Tonnis. And the reason none of these women were ever present. Was simply due to the fact that the five lords knew of their total loyalty to the Prime Commander. These women were now either growing old, widowed, or as yet unmarried which was why they held the title. What they all may have thought about the Garen Royal Family mattered very little. As just like themselves, all of them also had very little power to control anything at all.

These lords had known for a very long time indeed of where the power of Haff actually lay. Not in the hands of the ruling classes, in the way they thought it should have been right from the very start. But in the hands of a woman who it appeared would never apparently *ever* lose this total control over all their lives. Yes, these five were all jealous men. Envious of the utter loyalty and devotion laid upon her . . . Loyalty which they thought would have been best served for they themselves and to their families before them.

Even if their own families from the many millennia which had passed had also been loyal to her as well. These five men were completely different in their hearts. They were hungry for power; in the very same way that Bork Gremplar was. All were now in their mid-forty life cycles, apart from Flent who was closer to fifty of them. Even they as Haffian's had had to do their military training just like everyone else. Something which they of course had thought was beneath them even then. Were *they* not of a different class on Haff? And if so, why did they have to waste so many countless life cycles of their own when there were so many others lower to them who more than happy enough to do it.

As with all people of such nature. This long duty to be done only infuriated each of them more. It had made no difference that even their own ancestors. Their fathers, mothers, brothers and sisters. As well as all those before them had all had to do the very same training too. As it had always long since been the Haffian way.

In the last decade however, they had all watched as Raxx's own growing age began to take its toll upon her. They were finally setting out on a coup to take this power from her. Their own personal wants, needs, and ideologies imagining what having such power could both offer and bring. They had imagined that they could rule their planet far better than this old woman who would never seem to die, ever could. Although, in each of their own hearts, they knew that what they wanted most was not for the benefit of their people - it was for themselves.

The one actual thing which none of them ever considered though. Was that when more than one greedy person was in charge, things could quickly change. It would just be like harking back to those ancient long ago days. When one ruler soon wanted much more . . . Then the rivalries would begin and possible civil war would break out.

Raxx herself had been chosen by their people to command them over and over again through many lifetimes. The one person they had felt would always do what was best for Haff to ensure their own safety and standards. This was the thing which they did not truly understand. Raxx herself had never actually wanted it. But due in no small means to her very able talents, was deemed the only one capable of doing it. For this reason alone it was a one woman show. She did not want it, and would happily step away from this extreme hold of power if the people asked for it. The five lords were quite the opposite. As to them, power itself was the be all and end all of what their own dreams were made of.

They were now purely and simply fed up of being her puppets to do with as she willed. Open this or that new building. Present these awards. Appear publicly whenever any upcoming event was due. They *were* the Lords of Haff . . . not irresponsible children who needed to be told what they should be doing all the time. What they all wanted was the power and wealth which should by rightly be due to them with having such family names.

'That old bitch has to die!' stated the first speaker.

'Can it work though?' asked Lord Wynoc of the speaker. 'Can we actually do this without being found out?'

'Only if we plan it well. Very well indeed ' said Lord Arne. 'She hasn't the strength she once used to have now.'

'Perhaps not,' stated Lord Flent, the eldest Lord there. 'Though we do also have to remember that she was a supreme master of all weapons, including even that of unarmed combat!'

'True,' said Lord Arne. 'However, she does not carry any weapons around with her. And her actual age now has also caused her to become far slower and infirm in her movements. You only have to watch her move to see that.'

'Again, what you speak is true, Lord Arne. She does indeed look very frail, and even looks all of every one of her three hundred and thirty plus cycles now. But to capture her where it would not be seen happening by anyone? . . . That will *not* be an easy task to manage, of that I can assure you! Even if the actual dispatching of her would be.'

'True, Lord Flent. The only places available for us to do this is her office - which as we know, would have no merit of success at all due to the many staff working there around her. Or when she is travelling to and from her office in her pod. She is alone almost every time like that. So I am saying that this is our most optimum chance of taking her.'

'And what of the Garen's? Without her, we know that *they* would be the first in line to assume command.' queried Lord Budle, who had remained silent up to now.

Arne just smiled at him. 'The Garen's will relinquish that same power to us. One way or another . . .'

'All of them as well?'

'If we must, then we must!' answered Arne. 'We are not doing this only so that those useless toadying Garen's of hers can simply take for themselves what we have made available. If we do what we have to do, then they will either have to pass over this power to us - or we'll just take it anyway when they are gone!'

'And if we fail with our capture of Raxx? Or, if we miss our chance and she dies only to come back again as a younger Raxx.'

'In which case we will likely have failed to gain our reward within our own lifetime, Lord Budle.'

'I am only worried about one thing myself,' said Lord Wynoc to them.

'Which is?' asked Arne.

'That if we do fail in our capture attempt of her, and she then knows that it was us . . . ?'

'You may have no doubt, Lord Wynoc. That if we do fail we will certainly pay for it! If she does not hesitate to attack entire *planets* who cause problems - then what do you imagine she will do to us few for trying to kill her, eh?'

'I am only wondering just how far her own retribution against us could fall, Lord Arne?'

'Meaning?'

'When it come to our planet, or the people here on it. We already know that Raxx has no kinder feelings for any off-world planet, system, or society who may want to attack us. So what I *am* now saying to you is this. That in a way, we are not only attacking Raxx herself, but also our own planet as well by doing this.'

'I am still not getting your meaning, Lord Wynoc? If you are actually making one right now, that is?'

'All that I am trying to say, Lord Arne. Is what the actual return repercussions could be in full if we do fail. Perhaps executing all of us for treason is what *we* would expect if we do in fact fail . . . But, and here is also where I place a very heavy, *but,* now . . . what if Raxx's own response is even greater! What if she not only executes us - but all those within our entire family lines for the same link to possible treason! If that takes place, then each of our own long family lineage will suddenly cease to exist.'

A lengthening silence then went all around the table at this unexpected query. As it was not something which any of them had even thought about, nor even wished to really dwell upon.

'She wouldn't do that. Would she?' muttered a shocked Budle. Now already imagining his wife, children, as well as any and all relations of his being put to death for their planned actions.

Arne gave a shrug. 'If we were in charge, what would we ourselves do if such an event took place? he replied. 'It would be hard for me to say. Only as we do not really know just how vindictive Raxx could be to our families in response to our own personal plans. She could place similar blame upon all of them just as she would us. As she may think they all knew of our plans to take over. So maybe we had better *not* fail in our attempt, eh . . . ?'

∞

As their plans to take her life were being made. Raxx still stood before her desk sifting through the masses of information upon it. She knew as always that it was up to her to plan any required tactics with her typical finesse. Yet she was feeling far more tired than she should be right now. All of this work only seemed to exhaust her frail body more and more as her cycles of life continued. Yes, she thought sadly, it is definitely time for me to go . . .

She had already dispatched half a legion to the planet Styros 5 in the Kinos system a few days ago. This was another planet which had lived under their protection for a very long time now. It lay a good fifty light years away from Haff.

They were a race of strange looking beings the Styrosians. Quite small in stature with a green hue to their skin and with rather a bulging eyed look. Although a population who had happily accepted such an arrangement after their android scout, and then one of their android envoys had visited their planet. They had only recently sent a message to her requesting some kind of military presence being nearby while they held trade and treaty discussions with the Macranians, a former enemy of theirs from another system.

Raxx herself was all for peace and peaceful negotiations if it was at all possible. So she had sent those ships and troops. Just to show those on the planet of Styros 5 that they had not been forgotten by her when their call had came in.

The only problem, was the distance away it was had now caused her to rethink the force of ships and troops that she sent. Troops who were already in place were far different to troops who would need to be sent. So Raxx had ensured that the High Commander she had sent in charge of this detail. Had plenty of ships and troops available to him if the need did arise.

With this, she also knew that half of Legion Ten may be unavailable for what would be sent to the Gelten system soon. It would also depend upon how quickly any of their discussions took place and were finalised. Only then would they return home. But for now, Raxx left their legion out of her plans for Gelten. She had plenty of ships and plenty of troops here on Haff for her planning anyway to cope with this Bork Gremplar. Even if he did have any allies he could call upon for help.

Although she had remembered when talking to Shrum in her office. That he had said nothing to her about any other planet or systems other than those in the Gelten system itself which he ruled over. So she was assuming that the Barathon system had been Gremplar's first chance to expand his personal empire. It was possible that his own space exploration was not as well organised as their own had been for so long already.

Over time, many scouts had returned back to Haff from their various long space travels. Some with no results, others with many. It was the one and only way in which they could find out exactly who was out there. And where? . . . Also as to whether they were friendly or not. As such, whenever a drone ship returned with its android pilot. Their own Space Maps were constantly being updated with any of this new information being incorporated into them.

But her own task at this very moment in time was of the tyrant Bork Gremplar of Briath. She was the one to decide just how many ships, troops and vehicles would be needed to cover all five of his planets. So as to finally free them all from his personal grasp.

Five drone scout ships had already been sent away right after Shrum and his men had been captured and questioned by her. So even while she was busy deciding what forces to use. She still awaited their return to offer her more knowledge about each of these planets. Only then would her final decisions began to be made, and the order to embark sent out.

Sometimes though, it was simply a waiting game. Yet as such a well known battle strategist. Raxx wanted to know everything she could before she came to any certain conclusions about what could be done - and also how.

∞

It was a full seven days before the first of her scouts began to return to Haff from the Gelten system. It and their language had already been known to them from earlier scouting. As each of them returned, they were detailed as expected to see Raxx right away. Not all were alike though, as none actually looked like a typical human right now. As with other recent general information gathered from Gremplar's captured troops by Raxx herself. Previous scouts, as well as by the some of their scientists.

Modifications had taken place on these androids to enable them to be able to blend in better. Three of them had the same appearance as that of Shrum and his men. The other two had body characteristics for two different species which lived on Nee and Pelus. The scientists even had to specifically order some parts of them smaller from the tech planets so that they could pass unnoticed. As Briath and the other two planets which Shrum and all of his men were from were quite different to them in shape and stature.

But, the sent scouts had blended in well. Observing everything very keenly and noting anything of importance that may be needed. Even to listening to exchanges between those living on these planets until they had sourced all their proper speech patterns correctly. On most, so they told her, unhappiness and general unrest was quite evident in the lowest of classes. Whereas only those who had attained higher placements and a far better standard of living appeared to enjoy their life upon them.

As each of them finished their reports, she asked if they would return again and see if their people would welcome an end to Gremplar's rule over them. She could only ask them as a request, as of course even as androids their brains were self-functioning. And just like every other android in their own system, each even had the right of refusal if they felt it was wrong. Except here on Haff for some very strange reason, even the androids had felt a kind of kinship to the planet and its people. So they saw this more as a duty to protect them. As if they did not agree to go, then they knew that humans who would not fit in as well as they could would have to risk doing it instead.

Those of them who worked in the service industries, or on the farming and mining planets. Already knew that humans only had a certain tolerance level to very repetitive work which could lead to boredom. And boredom of this kind could then lead to their not being aware - which could then lead to accidents. As androids did not have any kind of boredom threshold at all. They were happy to serve in these same industries where humans could be injured.

And so, Raxx had to wait. Not only for their new reports to filter back to her after they had agreed to return for her. But also to see if the troops which were now on duty at Styros 5 may return in time also. Which she assumed was quite doubtful.

As she awaited any of these things. The five Lords of Haff, had again and again set their capture plans in motion. Only for them fall by the wayside, as Raxx either did not appear on the ground route at a supposed time, or had used flight mode. Or not at all when she actually stayed in her office throughout the night, continually sorting through all the incoming information. At these times one or more of her maids would travel there to her until they could finally take her home to rest.

Any attempt to capture her with any of these maids in close attendance was also a non-event. As her own androids had the highest upgrades available already. Which meant that their own strengths far outweighed any of their own human ones. Even if knowing who they were, their own existing programmed personal duty and loyalty was to Raxx first and foremost. Just as it had been for hundreds, if not thousands of life cycles and former clones of her already. If they showed to be a threat to Raxx, then her own android maids would defend her to their own termination to enable her to escape. She would then know just who had been trying to get to her. And even the lords themselves knew that her four android maids were just as loyal to her as all of their troops were.

∞

General Shrum requested an audience with Raxx. A request which was unexpectedly, yet immediately granted much to his vast surprise. After being escorted up to her, he was then shown into her office as Morg departed, leaving them on their own.

'You wished to see me on some matter, General?' she asked, while inviting him to sit opposite her desk.

He gave a nod of his head as he took a seat. Still a little amazed to have been allowed here into her office so easily; and to be left on his own with her like this. It was as if none there had any worries over her actual safety.

'To be honest, Prime Commander,' he began by using her own known title. 'I am worried about what may happen to our planets whenever you decide to attack them.'

'In what way, General?'

'I am just worried about how many may die on them when the attack takes place. Many in our populations upon them may die when your troops start to kill.'

'There should be no need for you to worry, General. Have you not already been told this by Octavus? That only those who bear arms against us will be the ones to suffer? We do not kill those who are unarmed, only those who are armed after the first shots in battle are fired. We are very discerning when it comes to *who* is an enemy!'

'But how can you be so sure that no innocents will be killed as a battle is raging?'

'Because it has been our way for a very long time now, General. It is set into our teaching that any unarmed person, or being, who we encounter - even during a battle, will not be harmed. Only those who fight against us.'

'You place a lot of trust upon your troops to make no fatal mistakes, Prime Commander!'

'The troops of Haff already know that those who carry no arms are of no true threat to them, General. Our troops will only target those who act belligerent towards us.'

'Yes, although Octavus did say that if one person fires at you - all will be eradicated!'

'He meant troops, General. Which means an actual army, or even just a part of one. Typical citizens within a population would not be in an army so have no need to fear us. Well, unlike here on Haff, that is. However, if any of these said non-military citizens picks up some kind of weapon to use it against us . . . Then of course they must also pay the ultimate price, too! Anyway, we do offer terms of surrender as soon as we land so that they know what is possible.'

'That's what I'm particularly most worried about, Prime Commander. That some of our citizens may just think that you're attacking our planet for no special reason and so may wish to aid the army against you . . . '

'I cannot help that, General. If they carry no weapons upon them, then they will not be harmed. That's the most that I can promise you. We do not even hate your own troops for what you recently attempted to do here in our system you know. You tried in your attempt, and you failed, that is all. But that was not the most important factor either . . . It was because you were sent to do it! You and most others commanding your troops heeded the words of the Mayors and decided not to fight. That was your one saving grace that day. While two others in command must have ordered their troops to fight. That is when we take our role as protector very seriously indeed.'

'I understand that, Prime Commander. And also even to why so many of my men were killed now. But I wish to offer you a compromise regarding your imminent attack.'

'Which is?'

'That you allow me to go and speak to Bork about what will happen if he refuses to listen and seeks to fight. Only myself, the rest of my men will stay here as your hostages as I do this.'

She gave him a smile, but then shook her head. 'There is no need for you to go, General. Matters are already in hand about this now even as we are speaking of it.'

'In what way?'

'A few of our androids have already been sent to your own planets to gain additional information for me. Mainly as a precursor to my launching a multiple landing upon all of your planets at the same time.'

'Androids . . . for what reason especially?'

'Simply because they can blend in, while we cannot.'

'How is that possible? When they all look like you anyway? You know that you look very different to us, so they will quickly be spotted as being not of our world.'

'We took certain steps in order to make sure that they could blend in with your peoples, General. In other words - they have been adapted or modified. Some look like you, while others have been changed to suit your other worlds description. When they came back, they were also able to tell us if any additional steps were needed before going back again. Those that did, have since been sent back to find out what your peoples would think if your tyrant finally lost all of his power over them. My scouts will soon report back to me as quickly as they possibly can over what their new overall thoughts are. Mainly concerning Gremplar losing his tight control over them all. When they do so, then I will be able to finalise my invasion plans to suit.'

Shrum was astounded by the lengths in which she had gone to just to make sure beforehand. Which had been far more than their own scouts had done. Their orders had been to simply go and look, to assess any likely difficulties with any military units when they landed to conquer. While Raxx herself it seemed, had wanted to know what the actual peoples of his planets wanted most to benefit them.

'What if your spies return to say that those on our planets do not *want* to change from being under a single ruler to that of one your democracy things?'

'I follow what the people want usually, if I can, General. It is mainly how we work when reconnoitring any newly found planet or system. And just as I stated previously to you. Our initial android scouts who do our searching and language understanding. Will land on these occupied planets and then make a judgement after seeing what or who is there. As to whether their civilizations could indeed benefit from our help - or not.

'Some have been quickly dismissed by them, simply as they were too busy fighting amongst themselves as even our own ancestors once used to do. Or perhaps each side only wanted an agreement with us that would give them our help against the other side. In such cases, no actual envoy is sent there. We from Haff do not do this . . . We are mainly protectors of complete worlds if at all possible.

'On other worlds when they are finally approached by our scout. If any decision is made to refuse any help or trade deal which we may offer them. Upon any *stable* world I should have said, then we of course will accept their right to do so. We do not force any planets to become united to us. We simply make them an open offer. Their choice of refusal or acceptance is of course down to them alone.

'So, as I have said, General. As we continually seek out and find new civilizations, some new worlds, planets or even entire systems will agree, or disagree to unite with us. In some systems, one or more may accept while others refuse. But as you now well know, as a protectorate, our own military strength is there for them if its ever needed.'

'And what do you receive in return for offering this?'

'In some ways it is almost like a trade deal, General Shrum. We offer them our full protection, while they offer us whatever they can in payment in return. Here in our own system, the agricultural planets send food to us. Just as they sell more of it to other planets who do not grow it. From that revenue they will also purchase their machines from the tech planets.

'The mining ones may send us various ores. Some ores and metals may be quite ordinary - while some can be very rare. Also they will smelt these ores into ingots to sell. From the rarest of metals found they will maybe make intricate power circuits for androids, ships or machines. We pass most of our own given quota freely over to the technology planets in order for them to make us these kinds of things. That is what they do for us as part of our agreement. They are the ones who build our ships, weapons, and androids.

'The mining planets also sell to the tech planets to earn revenue. With this, they also purchase food and any technology they may also have need of. So as you can see, here in our system, one planet always seems to have what another requires. Any rare gems, metals, or such like which are found are sold to our creative planet called Spirit. They make jewellery or whatever out of these and then sell them again when they are completed as many other things.'

'And what does this Spirit do for you?'

'As I said, Spirit is known as the creative world within our own system. It holds the songwriters, film makers, singers and dancers. For us though, it also holds the most numerous of scientists too. For our given protection, these scientists are forever coming up with new ideas of ship designs, armour, weaponry, or upgrades to the androids. As well as a lot of other things which they have invented over time for us all as well.

'For instance, the bubble-pods we travel around in. Cryo-cells in which we allow clones of some of us to mature naturally. And even the newest ways of construction for our buildings, etc. Only as we have the most populated planet within our system, so we are always needing better ways of constructing buildings to house all of us. Apart from to ourselves where their work is offered freely. They sell their latest designs for mining, agriculture, or new technology to other planets who may wish that. As I said, some planet always needs something which it cannot do itself as well.'

'What about that creature planet I visited with Octavus? They don't seem to be able to offer any of you anything really?' he asked.

'As for the creature planet, it is simply a stock planet, General. It is the holder and breeder of any type of animal, bird, insect, reptile or fish that was once known to us before we came here. In some cases it can offer stock to the farming planets where all our meat derivatives come from. In another way, it is also a planet which any of us from the other fourteen can go to visit and enjoy the sight of all of these animals in a natural habitat. In a way, something like a holiday destination. So they earn revenue from stock sales or visitors to it. However, if they do not earn enough then none of us mind too much. We will all happily offer them something so that it can continue in the way that it does.'

'And how many planets are you protecting, Prime Commander?'

'Seventeen so far. With another four in discussion at the moment with our envoys,' she answered.

Shrum thought for a moment. 'Are you not protecting too many now? I mean it would be hard for you to protect so many if they all needed you at the same time.'

Raxx smiled at him. 'You only have to remember exactly how many troops and ships we have to use at any given time, General. Only one of our full legions is of one hundred million strong. In troops terms, our army is approximately four to six billion in full readiness at any time.'

She saw that he was struggling to understand the huge numerical figures she spoke. 'A billion strong army alone consists of one thousand million troops, General. We have anywhere between four and six times that number. I only used a small part of our First Legion to bring a halt to your attacks on our own system. Our legions themselves consist of one hundred million troops in each, General. We can use them as one single army, add them to each other - or break these into many options - like sections or units. They have of course been trained to work in any required number, from large to small.

'One billion troops though only means ten legions . . . we have between forty and sixty legions to use as or when required. Although this higher figure is also counting our reserves and newest trainees too - who are only non-adult children right now. Yet who would still fight for Haff if it was asked of them.'

'I do not doubt that at all!' stated Shrum, remembering the children who they had visited and watched on the training grounds along with Rist. Shrum was already overwhelmed by the sheer size of their army though. He could not even *imagine* there being forty legions like the one who had marched towards him on Jitrus. And as she had already said, that had only been a very, *very*, small part of one of them.

It was just then that Shrum reiterated his original idea, and solution to the forthcoming invasion of his own planet and system. An idea which he suddenly offered to Raxx.

'I think it would still be best if you sent me ahead of your invasion to speak with Bork Gremplar, Prime Commander?'

'For what reason now, General?'

'Well, if I could really make him understand *what* he is coming up against. Then perhaps there need be no fight at all when you do arrive.'

Raxx deliberated upon this for only about a minute. 'I thank you for your generous offer, General. But as is usual when we do land on any planets, the one who is in command offers the ultimatum. As he is on Briath, then so shall I be. And when I step on to the ground there, my ultimatum will be offered to him and also to everyone who can hear it said. I'm afraid that this is just our way, General. Just because he deems himself to be in charge of it, does not mean that he should be the only one to hear it.'

Shrum shook his head and gave a long sigh. 'So it's war then . . . there is no other solution possible?'

'My dear General, what you call a war between us - to us will only be like that of a skirmish.'

'I'm sorry but I do not know this word *skirmish*, Prime Commander.'

'Skirmish is simply a word that can in fact mean a very short battle, General.'

'Short?'

'Indeed, very short . . . '

'One of your weeks or months?'

She shook her head. 'It will probably only last for an hour or two at most.'

'Impossible!' he exclaimed.

'Really, General? Even after everything that you have seen here already? I can even set one legion down on each planet. How long do you imagine your troops on any of these planets of yours will last then against one hundred million?'

'Why so many?'

'Why not . . . ? We all use what we have, do we not? And we on Haff have a large force of ready troops. Did you yourself feel at all overwhelmed when Octavus and his troops landed on Jitrus to confront you, General?'

'Of course! I only had forty thousand troops of my own there with me and on the other planets to take them,' he muttered back.

'And I only sent out five million troops to each of our planets to stop you, General! But as you now know, there were many more all waiting here on Haff who were just as eager to be with them. You must always remember that as warriors, we have all been trained to fight. That we are a well ordered military society, General. Our sole purpose here on Haff is to train and learn to fight. In a way now, we are bred to fight wars. It is what we are here for. To live and to die is simply what happens to all of our bodies in the end. But for us - to die in an actual battle is the fulfilment of all our training. This is also why death itself does not frighten us as it perhaps would do others. In a way, you could say that we are each born to serve our planet.

'From first starting to train at only five cycles of age, you are already told that you may have to die for Haff. To possibly even *die* alongside those who you are training with at that time. That you may be called upon to offer your loyalty and life at any time no matter what your level of skill or age you may be if Haff needs you. This is why our training is so hard, General. Yes, after only two or three cycles at most our children could kill an enemy if required. But we have also, by then, attuned them as to what even a single well-trained unit of troops not only can, but would be able to do as one. However, our children being used in any such way as that is only a final option after all others have been used.

'The men and women that are in retirement and who we call reserves would come before them. And all of these were also former fully trained troops as well. They may have aged, even gained a little weight perhaps from not training as much any longer . . . but they will certainly not have forgotten how it felt to be in a legion for so long, General. That is one feeling which will *never* leave you no matter how old you may be! And if the call does go out to them, I already know that all of them would happily step forward if it was for Haff . . .

'So, I thank you for your kind offer to be an emissary for us to your tyrant, General. But I am afraid that he now has to learn what the actual cost may be when you attack another systems planets as he did.'

Shrum's head bobbed slowly upon his thick neck. He knew he had tried his best . . . But as the old woman before him had said, and which he already knew. Haff did not attack his system first - His own leader Borg Gremplar was the one who had chosen to attack theirs. Which meant that he could only fear the worst now . . .

8

It was close to being a long thirty more days before the five android scouts began to return. Raxx herself had surprisingly been incredibly generous in this same time too. As General Shrum and all of his men found to their amazement. That instead of being held under guard within the confines of the building where they had been placed; as they had thought typical prisoners would be. She had actually allowed all of them, by placing them on their honour not to cause any problems. To go outside and to move freely about in Haff Central; and to do as they wished - so long as they were all back inside again by nightfall.

Not only Shrum, but his men could not believe their luck really. Prisoners indeed they were, yet were being given such an offer as this and without actually being surrounded by any guards.

What they had forgotten in their actual excitement of course, was that none of them looked anything at all like the typical citizens of Haff. So of course those who they saw walking around knew them for who they were anyway; and many would still view them warily because of it. However, if their Prime Commander judged such a thing to be safe to allow, then who were they to question it. They were certainly not armed in any way, and they definitely could not hide anything even if they were. Since they were all just as bereft of clothing as so many of the local inhabitants were.

So, they walked, they talked, they peered, or even went inside some of their huge shops and stores just to look around. Mainly awed at what actually was inside them to be bought by anyone usually. As they had never seen any of the things on display being for sale on theirs before. Some were even asked by a helpful android shop assistant if they were looking for anything in particular to buy. At this point most felt embarrassed as they had nothing with which to buy anything with. Many of them though, actually only sat just outside the building in the open air. Just pleased to be allowed out of it and seeing daylight again. As none of them had expected to live after being captured. So they even began starting to compare Haff to their own home planets, and their own did not come out of it very well at all.

But that was Raxx at her very best, as usual. As cooped up prisoners held within buildings learned nothing. Whereas those who could go outside both to look, and to *see* for themselves, were also able to view and understand a lot better. Raxx was actually showing all of them, instead of just the first select few. Of what the benefits of trade were with being united to Haff and their fellow worlds.

It had all began when she had made one of her typical decisions and told Morg. From that short talk, word was soon spread all around Haff Central at first, and then graduated further and further afield. Her stated words to Morg to pass on were these:

'You do not need to subjugate an entire civilisation in order to try and make them agree with you, Morg. You only need to show *some* of them just how good it could be for them to wish to live in a different way. Perhaps even in a far better way than they are used to. And then *they* will be the ones who will tell others what they are missing out on; and so will soon want changes to happen.

'So, they will be free to move around Haff Central as much as they wish, so long as they cause no trouble anywhere. And as for our people, advise them to simply think of them as tourists from one of our own system planets visiting Haff for their first time. If they wish to speak with you, then you can respond to them. Simply remember that Haff is the best planet anywhere, and act accordingly so that they know this. That way, we are showing them just how wonderful it is to live like we do on Haff . . .'

Raxx had also heard soon after this. That Shrum had also informed all of his men in their various large groupings right after the message had came down from her. That if any one man caused any kind of trouble here, that they may all end up paying for it.

'Walk around the city if you wish, sit outside in the light of day and enjoy the fresh air also, if that is all you may need,' he told them. 'You may talk to some of their citizens - but only if they themselves will allow you to do so. Prime Commander Raxx told me earlier that these Haffian's of hers are a very fair-minded people when they are not fighting. So if *she* has allowed us to go freely outside without any restraint or guard - then no citizen here should bear us any ill will from what we tried to do.

'The reason for this being, is that they trust her judgement in all things. And so, all that I will say to you is this. To enjoy this freedom we have all now been given from her and do not ruin it! Do not cause any trouble with them, and especially do not start any fights with them. Even if it is with one of their small children - as you could well lose. Or else, you may even lose all of us these newly granted freedoms and privileges.'

∞

Raxx listened to each of the five androids as they began to return from their mission and went to see her. She took many notes, all adding to what she had already received or discovered. To all of them she said it had been a task well done and thanked them. While to two of them in particular, she gave her personal thanks. And then said that they could now go and exchange their vastly altered parts for their more usual ones again. When they had left, Raxx began to move all of her notes around her desk. Until she now had them all where she wanted them to be for each of the planets in question.

'Link me to Sherf Moll, please,' she spoke aloud in the empty room.

The auto relays in her room automatically turned on whenever her first words were "Link me to!"

'Prime Commander?' queried a male voice from a large holo-image appearing in her office.

Raxx looked at the display. Sherf was seemingly aging just as badly himself since his retirement.   However,   as   a   former   transport coordinator of some note, she had never found a better one. So retirement or not, he was more than pleased to continue his former role for her. But body-wise, that's exactly what could happen to you when you were not able to train as regularly due to doing another kind of task.

She could blame herself for his quite heavy looking paunch that hung there now, as he stood and looked into the many lenses in his own office. Although she could not be blamed for his completely bald head. In a few ways, some of their old ancestral genes still could cause some of her people trouble. He could also see her just as well in a similar way before him, too.

'Can you come to me with your latest ship availability update, please, Sherf?'

'Certainly, Prime Commander, I am on my way to you right now!''

'Thank you, Sherf . . .'

Less than five minutes later, Morg had shown Sherf into her office. In only one hand did he hold something in it, and that was a data tablet.

'How many ships do we have ready for use - and how many not available right now?' she asked him straight away. He'd hardly came through the doors as she asked him this while walking to stand back behind her desk and gestured him to a chair.

He looked down at this tablet as he sat. 'According to the data I quickly requested and received right after your summons, Prime Commander. We have forty of our main carriers noted as unavailable at the moment.' He saw her head rise at the amount. 'I offer my apologies for this Prime Commander, but most of these have engine problems and we are either awaiting new ones arriving for them, or very integral parts for others of them. Out of the forty, we could perhaps interchange parts with others to make some of them run. But----'

'Yes I know, Sherf. You hate to cannibalise one ship just to make another one work, as doing so could lead to other problems from switching them.'

He nodded perfunctorily. 'That is so.'

'So what *do* we have available then?'

'Our ship carriers are at full capacity. As for our main carriers for both troops and the usual machinery . . . enough for at least ten legions to use right now. With our smaller ships, only two are not space worthy. Again one is waiting for a replacement engine, while the other is having its weapons upgraded.'

'Ground attack vehicles?' she now asked, while making notes of all he said.

'No problems at all there, Prime Commander. They are so small compared to the others that any mechanical work required on them is simple by comparison. I'd speculate that with at least a day or more notice, there would be none missing for use.'

'You have between two days upto one week to see what you can do with everything, Sherf. After that, whatever you have I will be using many of them.'

'That is understood. I will do my best to have everything online as quickly as I can. And when you call me again to make sure, I can then inform you even more fully of what is ready to use.'

'Good enough. Thank you for your time as always, Sherf.'

'I am as ever, happy to serve, Prime Commander,' he said, ending with a salute to her before heading out through the opening doors as they sensed his approach. As he then headed back to his own much smaller office to get things started.

As he left and walked into the outer area. He was already thinking ahead out loud to himself. 'Only two to five days at most, eh? Then I guess it's time that I get the whip cracking!' he chuckled. Also knowing that with mainly only android technicians repairing them, a whip would actually be useless anyway! It was just a phrase that he enjoyed using now and again.

It was just then that Raxx made one of her typical instant decisions. Which was instead of a full five legions being sent out, one to each planet to both shock, awe, and to send utter fear throughout them. Her new choice was of only using fifty million troops per planet. Her new choice was made so as to limit the fear factor to the ordinary citizens on them more than anything else. As even fifty million to where Gremplar's three or so were stationed on his home planet. Should be more than enough to do the same thing. She nodded her head - her plans were now ready and finally all in place.

∞

Four days later as the first of the morning suns rose and shone down on Haff Central. Shrum and most of his men were already outside after having eaten. They rarely had anything to do every day, except to sit and talk or to walk about. But it was the feeling of freedom to do this which they now valued so much.

Many of them had walked around the recreational areas. Where many of the capitals population just sat and talked, ate, or passed time with each other in a colourful setting. These same areas were typically spotless. Flowers and trees bloomed just about everywhere, offering a variety of scents and perfumes to those nearby. What they did notice on these walks though, was the general lack of animals as were often seen on their own planets.

Haff, over time had found that what had been called pets were distracting. Training, eating and sleep were basically what they did almost every day. And if sent on missions off-world, it would be hard to find someone other than an android to care for them. Which did not have the same human feelings that a pet would attach to.

So pets of any kind had soon disappeared from Haff. In fact there were no animals or birds around, and only one type of insect. A hybrid kind of honey bee had been engineered which no longer had a sting. It was in fact only there so as to pollinate the trees, flowers, and perhaps some fruits which were being grown by people to enjoy. Though their hives were ran by retired warriors who did so to gather honey, since that was why they were called such a name A lot of which was soon being sold by them at home and elsewhere. Insect wise, that was it. There were no birds or other animal life. Because Haff was just so well ordered and clean, that there was no waste lying around for anything to feed on.

Everything they had was either recycled, composted, or placed into huge tanks where micro organisms would break it all down.

∞

And then, right in front of the building where they were all housed. The actual ground seemed to rumble loudly and then open up before them. Only to be followed by a huge sound coming out from it. It was then that one of their massive ships rose out of that hole and slowly made its way higher and higher as their eyes followed its quickening rise and shrinking details. They heard more of the same sounds, and watched as again and again yet another of their enormous machines took to the skies. In minutes, the sky above as far as their eyes could see - seemed to be full of them. And all were heading upwards with thrusting engines howling to lift their weight. These were soon followed by much smaller craft, and then the hole in front of them closed. Their sounds diminished well before they lost sight of them as they climbed higher and higher; even if they did only become small specks.

Their citizens must be very used to this happening, Shrum assumed. Only because as soon as the gigantic hole began closing, many of them were already walking upon it as normal again.

'Is it what we think it is, General?'

'I'm afraid so, Borth. Their invasion of our own system of planets may have begun.'

'May Aldur protect them!' Borth murmured.

'They will truly need Aldur, and as many more of our Gods as they can call upon I fear!' said a saddened Shrum.

Borth only gave a nod as the specks they had all been watching soon rose too high for them to see any longer.

∞

High above Haff as they began to position themselves in space in readiness for their jump. One by one the main engines cut-out leaving only their thrusters to hold their positions. Raxx sat beside Rist while holding a far larger viewing tablet in her hands. As her own ship had been first to take-off. She was watching the screen to make sure that all the rest of the fleet had managed to reach orbit safely. This was only because you never really knew as you lifted off. It took a large strain upon the engines to lift such a huge weight due to the gravity of their planet.

Whether any ship would suffer a major engine malfunction as it did so. There were also safeguards in place for any such event as that. Large snap-walls would then literally appear and crash around them as if from nowhere to seal them all into separated compartments. Either of the pilots could then activate a release button which caused the ship to quickly break-up into their own smaller parts. In space, they would simply float around until another similar skeleton ship could be sent to reorganise them and take them aboard.

On take-off though it was quite another matter entirely if they had to cause any separation. As with each sealed unit being far lighter than the entire ship, the safety thrusters would fire on each one of them, and hopefully return them to the ground no worse off. As for the main ship itself . . . it would quickly then become a skeleton ship. Simply to that of a cockpit at the front. Then the skeleton framework which had held the separate units behind it. And right at the back of the ship the massive drive system of the engines.

Without the extra weight, the skeleton then had a chance of safely returning to the ground again. However if it was actually a full failure of the engine systems. Then the only task of the pilots, was to make sure that they aimed it towards an unpopulated area of the planet. If they could do so *before* engaging their own cockpit release.

Raxx sat and watched her screen as the massed array of various ships rose safely up from their numerous locations on Haff into orbit. She knew from her own made plans of just how many there should be around her. At which point, when all seemed in place. Her face made a movement almost like that of a nervous tick. Which turned on her own hearing and speech implant.

'All Commanders report!' she spoke.

One by one, even including Rist beside her gave an affirmative to her question with one word. 'Ready!'

'Pilot's, you each have your coordinates with which to take us where we are going. So please set them into your Star-Nav now and then beep your beacon.'

Raxx watched as the ships upon her screen began to send a pulse wave out from them. She waited and watched until no more flashes on it were seen.

'My Commanders and troops,' she now said, as the entire army around her listened only to her voice. 'You have all been told of what to expect upon landing on this enemy ground. You have all been trained fully to expect the unexpected. So you must also use this training if need be now. Each Commander has been given their battle orders, and they will have passed my battle strategy and tactics down to all of you for this invasion. Remember that compared to our army, they have very few - so unless fired upon in any way, it should be a bloodless takeover. Yet as always, there may be a few who resist and as such cause much harm to others because of this. As you know, I trust every single one of you to do whatever is necessary to survive yourselves first above all. May our dear Haff be proud of us all! For Haff!' she ended her speech. 'All pilots, begin our jump!' were her final spoken words.

The warning tone in her ship sounded as it always did, and as it would in others around her. The usual travel field was generated around each of them, and then there was the jerk. They were on their way. In less than five hours they would be at their destination.

9

The first thing that many of the citizens on the five planets of the Gelten system knew. Was when some kind of a shimmering effect, which also caused loud crackles like rippling thunder took place very high up in their skies. From these same unusual things, appeared tiny specks one after another. As those very strange effects also then quickly disappeared.

The reason they could see these was only because as Raxx now knew, their gravity was far less than that of Haff. Which meant in her mind that tactically, her fleet could come out of their jumps at a much lower altitude here. Rather than doing so out in orbit as they would always have to at home.

As these ships gained in size the lower they came. The sound of all of their engines also soon began to roar above their heads the nearer they approached the ground. Naturally, panic ensued. The populations either ran into their homes to shelter and take cover. Or else they tried to hide in the doorways or inside buildings of any place that was available to them. On four other planets, the military commanders in charge sent urgent messages to Briath. To advise Bork Gremplar that huge fleets of ships were about to land and they desperately needed reinforcements on them.

On Briath itself however, Bork Gremplar already had his own problems and had his hands full. Their own defence systems were in no way comparable to those of Haff. As their own supposed detection equipment only picked up Raxx's fleet as it came out of its jump. The element of surprise had already been gained! Once again, being at a far lower height due to its lower gravity. Briath's detection systems only picked them up even as those below heard the crackling noise first.

He himself was prepared to dismiss it as only weather at first. As just then, he was laid prone on his side in very rich quality garments like that of an olden day Roman Emperor or potentate. Upon a long piece of

90

well-padded furniture while sampling various expensive fruits and treats. In the same room were his three wives and five concubines and many of his children to them. It was early morning, and their own first light meal of the day since rising from sleep. What they ate bore little resemblance to what many could afford themselves upon any of his five planet kingdom.

But as he repeated to his family quite constantly: *"Those who rule have - and those who don't, just have to make do with what they can get."* That any may starve while *they* lived in such a lap of luxury bothered them not at all. In fact they rarely even thought about the sufferings of anyone else at all. They were placed where they were due to who he was. And so they had always enjoyed their rich lifestyle. That was until the newer sounds of many straining engines could be heard.

Gremplar slowly rolled from his side into a standing position and then walked over to one of the unglazed windows to see what all the unusual noise was about. He could only gasp at what he saw, while his thickly squared jaw hung slack. What was all of this? There was even a nervous gulp in his throat as he watched each of them growing in size. He was actually stunned into silence by the sight.

'What is it, husband?' asked one wife.

He coughed to clear his throat. 'I think that we are under attack!'

'What! By who?' she gasped and rushed over to stand beside him. Followed quickly by the rest of his family members.

A door then opened and one of his military aides rushed into the room and over to him.

'They are not any of ours, Sire. These are far too large to be ours. We do not even know who they are or where they have came from. What shall we do?'

'Place everyone on high alert. Charge up all our defences and prepare to fight!' he shouted, finally getting his voice back.

'Yes, Sire. We gave also had incoming messages from our troops stationed on Goll, Nee, Pelus and Chell. It appears as if they are each also under attack too, Sire, and have requested help!'

Gremplar cursed out loud and viciously. 'We don't have time to send any of our troops to the others now . . . They will just have to do what they can!'

He had neither remembered nor cared that his wives and children were also present when he made his vitriolic outburst. He marched quickly over to another window of the room where his polarised viewer stood. A piece of equipment that he often used just to stare down into the capital itself. Sometimes for him to see what the lesser people far below were doing down there. Almost in a way like that of a voyeur. With his eyes to their lenses, he raised it from the city to look at the falling ships.

He gulped again. No matter that its resolution was set high for only watching people better. He focused on one of these landing ships. He had never seen anything as monstrous as these before and there were just so many of them! Who are they - and why are they here? echoed in his mind.

He pulled back from his viewer to gaze at his family. 'Head to the safe room all of you. Now!' he shouted. And as they all ran as quickly as they could manage to do so. Gremplar followed by the aide scurried to the highest point of his citadel to gain a better view and understanding of what was taking place right now.

∞

One by one Raxx's fleet set down outside the city wherever possible to her predetermined plan. Doors were opened and both men and machines quickly poured out of them and began to follow her tactics.

Gremplar looked down at his city, and all he could see were his people running around like scurrying insects not knowing what to do. Briath had never had a contingency plan in place in case it was ever invaded. Only as with four million troops usually stationed on it, he had never feared one taking place.

He used another viewer to stare across his city and out to its limits. This was where ship after ship were now settling upon the ground. His hands swung the viewer one way and then yet another as he watched the figures pouring out from each of them like a never ending wave. He was already dazed by the sight of so many of them being naked. Yet in his mind he was wondering why they were all out there mostly without a stitch of clothing on their bodies. In some ways it was almost immoral to his own sensibilities!

He looked around him. Many of his troops were already positioned on the citadel. Behind their laz multi-cannons or laz rifles. While a lot who were classed as the elite, only carried their Gan war clubs. Back to the viewer yet again, and he lowered his gaze. Some of his own troops were rapidly taking up defensive positions in the streets. Or overturning various vehicles to create barriers to stand safely behind.

His view went back up and out again. From one ship in particular, he then saw a naked old woman appear. Although the term *old* was putting it nicely after he had increased its magnification further. She was walking down a ramp very slowly from out of the nearest ship. Something of a gold colour was brought over to her, which she straddled and sat on. Then it appeared to rise a little and float. That was a new sight to him with it having no wheels. It then began to steadily head towards his city.

∞

As they all came out of their jumps. Raxx was not only watching her tablet closely. But also the countdown timer she had set in motion from when they had first jumped away from Haff.

'Descend now!' she ordered, only when noting that all the ships had emerged safely. Her parting words were, 'All Commanders, be sure to follow the battle strategy. And I will see you all after the battle ahead, if there is one.' Raxx then did a facial movement and her implant switched off.

The tightness of their restraints held them all securely in place as the entire fleet quickly dropped from the skies.

As soon as Rist beside her felt the shock of the landing struts touching the ground, he was already free and stood. 'Open the doors! Evacuate!' he called out. He watched as they flowed from the open doors like a river in full torrent.

'Have my hover machine brought around to the nearest door for me please, Octavus. After that, you will soon know what will need doing either way,' she told him with a smile.

He sent that message out, and then deactivated his own implant for just a moment. 'Derus . . . Please!'

Her response was only a sad looking smile to him. 'It *must* be this way if I am to finally rest and to have a new clone of myself activated, Octavus. I have already told you this. Take heart my dear friend. If this happens in the way as I expect it to happen. Make sure that you get a medic to me as quickly as possible so as to extract my final memories when my own life functions cease. Then send the red burst signal to Haff. My nearest aged clone will then be activated out of her cryo-sleep and be prepared. Only awaiting my memories to be transferred to her when they arrives home.

'It is the reason why I brought a few fast cruisers along with us for you to use one as a transport for my body and memories. Or just my memories if my body has been blasted to shreds. So you must do whatever you must to have them collected and sent to Haff as quickly as possible for me, my friend. In this, I am counting on you completely.

'You will be in total command of everything happening in this system after that. So please do your very best to follow my planned strategy now. And with luck,' she smiled again. 'When we do next meet on Haff, I will once again be a lively and vibrant young woman once more!'

With that, Raxx rid herself of her own restraint and rose to her feet. She raised a hand to his face and ran it down his right cheek. 'I have told you not to shed any tears for me, dear friend. I have been blessed with a very long life already, and my coming time of final release is now here. So please, do not make me feel sad as well. I have spent the past fifty cycles of my life wondering how my end will come. And now I have a chance to end it in the way that I would prefer. Leading my troops from the very front once more as I seal my fate.'

She patted his shoulder and then walked away from him down the ramp.

'Damn it, it's just not right!' he muttered while wiping his eyes. The deep sigh he then gave must have travelled up from his toes, and then he followed her while reactivating his own implant. Voices returned, all the commanders under him were calling out to their troops to form up.

As he came to the bottom of the ramp, Raxx was already at hover astride her personal machine. She smiled at him again. 'Remember, Octavus, it's only until we meet again!'

Then as he watched and moved into place to lead their troops, she began to move towards the city ahead of them - completely alone.

∞

This very same thing was now happening almost to the same moment on each of the five planets. However, where Raxx was very much alone, the other commanders all had a mass of expectant troops waiting behind them.

Raxx came to a halt and her machine settled upon the ground. 'Give me amplification, please.' On each ship on the ground, a single mast-like tower rose from out of them.

She began to speak in a very clear voice. 'I am speaking to you, Borg Gremplar, and to all the citizens of Briath. Just as the citizens of the four other planets which you rule over are being offered these same terms as well.'

Their amplitude made sure that she could be heard a long way off quite easily.

'My name and title is, Prime Commander Raxx. My own planet is called Haff. You sent your own troops to invade our system of Barathon. They failed! I am now here to offer you terms of surrender. Have all your army lay their weapons down and you will survive . . . if you do decide to fire and injure or kill any one of us, then you must all face the direct consequences of your actions. As all who *hold* or *use* any weapon against us will have their lives terminated immediately. If you fight - you will die! We do not take prisoners if you decide to do so. These are your only choices, so please make one quickly.'

Gremplar simply couldn't believe it. That ancient old hag out there was not only threatening him, but ordering *him* to surrender. He could not even believe that she, at such an age was in charge of all of them.

His next words were the biggest mistake that he'd ever make in his life. As he turned to one of his troops behind a multi-cannon and ordered, 'Kill her!'

∞

Raxx herself knew very little about what happened next. One moment she was on her hover machine waiting for an answer. And in the very next moment she had received it. As she saw lights suddenly approaching her which blasted her from it. While the wrecked machine lay on its side and its engine was now silent.

Rist gazed sadly at the crumpled and scorched figure lying prone upon the ground. Derus had got her wish.

'Medics to the Prime Commander!' he called out. and then. 'Legion One - Shield formation!' The static buzz from all their shields being activated at level ten actually sent a small shockwave out. At which point he shouted, 'Life or Death!' and began to trot.

'LIFE OR DEATH!!!!' chorused the fifty million voices in unison with a sound that shook the air itself as they all now followed him.

Even as he trotted past her body and its attending medics around her he asked how she was.

'She is dead, Low Commander.'

An enraged growl almost animal in nature came from the trotting troops behind him when they heard this.

'Extract her memories and take her body to a cruiser. Then have the pilot send a red signal burst to Haff. After that I want it to lift-off and take them both to Haff straight away.'

'Understood.'

His task for her had been carried out. Now he only had to concentrate on carrying out her strategy.

'Oh Great Aldur, save us!' exclaimed Gremplar's aide.

Gremplar himself could not have said it better, as he was now thinking the exact same thing after she was struck and had fallen. He hoped that at the death of their leader, her troops would now be lost and wondering what to do. He saw through the viewer a few of them had broken away from their huge mass to go towards their fallen leader.

'Should I shoot at them now, Sire?' asked the same man behind the multi-cannon.

Via his viewer, Gremplar saw that they only carried backpacks or small cases by their handles. With a gulp that almost strangled his throat, he also noted that the old woman had not even been armed. 'No, they are doctor's or medical staff who have gone to check their leader. Even I will not have unarmed medical people shot at - or they may do the same in reprisal to ours too.'

Then he gave an audible gasp along with the others as their voices all shouted life or death as one. The wave of sound reverberated, and carried to them, almost deafening in its tone. It was a fearful sound indeed! And then those same troops all began to trot towards his city and citadel.'

'Oh Great Aldur, what have I done!' he muttered under his breath. They were like a swarm of insects heading towards them, millions upon millions strong. Just how many he wasn't sure. But they certainly exceeded the entire population of his planet, in that much he was sure. Their trotting feet literally shook the ground beneath them. Yet apart from that, there were now no further voices raised.

Still at the trot they came, with Rist himself now falling back into the front line for the moment. At level ten, all their shields formed that same high concave barrier around each of them. Although now they were so close to each other that it created an almost impenetrable energy barrier.

Even as the cruiser was taking off with Raxx's remains and her intact memories being carried aboard it, Gremplar suddenly woke up to the oncoming danger and screamed, 'Well? - Shoot at them!'

And so they did - but to very little effect.

Their close shield deployment deflected their weapon charges again and again. The laser fire either rebounding or ricocheting. Yet none appeared to pass through their solid wall. Their training for this had been hard won over their many life cycles, and now they did it well.

'Split now!' ordered Rist.

The large trotting mass now disintegrated into six quite separate divisions. Each one heading towards an opening into the city itself. Those within the battle machines sped away at each side to head around to the rear of the city. In Raxx's own words as she told them her tactics: it was a noose they were forming, and they had to do this way so as to tighten it quickly and to cut-off any means of escape.

Gremplar's men continued to fire, yet none of those attacking were seen to fall. One Remplar decided to attack by his own decision instead, and urged his elite unit of ten thousand defenders to follow him. They held their Gan clubs ready as they ran at them. Rist saw this, and still had time to marvel at Raxx's earlier understanding of what might happen.

'Open the wall! Pincer strategy!' he called out.

Gremplar's men then ran into the opened gap.

'Close the wall! Unit behind, terminate!' said Rist.

The front line reformed at his command while still trotting. Gremplar's men ran into the following line which did not open for them. Where shield's were turned off to change them into weapons of attack instead. High energy bursts flashed everywhere even as they continued to trot without stopping. Then they were back behind their large shields again. Behind them lay all ten thousand, level ten settings had left none of them alive. Only ten naked men and women were on the ground, and they were already being tended to by the medics.

Gremplar cursed, yet he couldn't take his eyes off the sight of so many of his men dead and unmoving. Rist and his troops continued their steady pounding into the city, and upto the first of the barriers.

'Over and around!' called Rist, and gathering his own muscles, actually leaped over it along with many more. Landing amongst the defenders. Coming from a far heavier gravity planet had certainly helped with this. But how could Derus have even foreseen this happening?

With their Grem's spinning and changing from one option to another, They only left more thousands of dead behind them as they continued on towards the citadel itself.

Gremplar's heavy face was ashen, as if all the blood had drained from it. As all that he could see was so much death down there, and mostly all were of his own men. Few of these attackers appeared to fall whoever they met with.

From his own high point of view, he turned his gaze from the terrible sight below and began to look around. They were coming from everywhere. All of them were swarming to one place, and one place alone - his citadel. How can you ever hope to beat people who don't seem to die, he wondered?

'All is lost, Sire!' said his aide with sadness etched upon his face.

'Not yet, they cannot break through the doors with those things.'

'They already have, Sire. Some of them are now already inside the citadel as we speak.'

Gremplar almost fell due to his legs losing their strength. Just who were these people who could beat his troops so easily. And then also break into his citadel with such ease!

∞

As the sent signal was received on Haff and passed on. Shockwaves of anger, sadness, even despair echoed around the planet en-masse. Those who had been left behind could not actually believe it. That *their* much beloved Prime Commander was dead?

As always, the holo screens around Haff were waiting to come on for those on Haff to watch any battles in which they fought. But even before the short time delay allowed these received pictures to be shown. The red signal burst had already reached Haff to pass on the news.

Those in Haff Central began to gather around the Garen's Royal Palace. The three Ladies of Haff flew to the capital as soon as they heard the news. While the five Lord's all smiled when they heard about it and took their own sweet time. Yet even they also had to fly to their central city, too, as it was expected of them. Only they were far happier to hear of her death than anyone else was. All of them were expected to be at the incarnation of the next young Raxx.

Shrum and his men did not know what was actually going on for a long while. As with the attack taking place upon their own home system of planets. Raxx did not want any of them to be allowed outside to watch what may happen. She did not want them to especially see their friends and compatriots dying if a battle was to take place. So by her order, they were all being held within the building until the battle that would be showing upon the screens was ended.

They did though see the guards looking with utter sadness upon each other inside the building where they were all held at night.

It was much later when they were all allowed to return outside again; but only when the battle had ended upon the screens. That all they saw were hordes of people moving towards one building in particular.

'What's happening?' he asked of one of these passers-by.

'Prime Commander Raxx has fallen in battle.'

As Shrum and his men looked worriedly about them at these words. Wondering if her death would now also lead to all of their own. He could only ask, 'How do you know this?'

'A signal was sent to Haff confirming it.'

'So where are you all going?'

'With the battle now over, we are all going to the Royal Palace. We will then follow the Royal Family to the cryo building so that we can see our *new* Prime Commander Raxx as soon as she emerges.'

'What?'

'Her new clone will take over from where our dear elderly Prime Commander left off. We will again soon have a new Prime Commander Raxx to lead us.'

'May any of us follow you?' Shrum asked sadly.

'All may follow if they wish. Yet why you would wish to do so when you are not even *from* Haff . . . ' the rest was left unsaid.

'I liked and respected her,' was all he could think to say.

'You *knew* her?'

'We talked a few times before she left.'

'Then you are more than welcome to follow,' he was told, as the man continued to walk on.

Only Shrum and a few of his men in command followed. As few of their troops who had been captured had actually seen her as they had.

'I wonder what happened to her,' Borth asked of him. 'And because of this - what may have happened on any of our planets?'

'We may only be told if Octavus survives himself and will speak to us of it later, Borth.'

∞

The crowd continued to gather and enlarge as they awaited the return of the ship which they knew was bringing her home to appear.

At the immense structure which was the cryo building they all halted and now began to wait. The Garen's, the Lords and Ladies. And with them went four quite attractive young women who had been immediately summoned when the signal came in. These of course were her android maids.

The doors swung closed behind them, and they continued to walk to where a small group awaited them. These were some of the operators of the cryo building who were that at the time, one of the various teams who looked after its thousands of sleeping occupants.

King Jaaf, Queen Lerus, the Princes Toff and Serde, and Princesses Narize, Berla and Scarri led the way. Before this group they and the others came to stand.

'How long, Mecchus?'

Chief Scientist Mecchus looked towards the display as it counted down. 'Five minutes, King Jaaf. We are readying her twenty life-cycle clone as per our late Prime Commanders personal request. She herself preferred that one being awakened over the twenty-eight life cycle one.'

'She told you this?'

Mecchus gave a nod. 'As she told us before leaving. In any battle it is always possible that I may fall, Mecchus. So she asked which clones were nearest her own starting age - and she chose the youngest.'

'Why the youngest one?' asked Queen Lerus.

'As she said to us, 'The younger I am, will allow me even more time to devote to my dear Haff again'.'

They all began to nod. That was certainly the way that Raxx would think. Always about themselves and their planet. They all now stood there quietly and began to watch the timer now. Three minutes and twenty-two seconds to go.

Princess Narize had a sudden thought and so looked to the four maids for an answer. 'You must have seen this happen before many times I am sure. Yes? For all of us it will be the first time we have ever witnessed such an event. What will it be like?'

Leenis was the first of them to speak. 'For we four, Princess, this will be the twenty-third time that we have witnessed a new Prime Commander emerging. None of you will have ever seen her in her youth before as we have. She is a rare beauty indeed. Although when she first does appear she will feel very lost; almost like that of a child at the beginning. Due to this, she must be treated both cordially and gently. As she will not even know who *she* is herself fully until the old memories are implanted into her. Even with her brain only just starting to function as she emerges, she will only see herself as a young woman with no true idea at all of what or who she is yet.

'Right from the opening of the slot of her cryo-cell, we four will once again slowly help her to understand her new role. We will also take her home as soon as possible, so that we can to get her bathed and prepared for when her memories do finally arrive. Then we will return back here with her so that this can be done.'

Their eyes all checked the timer, only one minute and fourteen seconds to go.

Leenis quickly continued while there was just enough time. 'For many incarnations previously, which was both began and accepted by all the Royal households in the past; including each new Prime Commander herself. Deference must be shown to her by kneeling. This has been done simply so as we are not just standing here as if waiting to attack her en-masse as a group. As doing this will also take any possible stress out of her initial awakening.

'This is only because as the slot on the cell opens up on her, we would already be stood here, like this. That can be a somewhat frightening experience to some of them as they emerge from sleep. Whereas if we are kneeling when her eyes first open, then there is much less chance of her becoming agitated by the sight of all of us here.'

The countdown timer was already down to twenty seconds and counting. At which point, Mi, Leenis, Dorro and Parri all sank down to one knee and lowered their heads.

All of this was also a very new event to any of the others, of course. Seeing as none of them were born when she last emerged over three hundred years ago. Quickly they all followed suit and knelt alongside the maids. While all those from the building itself, except for Mecchus, did the same. He could not as he still had to operate the controls.

∞

With only five seconds remaining, a low beeping began to count the final five of these down until a final steady beep turned off. Mecchus began to flick various buttons and switches and the slot of the cryo-cell slid around upon itself and opened.

All of their heads may have been lowered. Yet all of their eyes were raised as high into their sockets as was possible to look upon something so very new to them. The pair of closed eyelids before them then opened.

Mi then lifted her head. 'Please do not be alarmed, Lady. And please do not move at all until this man.' She slowly gestured at Mecchus. 'Removes all of the life sustaining equipment from your body. May he do this for you now?' she asked.

The young woman before them licked at her dry lips. Her eyes swivelled to look at the person the one who was kneeling had signalled to. She them offered a somewhat hoarse, 'Yes.'

Her voice even sounded the same, apart from only its far more well known elderly tone that they knew so well.

Mecchus himself knelt and then bowed his head in deference to her. Before then rising to his feet and saluting her before walking towards her.

One by one each of the electrical contacts upon her were removed. These over the many cycles which she had been in the cryo-cell had continuously kept all of her muscle groups flexing and relaxing. The main conduit connection from a computer to the tiny slot on her head to her brain was now unplugged. This connection had kept her in a REM state over all this time, as if she had been in an everlasting dream. The final two connections to her body were the sustenance feeder and to her waste disposal unit.

She had no idea that for all her lifetime she had been laid flat as all these connections served to keep her alive. While just before the slot opened, one of the switches had raised the apparatus she had laid upon for all this long time into an upright position. The last things to be removed were the restraints holding her body to the table.

Standing there upon her own feet for her first ever time, she wobbled dangerously. It was then that the four maids quickly rushed to her side to steady her.

'Thank you.'

'You are welcome, Lady.'

Her black eyes peered at the four of them very slowly. As she licked across her dry lips once again.

'Liquid please,' Dorro said to one of Mecchus's assistants.

As they held her steady, Dorro took the offered drink and raised it to her mouth which she slowly drank until it was empty.

She looked around her even more now. Seeing all those who were still upon the floor slightly below her and as yet on one knee.

'Who am I? Where am I? And why are none of us wearing anything?' was her opening questions.

Leenis gave a light trilling chuckle. 'You ask us that every time you know,' she replied.

'You, my Lady, are Derus Raxx. Prime Commander of Haff, and now in your seventeenth incarnation. We four by the way are your maidservants.' As she pointed at herself first and then the others, she said, 'I am Leenis, she is Mi, she is Dorro, and she is Parri. We are the ones who will be taking care of you at your home.

'You are of twenty life-cycles in age. You also have black hair and eyes. We four will see to all your grooming requirements just as soon as we get you home. As here in this capsule, your hair grew without any restraint. But that will soon be rectified for you by us. And to remove all the gel which covered you to keep your skin both supple and hydrated whilst you slept. We will also remove any of this by bathing you, then we will dry you and massage you.

'As to where you are regarding your questions. At the moment you are in the cryo building, where you have just emerged from your dormant sleep. And as to why we wear little or no clothing? This has been the way on our planet named Haff for many thousands of years, my Lady. Very soon you will have regained all of your memories and know all of these things yourself anyway.'

Having attained her balance finally. Raxx could now look down and around at her herself. The first thing she noticed was that her hair behind her was so long that it almost reached to the floor on which her bare feet stood. She looked down over her breasts, not yet understanding why each of her nipples were so stiffly protruding like that. Although this was only due to the actual temperature chill inside the building. She quickly noted that the maids did not have this same problem. Whereas those women who were still kneeling lower down there from her were. So that was very strange . . .

She used a finger to touch the erect nipple of her left breast, only noting that it was very firm, almost hard; even her doing that left a single small cleared patch in the gel behind.

'Why are yours not like mine or theirs?' she questioned.

'We are your android maids, my Lady,' said Mi.

'What are those?'

'We are not human like you and they are, my Lady. We are not real life forms. Our bodies are built in factories to resemble humans. Within and upon your own body are skin, blood, tissue tendons and muscles. While ours on the outside are made with a prylastic material. Which is a formula created and used in an attempt to match the same as your own. Inside us, we are simply servo's, circuits, hydraulics and fluids. And while your own brains are certainly human in origin, all of ours are biogenic.'

But it was the sight of her own black pubic hair that caused her to gasp. Even just from looking down at it as it was like a wild untended bush that stuck well out in front of her. Not only that, she was also feeling a little itchy under her armpits. Raising her arms, there were also long haired bushes under these too.

'Do not worry over any of this, my Lady. We will soon have everything trimmed, cut, shaved and tidied just the way you have always liked it.'

'How could you know what I like or not, when I've never met any of you before?' she asked with a singularly fuzz-haired dark eyebrow rising quizzically. Which was also another Derus Raxx trait.

'When you do have your memories, then you will soon remember everything that you need to, my Lady.' The young Raxx only emitted a low sigh in response to that response.

∞

As the slot slid open before them, the Garen's, as well as each of the attending lords and ladies sucked in their breaths at the sight which befell their eyes.

They all then knew that the tales of their own earlier ancestors had been true, when they had spoken of her lustrous dark hair. As to each of them, they had only seen it when being that of a greying-white, or just a white haired old woman depending on their age. Quite similar to that of all the very old long retired Haffian's.

Yet as a young Raxx, she was indeed quite a stunning young woman for them all to gaze upon. Though the coating of gooey gel, and the highly unexpected amount of hair growth upon her body could still not detract from her actual beauty. A beauty which was very much apparent to them all.

They had listened attentively as the four maids had quickly ran up to help her newly released and teetering body out. And then as they slowly began to answer her first questions. She was female, of course, just as every Raxx had been for about as long as any of them could remember the stories about her. Only twenty cycles in age this time. Barely much older than Prince Serde himself, or the youngest Princesses Berla and Scarri; and of course Lady Yu.

Now though, they were also able to just see the slight colour tone to her tinted skin under the gel. Her almost oriental in appearance eye folds. And that even now as a young woman, she appeared to be both strong and fit, as well as having firmness of musculature all done through generations of gene manipulation.

The sheer mass of hair which she had upon her body had certainly been unexpected. Her figure itself was unquestionably exciting to a male eye. As her waist narrowed in so much to offer her an hourglass figure. Not that her hips were as large as many women they all knew. They were simply offset by her very small waist and completely flat stomach. Her legs were longish, although not too much. Yet they surely had a muscular look to them.

Her arms were the same, and were certainly nothing at all like the spindly affairs which they had all known previously and were used to seeing upon her older self. From her waist, her upper half tapered outwards towards her wider shoulders. And in the centre mass itself were two quite amazing mounds of flesh, each with nipples which stood out quite prominently due to the chilled air. Once again, the only thing which any of them had know before, was that of a Raxx who had had almost ancient flattened breasts. All in all, she was now a woman who would surely cause anyone's eyes to want to look more than once at her!

They also knew that she was also imbued with far higher brain functions than any of them. Also caused through various genetic balances over a long time. Which was indeed what had enabled her to carry out her task of Prime Commander for so long, and also so adroitly for them.

'So who are these other people down there?' she asked of her maids as they had made themselves known to her.

As Mi spoke their names, each rose to their feet and saluted her in their usual military style. 'King Jaaf, Queen Lerus, Prince Toff and Prince Serde. The Princesses Narize, Berla and Scarri, my Lady. They live in the Royal Palace which is here in Haff Central.

'Then from the eight main cities on Haff you have the Lord's Arne of Bollus, Budle of Ceday, Dacras of Erin, Flent of Golgos, and Wynoc of Humme. These are the Ladies Mell of Nerv, Winsher of Sereth, and Yu of Tonnis.' Each of these also came to their feet as their names were offered and saluted her as well.

'So why if they are royalty were *they* kneeling? When surely *I* should have been the one who is kneeling before them to offer respect?' she queried.

'It was only because you have just came out of your long cryo sleep, my Lady. None of us wished to alarm you by simply standing here while looking at you when your eyes first opened upon us. And, you are also our very own *Prime Commander* too.'

'I do not even know what that means ... Mi wasn't it? Am I right?'

'Yes, my Lady, you are correct. And as you are our Prime Commander, so you are in charge of Haff.'

'And Haff is what exactly, a village, town or city?'

'It is a planet, my Lady.'

'But why am I in charge of an entire planet when there is Royalty? I find this very difficult to understand, Mi.'

'May I speak to you, Derus?' asked the King.

'*Derus?* Who is, Derus ... Oh yes, that was my own name you told me, didn't you!' She gave a slow smile. 'And of course, please speak to me if you wish your majesty.'

'Haff, as you will soon come to learn, Derus, is a military planet. Even I myself, my wife and our children here. As well as the other Lord's and Ladies families who you see here have all been through military training-'

Raxx turned her head. 'Really ... I wonder why you have done that due to your own status. You four as well?' she asked the maids.

'Oh no, my Lady. We, as we are androids are not trained as combat machines - more as service machines.'

Raxx sighed. 'I'm afraid I'm quite lost again now!'

Queen Lerus took over, being something of a historian herself. 'It has been well over two thousand years ago now, my dear Derus. Since the first androids came into being. And it was decided even then that they would not, nor ever be created to fight for us. They were created as helpers, or as Mi has said, service androids.

'We as the humans on our planet all train to our utmost to become our own military. This also includes those of us you see here before you, too. We may indeed come from a different bloodline which allowed us these titles. But due to a very early Raxx decision, *we* also had to train as well. The reason for this, was simply to show the rest of the people that it didn't matter who we were by title. Only that *we*, just as they, are all Haffian's! And so, we also began to do our own training alongside them. This showed them that no matter who we all were, we were given no favoured status because of this. We *also* followed the Haff route of military training and so could function just as well as they could as troops.

'While those who are androids, such as your four maids here. Have been programmed with many options available to them. Such as doctors and medics, repair technicians, builders and maids, gardeners and cleaners. As well as in all of the other kinds of service requirements which Haff itself needs.

'You see, Derus, we on Haff have always been far too busy training to be able to do what those like your maids now do for us instead. So in this way, they are not allowed to fight, but, they *can* protect any of us from harm if the need ever arises.'

Raxx again looked at her maids. 'Are you happy doing all those things? Do you not get bored sometimes?'

Parri gave a gentle laugh. 'We know nothing else, my Lady. It is simply what we have been created to do. The human's of Haff like yourself only know what is basically military things. You could even say that we are luckier. As we are able to do many more things due to our constant programming. We can cook, clean, repair equipment, help to heal your bodies if possible. We can serve in stores, offer beneficial aids to any of you like massages. The reason we *are* required, my Lady, is simply because *as* androids boredom means nothing to us. We are never bored in the way in which a human can be . . .

'On other planets which are near our own, androids will happily do the most repetitive of tasks which humans themselves find far too boring to want to do. Likewise, what may be considered as being far too dangerous a working task for any human, we happily do so also. You must remember that a serious injury to a human is not seen in the same way as it is to us. Where any of you could perhaps lose a finger, hand, or even perhaps an arm or leg. While we would simply remove the affected part, replace it and then continue.'

'I see . . . Well, at least I think I do.'

'You will know all this, when you---'

'Get my memories soon?' she finished for herself.

'Yes.'

Raxx then just offered another low sigh. 'All of this is going to take some time for me to get used to!'

10

Eventually after she had met them all as well as she was able to, except with not really knowing any of them. Her maids requested that she followed them to her personal bubble-pod. Which led to yet more explanations of whatever *that* actually was as they made their way to the exit. Followed behind by those who had first greeted her.

'There is quite a crowd gathered outside to see you, my Lady. Some of them may even offer you strange comments. Please do not be offended by anything which may be said though. As the Haffian way is a very frank and outspoken way of speaking, even to speaking ones mind out loud.'

'Why are they waiting to see me?'

'Because you are their new, Prime Commander, my Lady. Or at least you will be when we return later for you to accept your memories.'

'If I am the new one - where is the old one?'

'She fell in battle today just as many other Raxx's have done in the past, my Lady. Some who were a little older than you are now. While others were far older when their time came. So when this news was sent to us here on Haff. At that time, you were then being prepared to be awakened to become our seventeenth Prime Commander. It is her memories which we are now waiting for to arrive to place within you. By then though, we will have taken you to your home, cleaned and bathed you, massaged you. Fed you, and we will have certainly sorted out all of your body hair for you!'

'Very well. Although I am still understanding very little of what you are telling me right now.'

'You will recall everything you need to know as soon as we return back here with you. By then you should not only feel, but look like a completely different person too. Everything neat and tidy. None of this gel still all over you. And hopefully we'll also have enough time to serve you a nice meal as well!'

'How? When I don't even know what I like to eat?'

'We already know what all your favourite meals and drinks have been for a long time. So we will make a few of those for you, so as to offer your body some proper sustenance for it. Instead of what you have been receiving via the tube for so long. It is just something to which your taste buds and stomach will have to become acclimatised to from now on.'

As they approached the great doors, they as usual began to swing open on their own due to sensing someone nearing them. It was as they opened and they could see some of the people outside that a rippling exclamation began to ring out.

'She's here!' one woman voice screamed.

'We have our Prime Commander again!' echoed a deep male voice.

'Hell, she looks a right mess!' said another woman.

'And so would you if you just came out of *that* place!' stated another woman in response.

'Well I know that, Edris. But I mean to say - could they not have done *something* about tidying up her wild forest down there before allowing her to come outside? I mean to say, it's not very womanly to have as much frontage as *that* showing down there upon you, is it?'

Leenis then held her hands aloft until all the excited and expectant furore died away.

'Please pardon our new Prime Commander as to her body state right now - or if she does not seem to recognise any of you at this very moment. You all must remember that without the memories which are on their way here to her as we speak. The only things that she does know are what she has been told in the past few short minutes since her newly awakened incarnation. Only when she has received these memories will she once again become our next Prime Commander in all ways.

'Before those do return here, we have to take her to her own home to see to her personal needs immediately. She will then return here again very soon whenever that news is delivered to have these same memories implanted and restored to her.'

With that statement, her maids began to lead her through the throng almost like that of having a security detail around her. Many hands were quickly reaching out simply to touch her. While one very old looking man with short white hair appeared to block their way to the bubble-pod completely.

'Raxx you slut!' he bellowed. 'If I'd known you were this good looking. I would have asked to be cloned myself so that I could marry you just for the sex itself if nothing else!'

Laughter rippled all around at his words. For Raxx though, whatever he said went right above her head. Yet she deduced that it was about her anyway by the way it was said, and she flushed slightly.

'High Commander Tarsk, I am very much ashamed of you!' Mi bridled and wagged a finger at him. 'You are taking advantage of a woman of whom has no former memories as yet. She does not even know who you are right now; or even *why* you would even say such a thing as that to her.'

The old man looked into the very much younger woman's eyes only to see a complete lack of recognition in them. In fact, there was only a hint of embarrassment.

'I can only beg your pardon, my dearest Raxx. We have known each other for so many decades that I was simply overcome with excitement by the sight of not only your return to us, but also your very loveliness at this age. I can only ask for your forgiveness right now - and to ask if you will kindly allow me to say the same thing to you again later when you do remember me.'

Mi nodded at his apology. 'You can agree to do that, my Lady. As with your memories returned you will certainly remember *this* High Commander again - and knowing you as we do. We also know that you will certainly be able to make a *very* suitable reply to him, too. Of that I am sure!'

'Very well, High Commander.'

'I give you my thanks,' he said, saluting her even while stepping aside. Shrum and some of his men were also near enough to see her from their vantage point. But they did note that even as her eyes passed over them. There was no hint or sign of any recognition for them either.

As they continued on they heard him say to further laughter, 'It's true - I'm not lying! Even I had no idea that she was as beautiful as that when she was young woman.'

When they at last reached the bubble-pod and helped to seat her inside, they then climbed into it themselves. At this point, they informed her of what she needed to know about what would happen next, and asked her to simply say, 'Home by flight', when her vehicle asked. As of course no matter even if she was a new Raxx. It would still sense all of her own body's life signs and traits. As well as detecting her own personal gene structure. Which meant that as she was in it, she was also in command of any of its functions.

The display on the bubble-pod lit up as it checked over its own preparation status throughout as usual. And then the voice asked its question of her personally, and Raxx answered it with the words she had been told to say. The twin doors of the bubble-pod slid down and closed as its engine turned on.

It then said the usual things which all inside the vehicle but Raxx already knew. The I.I.S.S. activated and she found herself unable to move as it began to rise from the ground. She felt a touch of fear at her inability to move, and from seeing the people around her suddenly disappear downwards. And then it whisked them away while the four maids talked together as they awaited their destination being reached.

∞

Even long after Rist and his troops on Briath had stormed the citadel. And the other commanders fought, or simply took prisoners on the other four planets. Raxx was just wading into the hot water of a sunken bath. All four maids followed her into it as they would usually do. And as one began to brush out her extremely long wet hair. The other three used various implements to gently scrape the gel from her body.

'I could really get used to this!' she sighed loudly, very much enjoying the pampering she was being given.

'You have enjoyed it like this for a very long time already, Derus. Which is why we still continue to do it for you like this each time,' said Dorro.

'You do?' she murmured, eyes now closed in pleasure.

'Our sole task is to look after you in any way that you require us to.' said Mi.

'You honestly don't get bored with looking after me?'

All four maids trilled with laughter.

'We are not susceptible to boredom, Derus,' stated Parri. Again repeating words which had been spoken to her earlier. 'Yet I must say that for us over the many passing centuries. We have actually enjoyed caring for you.'

'Why?'

'In one way, whenever you begin to become a great deal older you start to see us almost as your daughters, or at least very close friends.'

'Is that not usual?'

'Oh no . . . as androids we are simply seen by most humans as task completers. We four are, I suppose we could say, have been very lucky really in serving you. As you will happily talk to us just like you would to another human.'

'Don't the rest of you do this?'

'I'm afraid not. Almost all the rest are programmed just to complete the various tasks which are given to them.'

'So why are you four so different then?'

'Well, that was actually down to you. Well, a much earlier version of you that is. So you were the one who made the request to our creators on Klimm before we were each energised and brought into being. You were the one who requested that the parameters of each of our programming was altered and adapted. This was so we would all suit what it was that *you* personally wanted us to be like.'

'But what did I want?' Raxx asked.

'Company and friendship mainly,' said Mi from behind her head still brushing away.

'Are you saying that I don't have actual friends?'

'Not in the way that you may think of friends, Derus,' now answered Leenis. 'To those on Haff, you are seen as the exalted one. The beloved one of all the people. I'm afraid that most are so in awe of you that they would not even *dare* ask you to be their friend. So, you typically only have what are called work friendships with others. Which also means that when you leave your office, you leave those all behind you until the next day. And then, when you return home . . . '

'You always come home to us!' said Mi.

'For which I must be extremely thankful for?'

'Oh no, we are the ones who are thankful,' Parri interjected. 'Simply because you choose to talk to us so much at home, when you never really have to.'

'My life still to come must be so terrible!'

'Oh, I did not mean for you to see it in that way, Derus. I am sorry for making you think of it as badly as that,' Parri quickly added.

'Why, when it sounds so - well, sad!'

'We think it is because your own brain is always questing for answers at a far higher function level than everyone else, Derus. You must remember that you are a seeker of solutions. A planner, a strategist. One whose memories can recall events from hundreds, if not well over a thousand years ago. If only to compare one against another.'

'Do you mean to say I frighten them?'

'Some. Well, perhaps most of them actually . . . For you, Derus, life is forever a series of moves - like those in a game of Ringee. As in, will this benefit Haff. Or will this way make Haff different, or better, or stronger than it ever was. If I do something that way will Haff not work as well as it has. This is only because you are always doing what you think is best for

Haff. Simply because as you *are* their Prime Commander, and so all the decisions for our planet come from you.'

'What's Ringee?'

'It's a very fast game of strategy playing, Derus,' replied Mi. You play it a lot with us, only because we have a chance to beat you at it due to the speed of our own biogenic brains. This was another option you personally allowed us all to have. An actual chance to beat you at it, so that you would not become bored by winning all the time.'

∞

By the time Raxx was having her hair cut, trimmed, or lasered off where needed. Rist many hours earlier had already battled his way up through the various floor levels of the citadel. Bodies lay scattered everywhere on their upwards charge - although only those who fell had held weapons. Many of the citizens had openly cringed as they came trotting up to them in such a surge. Only to almost pass out in relief as they ran straight past them. It was as always, that those who were unarmed or had not fought were completely ignored unless they did something that was very stupid!

Rist, as the man in charge of this attack now since Raxx's death. Was also now the one on the ground who had to request information updates on a regular basis.

'Report death and injury counts,' he asked continuously via his implant, even as his own Grem switched instantly from shield to energy burst and left yet another lifeless body behind. The selected officer in the command ship who was gathering this information, sat in the ship which both he and Raxx had landed on the ground. As any ship which Raxx was in had naturally became their main command ship.

Before him was a bank of screens in order for him to do this. Screens which updated their flow continually whenever the medics on the battleground ran their scanners over one of their own fallen troops. The medics would then do a quick triage upon any injury, and then load them onto one of the many hover stretchers which always followed behind them. These would then return by whatever was the quickest route, back to what by this time to whichever one would have been set-up as their medical ship.

The army on Briath were dropping like flies. Even with many of them using weapons that reached a great deal further than their attackers. Nothing rarely if ever got through those things that they wielded so strangely in front of them.

'Fourteen dead, sixty-three injured but safe.'

'Seventeen dead, eighty-two injured but safe.'

'Twenty-three dead, ninety-four injured but safe,' reported the officer as each update filtered in to him.

The word *safe* at the end, simply meant that these troops would fully recover from any injuries which they had sustained. The reports as they came in each time he asked, also kept him in touch as they were updated. As they were already now inside the citadel itself, Rist could only marvel once again at Raxx's supreme strategy planning.

∞

'From what I expect at this upcoming encounter,' she had informed him as well as four other High Commanders at their final meeting before leaving Haff. 'And with the way that I have planned it. It should allow us to overrun their first defences quite easily. If we attack correctly. I also envisage very few deaths of our own troops all the way right up to the citadel itself. As Gremplar will no doubt hold back most of his own main force in order to guard that.

'As you yourselves know, I have already tested their weapons we captured against one of our own shield walls. So we know that they cannot penetrate our shields with them when ours are so close together. But it will be where their energy bursts may go *after* being deflected is where our troops may suffer most. On Briath they must attack in a united line until the actual break-away is done to enter the city in more than one place. As to any of their larger weapons which they may have to use. I have no way of comparing them to our shield walls yet. You will only see this to understand better what further tactics to use, Octavus - as by then I expect that I will no longer be alive to decide anything.

'After the split when you then begin to enter into the city itself, is where I expect the first danger will appear. As shots from them will deflect off those shields ahead and can go anywhere. Which means any troops using their Grem in attack will be open to being hit from these deflections.

'However, in the way that I expect to see it happening. We should lose no more than two hundred dead and possibly around a thousand injured before you can actually reach Gremplar's citadel. After entering, this is where more of our troops could be lost than outside.

'According to some of the designs of the citadel which I managed to attain from the captured troops. It is like a maze, which leads upwards to the very top. They will, or *should* know this maze of theirs perfectly. Whereas you will just be going off what you can see at each turn. But have no doubt that Gremplar will be right at the top of this building, with the main force of his own troops fighting every inch of the way against you to reach there.

'From what knowledge I gathered from Shrum about him. He will be far too proud and stubborn to have his men lay down their arms. Unlike the Mayors on our own system or planets, they had nothing to lose. Whereas Gremplar may lose his empire! So he will tell them to fight until there are no more left to do so. You can be sure that *he* himself of course, will *not* be holding any weapon when you find him. Tyrants such as he is you see, will rarely put themselves at risk in a battle. They much prefer to lead from behind and to send their own troops ahead to fight for their own empire. This is where we have always differed on Haff. As when I was still able to do so, I, just as all of you also do, *always* lead from the front. For us, it had always been a matter of principle. For our troops to see us fighting alongside them in the danger areas too!

'For quite a long while now though, my own age eventually failed me to allow me do this. To the point where I knew I would have been unable to keep up even in one of our battle order trots. That was when I came to rely on Commanders like yourselves to do this for me. And also why I planned any tactics so painstakingly. Only because I could not join you any longer. Yet still wished to save as many lives of our troops as I possibly could. By the end of our invasion of all five, my worst expectations are of there being one thousand dead and five thousand injured. I am hoping that those results will come out to be far fewer than my own personal assumption though!

'In my plans for this upcoming battle. I expect two or perhaps even three of these planets to surrender peacefully. Especially after seeing the size of the force being set against them. The tyrants own planet will fight, simply because he will be there himself; and for that reason alone - he will order them to do that. This is where I see my death taking place, Octavus. I will go out before all of you and offer both to him and his other planets terms of surrender before any fighting even begins.

'What you will then see is either just how smart a man he might well be, or else of how stupid he may be. As he will know immediately by the size of our army that he cannot win Yet will he try to save his own troops, or send them to their deaths? You will soon know this by how he answers me. Either a messenger will be sent out by him to discuss this, or I will be killed. After that, you must remember my personal instructions - as then you will be in charge of capturing his planet for me.'

∞

'Thirty-six dead, one hundred and two injured and safe.' Was the next report offered to Rist.

'Height achieved so far?' asked Rist of the same officer. Who would then check another display which showed his transponder against the building they were moving upwards within.

'You are approximately thirty metres above base ground level, Low Commander. While still forty metres from its highest point,' he was informed. Then, 'Thirty-nine dead, one hundred and ten injured but safe,' was lastly added to the message.

By the time Rist and the men and women who followed him finally reached, and then broke through onto the final level of the citadel. The count was by now up to fifty-two dead and one hundred and ninety-six injured but safe.

Only one man stood alone on it. Dressed in clothing far more colourful and richer in fabric than any they had seen so far. Except the rest had been wearing a similar style of body armour to that which Shrum had worn when they'd first met on Jitrus. And of course, just as Raxx herself had told him. Gremplar stood there without any means of fighting them either.

'You are Bork Gremplar, I assume?' asked Rist.

'I am. I am also the ruler of Briath and four other planets!' he stated somewhat pompously.

'Full Report!' Rist now requested of the officer.

'The word from Nee, Pelus and Chell . . . was that there was no fighting and we are in full control, Low Commander. Those on Goll who fought . . . have been terminated. We only lost fourteen dead and seventy-eight who were injured but are safe there. Our own count right here at the moment is fifty-two dead and one hundred and ninety-six injured but safe.'

'Thank you.'

He then stared at the wide and rotund body and sweat laden features of Gremplar, his eyes becoming mere slits. 'I am Low Commander Rist of the First Legion of Haff. Your own former rule now consists of absolutely nothing, Bork Gremplar! As we have taken all five of your planets.' Rist saw and heard the gasp he emitted.

'Three planets wisely surrendered without any bloodshed . . . '

'The cowards!' he spat.

'*Cowards* . . . ?' barked Rist. His own mouth curling in not only disgust, but also distaste at him. 'You actually *dare* to call all those who foolishly fought and died for you, cowards! All of your troops who fought for here and on Goll are dead just because of *you*, Gremplar! And what of those who did not wish to die as eagerly for you? Were they cowards, too? When you yourself are not even armed to fight!' Rist's head shook from side to side. 'I'm surprised that you ever became their leader if that is the most you can feel for them!'

'As their ruler I had no need.'

'Our own leader, the Prime Commander . . . who is the one you killed yourself which began this - or who I should say you had killed by your order, Gremplar. She always led us, and fought as well, but always from the front when she could. Yet she was unarmed, and had even just offered you terms of a peaceful surrender when you killed her.

'As for you yourself now; and your family who we also found hiding below. Along with any of your troops that are still alive. You will all now be escorted to one of our ships as we return home. I will be leaving five million of our troops stationed upon each of your planets until further decisions are made about them by our new Prime Commander.'

'What will become of us?' Gremplar asked.

'By *us*, I'm sure that you only mean yourself and your family, of course? Not your troops, or the people who live on these planets!' he said viciously. 'I personally do not care at all what may happen to you, Gremplar. Due to your own cowardly action against our late Prime Commander. I only hope our new one will have you executed!'

He stared harshly at him. Then as if to remind him again, said, 'By the way, just in case you were wondering, although I very much doubt it after talking to you. *All* of your troops here, and those which were stationed on Goll are dead. By that I mean there are no survivors.'

Rist then spoke to the officer on the ship. 'Reform, embark, and be ready to return home. Follow the plans set out by the Prime Commander before we left Haff. Advise those being left behind when we go - that their tasked duty is to clean-up and offer security until we know more soon. I will see you all back on Haff! Rist out!'

To a small group of his men and women he pointed at Gremplar. 'Escort this *thing* here to our ship along with his family!' As Rist felt no compunction whatsoever to offer Gremplar any titles or good tidings at this time.

'Yes, Low Commander.'

As Gremplar was led away, Rist had himself put through to the commanders who would be staying behind for the present time. He made sure they knew what their orders were, and even to how they must carry them out. Only when he was sure they each understood, did Rist begin the long walk back to the ship.

∞

After the new clone of Raxx had left the cryo building and they had finally been able to escort her away from the crowd. Her four maids placed her into her own waiting gold personal bubble-pod. The elder Raxx before leaving on the invasion had sent it home on auto. They had then used it to reach the cryo building after receiving the sad news about her. With all of them quickly inside, it left as it had arrived. Using its flight mode as a faster means of returning home.

The Royal Family and all the Lords and Ladies had gone straight to their palace for a meal. Having had this, and being informed that the expected ship was almost home, they were also now standing outside the palace. They were waiting along with the crowd of many millions, who were all still in attendance to offer their farewells to her older self when it finally returned home to them.

After Raxx had been well and truly seen to and had had something quite enjoyable to eat. They all climbed back into her bubble-pod and returned to land just outside the cryo building again where it had all begun for her.

As the fourth hour passed from her being awakened. She, her maids, and the still waiting crowd all began to look up as they heard what could only be a ship preparing to land. It came down slowly, as they always did, until settling upon a single grid with flashing warning lights. Which had for that same known reason been left empty by everyone.

As its engines spooled down and finally went just as silent as the mass of people waiting around it. The ramp on its side then came down. From out of it came only five people. The two pilots, the load master, and the two medics. Between four of them upon a hovering stretcher was the mostly covered body of their Prime Commander. The two medics, with one carrying the memory probe as if it were a priceless object walked only slightly behind them.

Only her head was visible, her white hair moving slightly in the breeze as if she was still alive. Though they all knew in their hearts that she was not. As they passed by the Royal line, they all saluted and then followed behind. It then began to pass through the multitude of people who had waited to honour her. They all began to salute her as well.

Shrum and his men who had also waited for such a long time even gave her their own salute by offering her a bow from one warrior to another. Yet they had been quite shocked earlier when they seen the emergence of a dark-haired and much younger woman a long while ago. Hearing the same name of Raxx being spoken again by them until her pod finally rose and left.

All their salutes had a ripple effect as she passed by them all. Until more and more of them now continued to follow the moving procession.

'Who is that?' asked Raxx of her maids.

'That is sadly *you* when at a much older age than you are now, my Lady. This is the Derus Raxx who you have just replaced due to her death. It will also be her memories which you will have implanted within you very soon now too.'

Raxx's body entered through the open doors, as did the still tightly clasped memory probe. Behind them now walked Raxx being ushered inside by her maids, as well as the Royals following in turn.

Shrum and a few of his men actually braved the huge crowd. And slowly but steadily made their way as near to the front of it as they could. As everyone now waited outside the two immense closed doors.

'Thank heavens that she's been nicely tidied up now!' said that very same female voice from many hours ago. 'At least she looks a bit more like the Raxx we all knew.'

'How can we possibly even *know* what she looked like as a young woman,' said her friend Edris to her. 'When she was already reaching her three hundred's before either of us were even born!'

'Well, I was only saying.'

'Then stop doing so. We have ourselves a new Prime Commander again. And with the age she is, we can *all* now at least tell our children and grandchildren just *how* beautiful a woman she is when young. I actually feel like celebrating right now and not complaining!'

∞

Back inside the huge building, the followers trailed the moving body of the late Raxx right up to where the same scientists stood as if they had never moved from earlier. At the bottom of the step they all came to a halt.

'What happens now? asked the young Raxx.

'Chief Scientist Mecchus will insert the probe and implant the memories within you,' answered Mi.

'And what about her now?' asked Raxx, offering a hand gesture towards the almost covered remains.

'Our former Prime Commander Raxx will be cremated, as we all are. And then her ashes will be placed into our wall of honour,' stated Mecchus. 'It is where many of our most revered warriors, or those who fell in battle heroically are entombed for all time. Our people can then visit and honour any of them at any time they so wish. There are many ashes of other Raxx's there, only as they have each served our planet so well.'

'Very well. So what must I do now?'

Mecchus pointed. 'If you would please stand just there below the step, Prime Commander. I will then be at a slightly elevated level than you are for me to insert the probe.'

Raxx walked a little further and turned around to face the way she had just came in. And then almost unthinkingly before Mecchus could do this task. Raxx bent forward and stroked the side of the cold and old shrivelled appearing face before her. 'I can only hope that I can do as good a job as you have for so long!' she said quietly to the cold-skinned corpse. Having done this, she now stood very straight and waited for whatever it was that was about to happen to her.

Her maids held onto her to keep her very steady as Mecchus took the offered probe which was still carefully cradled within the medics hands.

As she felt his hands on her hair to part it Raxx closed her eyes tightly and took a very deep breath. As what they were about to see was a new experience for all of them really, except for the maids and one medic who had all luckily been at the last incarnation. For Raxx herself, it was about what she was about to actually feel!

Mecchus was already sweating. As if he got this wrong in any way at all. Then the past memories of each Prime Commander prior to this one would be lost forever.

As he now pressed a button on the probe itself, a miniscule filament came out of the end of it. He knew that he couldn't make a mistake. The filament itself was so thin, that even missing the tiny aperture by the slightest and its touching of her head instead could shatter the strand.

Beads of perspiration now rolled from his hairless high forehead and over his rippled furrowed brow in intense concentration. To continue their passage down over his eyes and face as he slowly, hesitantly, sy-second by sy-second, edged it nearer. His tongue even protruded from between his lips unknowingly as he did so, such was the feeling of intense pressure being placed upon him now.

They all held their breaths at this moment, knowing just how important it was. Except for the androids there, who of course did not actually breathe.

Mecchus had no idea his mouth was open rather wide now, nor that his tongue was constantly running around his dried out lips. Which were dryer than they had been before in his life at such an anxious moment. With their programming, androids were of course even more dextrous at such things. Nor did they feel the same stresses or worries as he did. Even when extracting them from the original Raxx while on an actual battlefield!

But he was human and not an android as they were. And this part of it had always been a human only task. So he felt the growing nervousness within himself. Nerves which at this very moment, were not helping him very much at all with what he had to do. As all he could see, were his huge hands and fingers trying to manipulate this very tiny piece of filament into its recipient aperture. It felt as if his own aiming hand was shaking uncontrollably now. And then as it slid in, and he quickly depressed the necessary switch.

After he had extracted it, he almost passed out. Sat down upon the step and his entire body shuddered with utter relief. He had not screwed it up just when he though he might. His body still visibly shook while actually now covered in a sheen of wetness, from only just those brief few minutes of utter trepidation.

Raxx opened her eyes. Blinked once, twice . . . three times. Only to then offer a slow smile at the worried looking faces of her maids.

'Hello girls,' she said with a smile. Then her eyes took in the rest stood before her. 'Your Majesties, my Lords and Ladies, it is good to see you all again!' she said and gave them a salute. Fifteen collective breaths whooshed from their mouths after holding it in for so long.

'Derus . . . ' said King Jaaf in a slightly panting breath, 'It is so good to know that you are back with us once again!'

She smiled at him. 'Back indeed!' and then looked at herself. 'And thank the stars I even look a great deal better than I did not so long ago, too!' she remarked.

He nodded. 'None of us have ever actually seen you as young as you are now before, Derus. As a very beautiful young woman in her own prime of life.'

'I thank you for your kind words, your Majesty. It is even hard for I myself to recall how I looked when so young after such a long a time has passed again.'

Raxx now turned to the still sitting chief scientist. 'I must also thank both you and the medic responsible for saving my memories and giving them back to me. Has this new body been given what I asked for it?' she asked of him.

He dragged himself slowly back up to his feet. His body still carrying that wet sheen, although at least it was drying now. 'Yes, Prime Commander. The new attributes you requested were added to it before the new body was awakened.

'*More* attributes, Derus? Did you really need any more?' asked the Queen.

Raxx gave a nod to her. 'I did not ask for more longevity, as I think my past life was more than long enough, Queen Lerus. In fact, I think I would have preferred it being shorter actually! However, I did remember what I was like on my last awakening. That my muscles had only been kept in balance by electrical impulses throughout my cryo-sleep. But not through actual life cycles of training which all you had. So, I asked for far higher muscle strength to be added again. My brain was also still not quick enough yet for all the knowledge which I already knew, and had to run through to ascertain instant fact correlations.

'So I also requested that my ability to think and make faster conclusions and decisions had to be heightened as well. Hopefully these will now help me more as we go ahead in time. As when I have my first training session, I am hoping that my muscle groups will recall far easier how it should be carried out. The extra speed of my brain will, I also hope, allow me to work out tactics and plans at a even greater level than before.'

'We all do!' said the King. 'If not, then yet more will be needed to add to your next future self all over again . . .'

The Queen smiled at her again. 'By the way, our citizens are waiting outside to also greet your return to us, too!'

Raxx nodded slowly. 'In that case, your Majesty. It would be most inappropriate for me to keep them waiting.'

11

At the entrance to the building as the doors opened to let them out. A tumultuous roar went up as Raxx came to the top of its outer steps and raised her hands high into the air.

A trio of floating holo-cams swarmed around her as she did so. Causing the sides of many buildings to turn into giant screens to project her to everyone on the planet.

An android newscaster then appeared upon all the screens. 'Good day to you all. I am Tufas, your news reporter today, and I greet you all at this historic event which so many of you are now witnessing for the first time. This is a full system-wide broadcast to all citizens of Haff from outside the Cryo Building. Where our very recently awakened Prime Commander Raxx has just emerged from her incarnation implant.

'This broadcast is also going out to any interested protectorates, satellites; or to those of our troops who are stationed anywhere else at the moment through using our military pulse waves.

'If I may ask on behalf of us all, Prime Commander. How are you feeling?'

Raxx spoke and the holo-cams automatically scanned both her and her voice and relayed them via its network. 'I am feeling fit and healthy once again thank you, Tufas. A little sad of course that my recent old body had to make way for this wonderful new one that I have now. But, speaking as the much younger woman that I am right now. It only means I can once again begin to serve you all to the best of my abilities for a long time again.'

Again the roar that erupted was deafening and took a good long while before it calmed enough to hear anything further. Unfortunately, this next calm was also the time when High Commander Tarsk also now chose to repeat his earlier remark live on air, which was heard everywhere.

'Raxx you slut!' he shouted out before the cameras and all who were watching. 'If I'd known you were this good looking, I would have asked to be cloned myself so that I could marry you just for the sex itself if nothing else!'

'Masurik Tarsk, you old fart!' she replied instantly. 'Even as a clone you would likely still need a robo-crane just to try and hold it up long enough to try and please me!'

Tarsk let a loud howl of laughter out while he slapped at his bare thigh in happiness. 'Welcome back to us, Prime Commander! It truly is a great day for Haff to have you ready to take care of us all again!' he called out rather too loudly to acknowledge her properly while actually saluting.

For any of those near enough to see a screen. Whether on Haff itself, planets which they defended. Ships on patrol, or returning home like those which now carried Rist. Even the troops who had for now been left behind on five new planets. And who had already erected many portable screens so as to keep in touch with any news from their home planet. So all of these were laughing at the byplay between the very recently retired High Commander Tarsk of the First Legion and Raxx, whenever it reached them.

'It is good to see you again too, my retired former High Commander,' Raxx now responded. 'I can see that you are enjoying at least *some* of your retirement now. Since you appear to be out chasing after any young woman so as to bed her?' she chuckled.

An even larger ripple of laughter from the gathered crowd followed this statement from her. Then she continued on chatting to a lot more of them as she went. Until she came to a rather sudden halt while holding a hand to her ear. The silence now grew around her and became palpable. As all who were there knew she was receiving some kind of incoming information.

'Yes, I can hear you now, Octavus, please go ahead.'

Raxx listened as Rist first welcomed her new arrival. As well as offering his thanks that the ship had returned to Haff safely. He then went on to tell her all that had happened since the attack began, and how it had all ended up.

'So you are on your way back now then, Octavus. With enough left behind to secure all of them?' She gave a nod as she listened to his brief but concise report. 'In which case I will see you after your return and wait to hear the full details from you. Raxx out!'

She then began to walk and talk again as she headed to her pod. Although this was only until she reached a face which she had only recently come to know.

'General Shrum . . . I hope that you are finding me far more palatable to your eyes now than you appeared to do previously?'

'Indeed, Prime Commander,' he responded while offering her a bow. 'Although I am sorry that you lost your life not long ago . . . '

He had to stop there only as it sounded so stupid really. As he was welcoming a woman who was actually dead, and who was now back to life again. But yes, she truly was a much better sight to his eyes now - even if it was in a strange way.

'Can you tell me how it occurred?' he asked.

She gave him a nod. 'The invasion went just as I had envisaged, General. Three of your planets surrendered without any trouble. Whereas I'm afraid both Briath and Goll did not. As for myself, I rode out in front of my troops to offer the same terms of surrender to Gremplar as was being done on the other four at the same time.

'As I awaited his response to my offer, the very last thing I knew was that I was thrown from my hover machine and died then, or shortly after. According to Octavus, Gremplar had fired at me - or more than likely he had ordered someone to do so. After that, well . . . I will only know a lot more detail about what occurred afterwards when Octavus returns to complete his full report to me. However, I am sure you will recall what I told you a while ago? That in one way or another through him, those on Briath fired the first shot. As I expected, the battle itself did not last very long at all after my troops saw me fall.

'What I *can* tell you though, is that very shortly you will be joined here by more prisoners. This will be Gremplar and his family, as well as all those troops who did not resist. Where they did - well, you will already know as to what the outcome of that would be yourself! Anyway, I'll also let you know more later when I do myself.'

She gave him another nod, which he returned with yet another bow, as she again continued towards her personal bubble-pod. Where once she and her maids were inside, it rose into the air and set off for her home.

∞

Lord Arne and his four fellow lords left together and walked away from the heavy crowd even before Raxx had managed to reach her pod. The three Ladies of Haff did not even know they'd gone. So they returned with the Garen's back to the palace for a late meal before returning to their own cities.

Where around a large prepared table, quickly added to with another three place settings. The Royal Family and the three ladies began to talk about what events of the day had been like for all of them.

'Wasn't it amazing that after that tiny probe was given to her, Derus had all those memories back again so quickly?' offered Princess Narize.

'It certainly was!' stated her mother, the queen. 'Personally speaking though, I still cannot get over seeing her emerge from that tube with all of those connections upon her body; as well as being covered all over in that slimy gel when the slot first opened. She just looked so lost and so vulnerable at that moment that I just wanted to hug her.'

'I have heard that they are all like that after first being awakened,' King Jaaf said to those around the table.

'How so, my husband?'

'Well . . . this is only what I heard passed down from my father to me about it, mind you. Because as all of you here will know. Not one of us were even born when the last clone came out of one of those. And he was only just a young boy himself when it happened,' he told them.

'Who exactly *was* the last one now, as even I cannot remember who that was now?' asked the Lady Yu.

'Malk Veleronis, somewhere around eighty-four cycles ago now - or thereabouts,' he imparted.

'The scientist from Spirit?'

'The one and the same.'

'But why here on Haff?' she queried. 'Surely coming from the planet Spirit. It would be much easier for them to be brought out of cryo-sleep on their own planets?'

He shrugged his heavy muscled shoulders. 'It was I suppose, a decision made by another Raxx a very long time ago now is all I know.'

'For what reason though, Father?' asked his youngest daughter, Princess Scarri.

'Perhaps for the very reason why she invaded that tyrants system, Daughter. Imagine if the other planets of our system all had their own cryo buildings for their own important or highly regarded people. And that *our* planet of Haff were *not here* to protect them as we do . . .

'So, unless they each of them had their own armies, then they would have been taken over. Which could mean that any of their clones in a similar building to ours on their planets. Might then simply have been switched-off or shutdown by the new rulers of them.'

'So what you're saying is that by their being here with us on our planet. That we are keeping them safe in case that ever happened?' she asked.

'In a way. Perhaps that was even the earlier Raxx's own thoughts at the time of instigating this measure. But again, you have to also look at the larger picture. Being a military planet as we are, we are also likely more capable of protecting them than they are. Just as we are also protecting our own cloned people here, too. Since we first arrived in this system, we have always been the main protector of all of them. At the time of leaving our home world long ago - it had also been decided before they did that each of these planets would have their own uses,' he said reciting from his own earliest taught memories.

'Where instead of every type of person living together on only the one as we once used to do upon a planet by the name of Earth. We broke apart to make the various planets here in this system suit the requirements of all the different people. Which is why we have planets that only grow things. Then there are those who mine for the metals and such we all need. The ones which are mainly water based which offer us a differing form of fish type food. To the technology planets which make just about everything we all use. There is also the creature planet, where all known forms of life not too hazardous to human life by carrying diseases were brought in cell form to inhabit it. Some which were classed as not being wild are also bred there for our use if we wish to do so.

'And then there is, Spirit, which as we all already know, has the best scientists, thinkers, musicians, writers, and so on. Those who are there to create more than anything else. Something which we ourselves typically do not need to do now. If I remember what is now a very old Earth term correctly that I heard said by Derus once. We are keeping all of our eggs in one basket. which is here on Haff. Where we, with our military forces, have a much better chance of keeping them all safe for future times and needs.'

After a few more varied topics were discussed between them. They began to consume their incoming meals.

∞

There was no such similar happy feeling being shared between the five lords though. As they by then had headed off towards their own transports to return to their homes.

'So we have no chance now?' asked Lord Budle.

'Very little,' answered Arne. 'Unless we manage a stroke of luck at some time to come.'

'In what way?'

'Well, as a new clone of Raxx, she will have to do some training to make sure that her own skills are more than sufficient due to who she is, Lord Budle. Which also means, that during any of these training sessions . . . an accident can always happen!' He smiled a sly smile at them with eyes that appeared to glitter.

'We've been patient for long enough,' said Lord Wynoc to them, 'so a little longer won't make any difference.'

'Not until she feels that her skills are complete,' stated Lord Flent. 'After that, we may have no chance at all. You all must have heard what she said in the building just as I did. That not only has her muscle strength been increased again, but even her ability to think too. She'll be even more dangerous to attack now than she ever was before!

'Just how much extra strength *has* she been given though? And how quickly will her mind work now? We will all have to be even more careful from now on. As if she is even able to sense, or perhaps even *feels* that we are plotting against her . . . then I dread to think of the outcome.'

Lord Arne's head was nodding as they reached the place where all their own personal pods were waiting for them. Just loud enough for them to hear, he said, 'We'll meet again in a month - if not sooner if there is any good news to share. Lord Budle will be our host next time in the city of Ceday.'

With salutes offered to each other, they climbed into their own personal bubble-pods. One by one they started up, then rose slowly. They then headed to an access port far different to those for the larger ships. It was like a lift shaft, but without any doors underground to enter through with it being hollow. Once inside their pods would simply rise up inside the shaft itself until reaching the small inverted L shaped opening at the very top. Only there would the outer doors part for them to exit. The doors there were only to prevent heavy falls of rain from entering down inside the shaft and causing any flooding below.

∞

'Well, she certainly remembered you *this* time, General,' said Borth as they re-entered the building in which they all lived as captives at the moment.

'According to what they were all saying out there, she had her memories back again.'

'Just how *does* that work, General, do you know?'

'Not really. I would not even be able to guess at how such a thing could work. It just shows us how far advanced they are over us,' answered Shrum.

'And all of our men on Briath and Goll . . . '

'I know. If it happened as she told us it did. And I for one certainly believe her. Then the actual main force of our army on Briath were wiped out to a man. As well as those few thousand who were stationed on Goll. Yet I am unable to work out why it is that *our* Leader would even shoot at any unarmed speaker - never mind that it was an old unarmed woman! But if that *is* what he did, then it is no wonder that their army responded in such a way.'

'We may find out what happened soon enough for ourselves, General. Especially if Bork Gremplar himself and the remaining small number of troops from the other three planets are all brought here just as we were?'

Shrum's head nodded slowly. 'I can almost imagine what our Leader's response would be if he captured their Prime Commander during an invasion. Yet with them capturing him, and now bringing him to actually stand before the one who he had killed . . . I cannot even begin to think what justice *she* may meter out to him for that.'

∞

As Raxx settled herself on her usual softly cushioned chair at home. She was asked what she would like to eat. As in a starter, a main meal or even a dessert. From the floating memories going around in her head, she set her own menu.

'Do we have any of that Kerrisof meat from Styros 5 to use? Or has our latest offering from their Minister been given away again? As that even on its own, or with some vegetables is a good meal in itself.'

Mi gave her a smile. 'Seeing as you told us that you were contemplating your upcoming death. We held on to the newest batch that was sent to you by him in readiness. Although many will soon wonder why they aren't receiving it from you any more What with it being so expensive a luxury. I suspect that they will just have to order their own supply of it now seeing as you have now returned back to us with a healthy appetite once more, Derus.

'Although, none of us as yet know what type of creature it is from. Except all that we do hear is that it's the tastiest meant anyone has ever eaten! We think that if you ever visit Styros 5 again, Derus. That you will have to ask them, to see exactly what this Kerrisof creature of theirs actually is. Anyway, what about a starter before it, or a dessert after it?'

'I really enjoyed that thick Coufre soup that you made for me, so I'll have that first, please. Lastly, and only as I haven't had it for a few decades now, one of your deliciously light Frombau desserts would be wonderful again!'

'All will be just as you wish,' said Parri with a smile.

Raxx smiled back. 'I'm going to gain weight terribly again, aren't I? Especially from eating all of these wonderful meals that I've missed out on for so long?'

'Not with the training you will have to do to make sure that all your muscle groups react as they should again, Derus. If like in times before, you'll be burning it off faster than you can take in all of their calories!'

'Great! In that case, bring on the food then!' she chuckled at them. While the four of them just laughed. As for them, it was actually good to be able to use all of their culinary knowledge again. Just so as to please her after such a long time of barely cooking her anything at all.

∞

As the following morning arrived. Raxx along with her maids left for Central just as the first stages of dawn brought light to the sky. After her very enjoyable meal of last night. She had then also remembered something that she must do. So had sent messages via a good many others who were still working on the floor of her office out across the planet. A further message from her was also conveyed to Rist while he was still on route home.

As word came to her from their tracking systems off-planet that their fleet was almost home. The screens in place all around Haff now came to life. Her planet-wide announcement had been carried out. All usual work or ongoing training came to a sudden stop everywhere due to her earlier message. With the holo-cams now showing her on the screens. She herself was already looking skywards.

The crowds had again gathered, but this time not only in Haff Central. As all the other cities also had people turning up as per her request of them. This time though, more than one underground lift had its lights flashing in readiness for imminent landings.

Even Shrum and all of his men were asked to leave the building and go outside for the event. Which the guards had answered at his question. That it was for a welcoming celebration ordered by the Prime Commander. And so as they had no choice in the matter, they all now either stood around or milled about just outside their own building as well. Looking at the nearest screens which showed her there up on them. And then which also made then begin to look up into the sky themselves.

As was usual from below, the cameras placed on top of the highest buildings anywhere on the planet. Now picked up what looked like dozens of meteorites falling from the skies. But that was only until the noise of their mass of engines came on to slow them down. Only when the intense heat build up of re-entering the atmosphere around them began to dissipate. Were they then able to be distinguished as being ships returning to land.

Slowly, but inexorably, the sound only grew louder and louder the nearer they came. As always, their own heavy gravity meant full power was being used to slow their descents, and also as an aid to then offer an easier landing.

Their clamour grew to an almost ear-shattering roar as each of their struts finally touched down safely. After that came the more high-pitched piercing whine as each of their engines were being closed down. Only then came the former silence back, before the many ramps began to lower.

Mi who had been keeping a very close eye on her personal data tablet for her, gave her a barely discernible nod. This told her that all ships had touched down.

'My fellow Haffian's, today we are all here to celebrate the return of our victorious troops - as well as those of our glorious dead!' she stated, which boomed out from all the screens upon which her image was being projected.

No matter where these ships had now landed, at Raxx's signal, a biodegradable confetti like material began to fall from the higher buildings as it was pumped out. The troops which now emerged from them walked out into this as it fell heavily not only upon, but also all around them. On the part of the planet where the city of Tonnis stood it was actually night now. So huge spotlights lit up the troops as they came out from the ships there. It also lit-up the hovering stretchers too. Having by now taken the tablet from Mi to do what was required of her. She spoke again to them all.

'My dear Haffian's . . . As always whenever we are forced to do battle. We ourselves know that there will also forever be casualties of war. I will now name those who died gloriously for all of us: Prime Commander Derus Raxx, being one of these . . . which was also my old own self as you all now know.' She then offered the sixty-six other names of those who had died for their planet.

When that had been done, she continued, 'Just as we all know from when we are taught as young children. To fight and to live, or to die for our own dear Haff is what *we* as a people are here for! No matter whether we do die, or are injured in some way or make it through any battle safely and unharmed. All that matters most is our personal honour of proving ourselves to our families for Haff. And as to this - I for one have *never* had any doubts as to the bravery of *any* of our men and women who do carry out these battles.

'Due to High Commander Tarsk's recent retirement, Legion One has been without one. For his work, I now promote Octavus Rist to that same open appointment. For those others who will gain in rank after this. I will discuss this with him and the other High Commanders of their own legions soon.

'For now though, it is all of you, and those who have remained behind for the moment who we are celebrating. To which I now say, that you who have just returned are all now free from any commitments for a full three day period, so enjoy it. Those who are still there and will return later will not miss out on theirs either. Of that I assure you! Finally, I again welcome all of you home personally for a task which has been well done!' And with that she offered a salute herself to the troops.

After that she had the holo-cams turn away from her to focus upon the still disembarking troops. Those who had emerged first were already well covered by the still falling material.

∞

Rist made his way from the nearest ship towards her. His face showing nothing of the inner feelings he now felt from been awarded such a promotion.

Behind him out of the ship came Gremplar and his family, along with the troops from the three planets which he had picked up before heading back to Haff. Being as there were only ten thousand on each, their totals barely made a dent in the huge carrying capacity of the troop carrier ship itself. But the one thing her most recent message passed on to him had already ensured. Was that they were all very much naked as they were escorted from within it. Behind Rist after he had walked right up to Raxx, they had all halted and saluted. While Gremplar and his family were all feeling very self-conscious about how they were now being paraded and looked at.

'I am not worthy of the honour, Prime Commander,' he said quickly to her.

'If you were *not* worthy of this rank, then you would not have been offered it, Octavus!' she answered back. 'But, as you have carried out my orders to the letter, it is also a well deserved reward,'

She then stared at Gremplar; and one of her direct stares could always make all others feel very uneasy. 'So Tyrant!' she said, 'Do you feel that it was worth killing me now for what you had to suffer?'

'Wha--?'

'You forget so easily do you? That I was the one you had shot off my machine after I offered you surrender terms.'

'That cannot be, it's not possible!'

'It is *very* possible, Tyrant - which is why I am standing here now and looking down at you. I will speak to *you* later though, Gremplar.' She looked at Rist. 'For now have all of them placed with the others until I do finally decide what to do with some or all of them. Just make sure they are taken to be all screened first before being put with the others though . . .

'As for you Octavus Rist, your new title of High Commander is effective immediately - but so is your own three day rest period. So I will call upon you after that is over to discuss those other things further with you.'

'Yes, Prime Commander,' he replied, saluted her and then walked off. He and his troops herding their captives over to where their earlier prisoners dwelt.

∞

Gremplar and the others were marched over to where Shrum and some of his men were stood outside a building. Rist called for the guards on duty to come out.

As they all lined up and saluted, Rist said to them, 'All of these newcomers require the scanning. After that, return them back to this same building where they will also be housed with the others.

'Yes, High Commander.'

Rist was taken aback momentarily, thinking that the female guard had got his command title wrong. Only then did he remember that he'd been promoted. He hid his own feelings, as he also knew that his family would be just as proud of his new promotion as well.

'After they've all had their screenings, they can join with the others in here for a meal if one is due.'

Having been given an affirmative to that order. Rist and those who brought them over began to break up. Their duty had been carried out and they were now all free to enjoy their three days of rest which had been offered to them by their Prime Commander.

∞

After an interminably long wait while they were all carefully screened and checked over. They were finally then led back to where Shrum and his troops awaited them.

Gremplar, whose own frustrations and rage had been building even before the ship had touched down. Decided now to vent all of it at his highest general.

'What kind of people are they? Making us strip off all our clothing before we landed! All of the finery that myself and my family were wearing stripped from us as if we had been wearing rags! And as for having been paraded around naked in front of everyone like this . . . do they not know as the ruler of the Gelten system that *I* at least deserve *some* kind of recognition and respect from them! And as for you failing in your duty to take over these fifteen planets for me - I'll be speaking to you later about that!'

'Sire . . .' began Shrum.

'He is not your Sire any longer. Nor is he the ruler of the Gelten system either!' said a voice.

'Who dares say that to *me*!' he screeched.

One of the guards stepped forward to stand in front of him. He stood almost a foot taller than Gremplar himself, and the difference in their stature was quite evident to them all. The guard was well tanned as so many of them were from their outdoor training. Just as all the guards were usually well muscled, both the men and the women. Who now watched with amused grins on their mouth's at Gremplar's face. While his stomach was flat, except for the well defined ridges to his abdominal area. In opposite, Gremplar was small in stature and his body was almost rotund from his lavish lifestyle and his lack of exercise.

'*I* said it to you, Gremplar!'

Gremplar's face began to purple in suffused rage and he made a step towards him while raising a clenched fist. At which point Shrum placed a hand to his bare chest and prevented him from getting any nearer.

'Take your hand off me you dolt!

'I cannot. If you carry out what you were about to do, then I'm afraid you, or perhaps all of us may pay badly for it.'

Gremplar even had to look up into Shrum's slightly higher eyes, and saw the very dire warning that they held.

He nodded, and lowered his hand, Then proceeded to plant both fists upon the side of his ample stomach. While again looking up into the face of the guard.

'If I am not its ruler, then what am I?'

'Now? Now you are nothing at all. You *may* have once been its ruler. But now you have as much power as all of your men here do . . . Which is none at all. You are all prisoners of Haff, Gremplar. What will happen to you, or to any of you soon will depend upon what our Prime Commander finally decides to do with you.'

The guard then slowly moved backwards until he had regained his former position against one of the walls.

Gremplar then spotted an aide looking past him, and on turning his head, saw where he was looking. 'You there!' he said whilst pointing a finger at him. 'Stop staring at my wives, concubines and daughters like that!'

'I cannot help it, Si---' he began, though not even finishing the title of Sire due to what the guard had just said. 'They are the only women in here, and we very rarely see any of *our* women so openly in this way.'

Gremplar moved towards him in a threatening manner now due to his freely outspoken words. Shrum saw the guards already moving forwards so again placed his hand upon his chest. Gremplar eyed him once again.

'We have been allowed certain freedoms here so far, but only if *none* of us cause them any problems. That same freedom also means no problems or trouble between any of us at all as well. If that happens, then we could all end up being locked away in here - for good.'

Gremplar's mouth issued a low exhaled hiss as he was forced to step back, yet again. He again stared at the disrespectful officer. 'It does not matter if they are wearing clothing, or not. They belong to me, not you, so keep your filthy eyes from them!' growled Gremplar, saying it as they were all just personal possessions to him and not actual females with minds of their own.

'There is also nothing that can be done about our own nakedness,' offered Shrum trying to calm him. 'Since being here, I've found that those who live on this planet think this to be quite normal. Neither the men or women who live here upon it consider being unclothed as of being any issue to them. And, being as we are *their* prisoners, we have even less options available to us, Sir.'

Gremplar gave the same officer a deep glowering look instead. Hoping he'd made his point anyway. Then to Shrum he said, 'We will speak more about this later, General.'

'I am at your service, Sir,' he replied calmly.

12

Later that evening, Raxx was out travelling in her bubble-pod to two of their medical centres. Each of these which were placed within all the cities of Haff were also huge buildings, just as most were. Only in their case, they were built so large in case they ever had to cope with very large numbers of wounded at any one time.

With only two hundred and seventy-four from the invasion. They were placed in the nearest one to where they lived and returned to land. Which was the reason why they were in two of these and not all in one. As only on Briath and Goll had any fighting ensued. So the majority were at Haff Central from the Briath battle, while a few more were at Lady Yu's city of Tonnis from the much smaller Goll fight.

For Raxx though, no matter if it was only two or two hundred thousand injured to visit. She had always made time for things like this, seeing as she was the one who had sent them. It was not a guilt trip though, as all the troops knew that this was what their lives had all been trained to do. In her own mind, it was simply a courtesy visit to see how they were. So she spent time with each of those who she was allowed to speak to. As a few were still in surgery, so she could only ask the staff to pass on her personal good wishes on to each of those.

Where any had lost limbs or any other such things, like damaged organs, an eye, full sight, or any hearing. The doctors assured her that with the technology available for them to use. That they would soon have whatever implants fitted or attached so that they would not be without that use of it for very long. The only thing they could not repair was death itself.

Raxx was always welcomed warmly by these men and women. No matter what may have happened to them on the field. She even spoke to some who were there only due to earlier training accidents as well. The one thing she always liked to see though, was just how well all these centre's were operated. There was never any panic or stress, alarm, cross words or arguments between any of the staff. The sole reason for this was simply because they were all androids. And each and every one of them knew what their particular task or role in the medical centre was that day. Whether as actual surgeons, or as more ordinary doctors to decide what was required, nursing staff, or artificial enhancement fitters.

In fact the only people who may have felt any level of stress at any time were the human Chief Medical Officer's, who ran each one of them daily. All of these were former troops but now retired; except that they each had remarkable coordinating abilities. Where instead of not having much to actually do since leaving their legions. They had more than gladly accepted a further role if only to fill their time.

Why had she placed humans in charge and not more androids - which could probably have done an even better job? It was simply really. A human being had feelings, whereas an android did not. It only had its precise logic to use. Another task of any Chief Medical Officer was to talk with those who were being attended to. As they were former legion members themselves who had been through the same training as they had. Perhaps even battles too. It allowed them to speak to each other in a way which no android ever could to them as well.

After the visit she returned back to her home to rest, to eat, and then to sleep a real nights sleep for her first ever time. And in a real bed, too. Even though her older memory knew what that was, her new young body had known nothing else but the cryo-cell's body formed and shaped surface for a long twenty cycles.

∞

After their morning meal, Shrum led Gremplar outside into the daylight. Where they sat beside each other upon a low wall or raised seating area. The sunlight glistening upon their darker grey skin hues. Shrum still wasn't sure what it was, except that it was not used as toileting facilities.

Gremplar was morose. 'So you failed me, Akras . . .'

'There was nothing that I, or they could do, Sir. We took fourteen of the planets just as you commanded. Remember, when we planned it, we thought that putting forty thousand troops on each would easily do the task. What we did not know at the time though, was that those here on this planet protected all of them - and that they could get to them so quickly. They had soon sent five million of their own troops to each planet to take them back.

'I checked their speed when we were placed on them to bring us back here. Within only ten creks, we had taken off from there, reached this planet of theirs and landed again. Our own ships by their standards are slow and all but useless. Where ours were also overloaded with only forty thousand troops, any of their carriers can each hold a minimum of half a million.'

'Speed, as well as a ships carrying capacity is not everything when it comes to conquest, Akras.'

'That is also true, in a way, Sir. But I have already seen the way they can mobilize their ships and troops. And *as* for their troops . . . I have seen nothing to equal them yet.'

'Troops are troops, Akras. Either they are well trained, or they are not. Ours simply were not good enough.'

Shrum's large head shook from side to side. 'You simply do not understand it, Sir. Their old Prime Commander explained it to me before she left for the invasion of our system.'

'I do not understand what?' he bridled.

'Sir,' he said patiently, 'our own total army was of four million in strength. Without conscripts. Whereas only one of their Legions is of one hundred million . . . and, they have *at minimum* forty of these here on this one planet! That's a four *billion* strong army to use. Then if you add in their retired troops, even their children who we saw training with our own eyes not very long ago. That gives them upto sixty Legions to use!'

'Perhaps . . . but you still could have fought! Just as the men did on Briath and Goll when we were attacked,' he said bitterly.

'And where are those men who fought now, Sir?' Shrum stated candidly. 'They are all dead - wiped out to a man only from *trying* to fight them. The same happened to those on two of the planets in this system also.

'Do you know the death toll of our own troops yet, Sir? I do, only because I overheard Rist on the planet I went to take. And a guard inside our building was happy to tell me of the figures from our system when I asked her of it.'

'So?'

'Sir . . . on just the two planets here, we lost eighty thousand of our troops! Do you know how many *they* lost in total? Well, do you?' he said a little abruptly.

Gremplar gave a negative head shake.

'Only thirty-one dead out of two thousand or so dead or injured in the fighting. Thirty-one, Sir! To our eighty thousand! And what about in our own system . . . ? Have you heard about *those* figures yet?'

Gremplar gave the same head motion.

'Of the ten thousand stationed on Goll, none survived. Of the just over three million who were left on Briath . . . again, none survived. Your only surviving troops remaining to you now, are the four hundred and eighty thousand who were taken prisoner in this system; and the other thirty thousand who were stationed on the three planets in our system who chose not to fight against overwhelming odds. Your former army of four million is now down to barely half a million. And how many did they lose to us on our home worlds through fighting? Only sixty-six dead and two hundred and seventy or so injured.'

Gremplar then asked just one word of him.

'Why?'

'Superior skills and tactics, Their Prime Commander planned everything right down to the very last detail even before they left here. She decided on how many troops and ships they would need to do it. Before he left, Rist told me that she was originally thinking of using one legion on each planet. But in the end decided that only fifty million per planet would be more than enough to complete it.

'Some of us have even been allowed to go around this planet to watch some of their training. To see my own Remplar, Borth, being bested by what was only a small female child told us all more than we needed. They begin their training when aged at only five, Sir. For our own troops it is at least sixteen. This girl may have only been about eleven or twelve who Borth was allowed to match weapons with. Yet even her skill with it outmatched his. And as to the way that they train . . . '

'Meaning?'

'When I saw their ways of training in regard to our own, Sir, there was no similarity at all. Pain is their natural element.'

'What do you mean by *pain*?'

'You saw the weapons most of them used on Briath?' At Gremplar's nod, he continued.

'Those things have ten setting's on them for attack. The children as young as five here start on level one. We all saw the marks left upon their bodies from hits they had taken from them. Their training can take from ten to fifteen years before they are judged to be full warriors. By that time they have had to have reached level ten on their weapons. And as Rist told me, levels eight to ten can kill an enemy instantly. Even when Borth fought her at only level one, he could feel the pain from the burns she inflicted on him.

'Before that though, he asked Rist if he could try a level five setting on him. He only knows now how stupid that was. But at the time he wanted to judge the power of it for himself.'

'So what happened?'

'Rist gently tapped him on the shoulder at that setting, Sir. The actual force of it actually threw him about ten feet and left him unconscious for a while. While he was like that, Rist then showed the rest of us what it was like when set at level ten! *Fearsome* is the only way I can explain it. As it not only completely shields the front and sides of its user. But at a simple switch of a button turns it instantly into a lethal killing weapon. His own display of skill and control of that thing was a sight to behold, Sir. And then, when he'd finished, he reset it at level five and tapped himself with it just to show us the result.'

'And?'

'Hardly anything at all. He only gave off a small grunt from its same force as it burned his skin. But, he was not thrown off his feet as Borth had been. He then told us, that over the years as they train they just get used to each new power setting and pain level as it rises. Even the young girl herself was already upto that one.

'And another thing . . . Death means nothing to any of them. They simply do not fear it as so many would. If a leader of theirs orders one of them to attack any amount of enemies - that warrior would do so without further thought; even if it meant certain death for them.'

'Ahhh,' murmured Gremplar, 'but what if our forces and theirs were matched equally, eh?'

'I feel that there may be not much difference in the end, Sir. Due to their own far higher training levels . . . and from their not being scared of anything at all. Well, except for failing any orders perhaps. That due to this long training they do, and a lack of fear at having to attack even if well outnumbered. I feel that their tactical advantage would still beat us very easily.'

'Not strength you mean?'

'Perhaps, perhaps not. I am given to understand that Raxx . . . Well, by this I mean their old Prime Commander and not the new one. Has an ability of somehow or other to almost guess what a enemy will do. So to know that, is already half-way to winning any battle!

'She told the Commanders in her pre-invasion meeting that she thought up to three out of the five planets in our system would surrender without a shot being fired. And expected you to order those on Briath to fight with you being there. Even to her being killed as well.'

'Well of course I ordered those on Briath to fight. It was their home world you know! Although I did not expect my troops on three of them to simply lay down their arms and surrender without a fight as they did!' he grunted unhappily.

'You have to be realistic, Sir. Ten thousand of ours on each pitted against fifty million? If Briath itself had no hope with the three million who were there. How could such a small number on the others when they saw them arrive, *not* be willing to fight?'

'Goll did!' he remarked.

'Yes they did. And all on it who bore arms against them paid for it, too!' stated Shrum.

'So, what are you telling me all this for Akras, eh? Are you suggesting that they are unbeatable!'

'Maybe . . . Think about it, Sir. Upto eight billion fighters who are not afraid to die? So many ships to carry them that you simply cannot count them! Ships themselves that our own weapons had no effect on. Yet one shot from their weapons could knock our ships out.

'I think the only thing which likely could beat them-'

'Yes?' asked a hopeful Gremplar.

'Is another race with either far more troops than they have. Or a race whose weapons and ships far exceed those of their own.'

'I see. So what you are saying is that they could go out and conquer the galaxy if they wished.'

'Yes, they could if they wanted to. But they won't.'

'Why not? If I had what they had then *I* certainly would do so!'

'Then that may be the main difference between ourselves and them, Sir. They see themselves first as protectors of those who they are allied to. They will, or would only attack another planet if this other one did so to one which was under their protection.'

Gremplar shook his head. 'What an incredible waste of such an army. When you could achieve so much more from having it!' he said as he rubbed his hands together almost excitedly as he thought about it.

Shrum just about gave up. Even as a prisoner now, all Gremplar could think about was an army that was not his own conquering everything in its path for him. He began feeling that the older Raxx he had spoken to was now right. That Gremplar was simply a tyrant who would always want more than he had, no matter what the cost to anyone else may be.

13

The king and queen, as they were also both now classed as being retired ex-troops; or reserves. Were the next to visit those in the medical centre in Haff Central the following morning. To their family, just like it was to Raxx, they saw it as their duty to visit any wounded. Their sons and daughters; the Princes and Princesses would have done the same if they had not had to leave early for training duties.

Whereas in Tonnis, due to it being night when the troops had returned to their underground home bays. And after only returning to her home herself very late. After sitting chatting with the Garen family and the other two ladies for far longer than they had expected. The young Lady Yu had made her own visit to the small number of injured in her city's medical centre before leaving for her own training. This late arrival to her own training was of course allowed, as she was the city's representative on such things.

This was the main difference between Raxx, the Garen's, the ladies - and then the five lord's. As all but the latter saw it more as their duty. A normal response to offer some of their people who might rarely see them otherwise. Just a small piece of their own time to shake a hand. Or to talk with them for a little while about whatever they wished to. The five lord's due to their own concerns about who they *should* actually be on Haff. To them it was thought of as more of a burden to them whenever they had to do anything similar.

To most of them though, if Raxx herself could spare some time from her own always very busy days to personally do this. Then they felt that it was only right to do so themselves. The king and queen with now being retired from the usual daily training. Like most used it as a means to combat having so little to do with their time. As if not for that, they would simply be walking around Haff Central talking to others who were in the same time of life.

With the ordinary people, as well as the injured. As they had both already served their military duties for their own army and planet. Which was also why they were well respected by all, but a few. Five to be exact. Lady Yu on the other hand was only nineteen, and only just reaching the end of her difficult training to become a warrior herself in name. Along with whatever could follow from becoming a true legion member afterwards. But like all who did so, even her being known to all of them as the Lady Yu. It still had not prevented her own body from receiving its many burns and bruises throughout the long years.

For herself, at only five cycles she had been a small and nervous child. Many thousands of children of the same age from her city had come together on that first day. Names were then being called out so they knew where to go. Her title of Lady Yu, even at that age was missing: now she was simply to be known as Celine to them all. Just as all of those there were at first name terms with each other. They were split into large sections first, and then into much smaller units. Each unit having its own much older retired trainers and teachers.

From that very first day, they were taught the very basics of Haff and its troops. How to act. How to show respect to all. Even how to salute properly. Only when those had been done to their trainers happiness, did they then have to listen even harder. As it was then when their trainers informed them of how all of their lives would now continue.

Their explanations of how only actual pain resulted in them both learning and understanding more as they reached new levels and ages. That both the carrying out and understanding of any given orders at any time was imperative. That not listening closely enough could lead to injuries. Which not only could sometimes be serious to themselves - but possibly even fatal.

As her early years of training then progressed. Celine had now found herself with friends who she would be with almost for her entire life. She was in a small unit, which could join with others to become a section. And all of these sections could become an entire legion. Her earliest fears of joining were gone, as she almost relished the regime which she had started. She was no longer just the child of Lord and Lady Yu of Tonnis. Now she was Celine, a small part of Unit 41. As a larger part of Section 8. And with these when they were all fully trained, would join whichever legion at the time of their full warrior status needed new troops.

On many of her earliest training days when she returned to her home and family. She would often sport a good few bruises here and there upon her small frame. Including the occasional black or swollen puffed eye, even to cuts to her lips. Her parents understood all of this, as they had both been through it. So they always made themselves available to explain anything she wanted to know.

They had been worried at first when she did return home in such states. And like most of the children there, due to whatever kind of clothing they had worn to begin with usually ended up either being well ripped or almost in tatters by the end of the day. This was when they all began to learn about how useless wearing anything at all was.

Yet her parents were still very surprised indeed to learn that she was actually enjoying herself; even when her body was suffering so much. They remembered the times prior to this, when if she fell over she would wail and cry and run to them.

The main difference itself now was, that over at the training ground, they were *not* there for her to run to. Many children cried after having been punched or kicked at the very beginning. But they soon learned that what they must do, was to rid themselves of such tears and carry on. It wasn't that easy with being only five, yet their training was as usual relentless. Tears from their being hit turned to rage and anger at those who caused it, even hate sometimes too. And this was where the trainers of them came into it. Diffusing such thoughts from any of them, and turning it into strength of will instead. Personal difficulties soon became things which they all had to master to enable them to not only learn, but to grow.

Her years of training continued like this on a daily basis. Until at the age of only fifteen, when both her mother and father had died on Garos. A planet in the Sembus system which was protected by Haff. It had been invaded, so as usual Haff was called. Her parents, both being from Tonnis area were in the same legion that was sent out. The fighting there had not only been bitter, but violent. As was usual though, the tactics used meant that the enemy suffered far greater losses than any of their own.

It was only when the Prime Commander herself personally came to her training ground. Where she then took her to one side to tell her of her parents deaths. Did Celine at first only feel hate for her for sending them there. By the time of her inauguration to the full status of Lady Yu of Tonnis. All of her new friends had not only consoled her, but also swore to protect her with their own lives even more. It was only at this time that she finally found what the true meaning of friendship from being in such a close knit unit was. Her hate for Raxx was suddenly gone as she recalled the sadness upon her face when she had told her the news. And from that point on, she was now completely loyal to the old woman.

As no matter if you were seen as being high or low born, Haff would always come first. This was what she had soon learnt as part of it. So training was training, and was necessary. And if you did not do something correctly, you endured the pain that went with it. Fighting for a cause, she also learned was just as important too. Her parents had always told her that the future of Haff was the most important thing in their lives. You are born, then if you are lucky you enjoy your life for a while, and then you die. It was what you made of your life that counted most. And as Haffian's, they had always made the most of theirs!

∞

The morning after the fleets return. Raxx had already made her way to her office to check up on everything. After an hour of this, she picked up her own gold coloured Grem from where it lay against her office wall and left. Those within it knew even before her recent incarnation that whenever she left her office with it. Exactly what she would be going to do with it for an hour or more, and also where she would be. Morg as always knew such details, so summoned a medic to be close by while she did this.

As just outside the front of the command building where she worked, was a small training area. The lift from her office came to a stop just one level above the underground area beneath the city. From where she exited this and walked through the auto-doors to emerge outside.

There was never really very much for any of the prisoners to do ever since their capture. So after an early breakfast, many did what they had already done for a while now. Which was just to leave the confines of the building to get out of it. As having close to half a million of them using the same huge building overnight just felt stifling to them. They did have plenty of room though it has to be said. As even with their having to use multi-rack beds, they still had a lot of space to move around inside.

That was one of the benefits of being in such an immense building. Yet apart from eating or sleeping, the only options were to stay inside or enjoy the warmth and breeze outdoors. Even some pleasurable rain falling upon them if the sky offered it to them. As anything at all made a change when you were a prisoner. Especially ones who knew not what their own fate may be. So far as they knew, Raxx had made no final decision about this.

And so, just as they had day by day, Shrum and his fellow prisoners filed out of that very same building to go outside and to enjoy whatever the day might offer to them. Some simply walked away from it, deciding to view yet another new area of the city while it was still allowed.

Shrum and his commanding staff, along with a begrudging Gremplar, who was allowing his family to go outside with him this time. Although as he had said to Shrum when he mentioned it to him.

'I don't want the people here to see my wives, concubines, sons and daughters like this.'

To which Shrum had replied, 'Sir, they really don't care at all about us, or what we even think. So I would suggest that we all make the best of whatever weather there is out there to enjoy. It's certainly far better than being in here all day long!'

So they sat, or literally perched upon the wall which was outside their building due to their shorter statures. Which by now had become more of a normal habit for Shrum and his staff. Except now they were joined on it by Gremplar and his entire family.

This morning though, as they all sat there and chatted quite amiably with each other about a variety of things. From the early morning heat, to the enjoyable breeze they could each feel upon their bare skins. Even to what yet may happen to all of them. Shrum's eyes narrowed as he saw a figure he thought he now knew emerge from the building beside theirs. It carried one of those Grem weapons, yet this was of a different colour to all the others he had seen at their training sites previously.

∞

The only thing Raxx noted as she began to warm up her muscles in readiness. Was the appearance of the expected android medic, who would sit on one of the long rows of resting blocks while she practised. Who was only there in case of any unexpected injury occurring to her which may then require instant treatment.

Due to this being her very first training routine since her new self had emerged. Raxx left it positioned on its zero setting. As this would also be the first time that her still unused muscles as yet would be testing themselves with it.

Her own earlier memories still retained her mastery of it, as expected. It was only because this newer body now had to become finely tuned to its weight so as to regain its usual levels of complete mastery. Not an easy task to accomplish with muscles which had been unused for a long twenty life cycles.

From a distance, Shrum then watched as she began to slowly twirl the weapon around her. He could even see her as she stepped forward, back and to the side as it continued in its rotation. He stood up from his seated position and began to walk to where she was doing this. Unaware that as always, he would be dutifully followed by his staff. Gremplar of course tagged along only as he felt a lot safer being with his general, while his family naturally followed him.

Raxx did not see any of them as they approached, as she was far too busy concentrating upon the task in hand. For to be at one with your weapon during training, you could never allow anything to interrupt or distract the flow of mind and body as you wielded it.

Shrum sat on one of the blocks not far away from what looked like a barely concerned medic and began to watch her very carefully. As what with him being a typical military commander, he wanted to see how their adults trained now. The others as they reached him, then sat at either side of him. Having watched Shrum departing to somewhere and then sitting down to watch some kind of a display taking place. Many more of his men began to make their way over to it too. This was only because to see something happening, was always better than nothing ever happening! Borth himself was another of the eager viewers of this display almost as soon as his rump touched the block.

∞

Octavus Rist, in his new and esteemed position of High Commander of the First Legion. Had been sat in a group around a table outside drinking. While talking with another eight similar ranked fellow commanders about the recent invasion and how it had all worked. When he began to notice the large movement of people . . . Well, not actual people like himself, but those who were held captive on their planet all heading towards Raxx's command building.

'I wonder what's going on over there?' he muttered, nodding his head in the direction he had looked.

'Perhaps the prisoners are planning to riot!' stated one to them.

'Without weapons?' said another, 'that would indeed be foolish!'

'Well it can't be much to worry about,' offered yet another of them, 'seeing as our own people are just continuing to walk by them.'

'I'm going over to have a look anyway!' said Rist. 'Seeing as it is happening at our command building.'

'Octavus, you are on a three day break now. So just report it and whoever is on Capital duty will see to it.'

By then though it was too late anyway. Rist was already on his feet and striding towards the area. The other eight reacted to him, slowly getting to their feet and following.

'I don't know,' said one with a low sigh, 'give them a day or more off duty and they *still* don't use it!'

∞

With his rate of walking, Rist was soon at the growing crowd and steadily made his way through them until he reached the very front. It was only then he saw the new young Raxx on the training area, who was performing a variety of moves with her Grem.

He saw Shrum and some others he knew seated on the blocks all just watching her closely. Making his way over to them, he looked down at him. 'What's all this about?'

'Oh, hello, Octavus. All what?'

'Why are you all over here?'

'All?'

Only then did Shrum turn to look, and so to find that around him were many thousands of his own troops. Who must have also decided to come over to watch whatever she was doing as well.

'My apologies to you, Octavus, if the sight of all of us here now caused you any worries. We meant no harm, or pose any threat to your leader. It was only because I saw your Prime Commander come out of this building with her Grem. And then she began to swing it around. Well, since I'd never seen an adult using one, apart from yourself that is. I decided then to come over to watch her.

'I honestly had no idea that so many of us would then do the same. But you will likely know yourself that our days here are quite bland, Octavus. We can either walk around outside, or just sit around, having being allowed to do so. But there is also very little else in the way of entertainment for us. So perhaps like me, seeing something actually happening out here instead of nothing. Has simply offered us all a variation to one of these days. Although,' he said now smiling up at him, 'we have no true idea what it is that she's actually doing! Yet it is better than just sitting on a block outside our building and staring at nothing!'

Rist looked to where Raxx was already in full flow. Her body already covered in a sheen of perspiration from the non-stop exercises. At the moment, she was also on one of the many repetitive exercises used for Grem movement.

'Our Prime Commander is simply retraining herself in its use.'

'Why? When surely she already knows how to use one?'

'The *old* Raxx did, General. Whereas our new Raxx has never used one before.'

'Are you sure about that, Octavus? I mean just look at the way she's spinning that thing out there!'

'I see what you mean, General. But really, Raxx is simply having to train her new body in order to reach what her old body already knew for a long time before. Her clone at this time does have the instinctual muscle memory of what is required. So, just as we train regularly to keep not only fit, but to also keep our own muscle usage in line. She is simply doing the same right now - except that she has had to start from the very beginning again.'

'You mean she is like one of your children who is just starting to train for the first ever time? It doesn't look like it to me,' he said honestly.

'Not actually like those of our first stage children. She has the memories of what to do already, General. It's just the muscles that need optimising. As a new and young Raxx, she has never trained before. You could even say that she was only born yesterday in this new form. So her memories *can* tell her what she should do. But to put it simply for you. Her body has as yet never had to do any of this before. That is her only difficulty at present. This is why she needs to train with it, you see. In a way her muscles need to be upgraded into what is needed to once again become a master of the weapon she now holds.'

With that, Rist fell silent as he, the other High Commanders who had made their way to stand beside him. And the extremely large crowd of non-Haffian's all watched her quietly. Any Haffian's who did pass, already understood what she was doing, as they had all done it themselves. So this training she was doing held no actual interest to them. For to them, unlike the others, it was simply a normal thing.

∞

For a good hour the silent crowd sat or stood there watching her. Even the king and queen out on one of their habitual walks came by, and they also came to a halt simply to observe as well.

The cool of morning was constantly warming to an even higher temperature as Raxx continued. By now though, she was already well and truly into it without much conscious thought being needed.

'She's in the zone now!' Rist remarked to the other High Commanders when he saw that her eyes were closed.

'What zone?' queried Shrum.

'The zone of being at one with your weapon. You can always tell this when the eyes close, General. The Grem which she holds is now almost an extension of herself. She does not need to see it to know what she is doing with it. That's what being in the zone means . . . '

A gasp ran around them all as it seemed as if she then upped her own tempo. Not only wielding it as a weapon, but using it as a lever sometimes to throw her body into the air. Making fast outward kicks from it, as if an enemy was right on front of her. Even to using its own weight as a balance to leap into the air, with her head nearest the ground, until she returned to her feet to carry on.

'She's gone now!' said one High Commander.

Shrum looked at the speaker. 'Gone? She's right there!'

'Not in that sense of the word, General. What High Commander Ege actually meant, is that Raxx has just surpassed the tenth level now.'

'I thought you said that it only went up to ten, Octavus?' asked a wondering Shrum.

'For *us* it does . . . whereas for her . . . she can attain level fifteen or more when she has fully trained herself.'

'By Aldur!' he stammered.

Just prior to the second hour coming up. Raxx was moving around so freely that it was sometimes hard for any of the watchers to see what she was actually doing now. Her spins, kicks, even to the way she was throwing herself into the air off her feet grew ever faster. The twirls of the actual weapon itself were so fast that it often became hard just to actually see the weapon itself held in her hands.

'That must be either level thirteen or fourteen now, surely?' said Ege.

'Only thirteen I think, ' said Rist, 'but she's very near to reaching fourteen.'

At that same moment, Raxx did yet another much higher and unexpected leap. Which of course only caused a new low gasp to come from them all. This time landing with one bare foot and knee on the ground, the Grem pointing ahead of her. She had ceased all her movements.

They could each see that she was breathing deeply though from the way her breasts and stomach moved in and out. Which to them was not surprising after almost two full hours of her doing that, they all thought. Her head was still lowered since she ended. Her now much shorter jet black hair, though still a good deal past shoulder length. Hung straight down, quite wet from her own recent exertions. It, along with the rest of body had drops falling down and beginning to pool upon the ground below her.

The watching audience would have clapped or cheered. If only they had known just what to do at the end of her long and amazing performance. But as none of her High Commanders made any such effort and did nothing, so they followed suit.

It was a good minute before she began to stand up straight, her heavy breathing now becoming normalised. And was also where she now saw so many there around her.

'What's the matter? Am I needed?' she immediately asked of her group of High Commanders standing there.

'No, Prime Commander,' answered Ege. 'For us, we are all just truly amazed that you have reached so high a level already. As to the others here, I think they were just happy to have watched your training efforts.'

She gave a nod to them. 'Not too bad for my first day of training, in that I concur with you. I almost reached fourteen, but not quite. Maybe when I try tomorrow I will.'

'It looked very close to me, Prime Commander,' responded Ege.

Raxx gave a small tight grin. 'Would any of you like to partner with me for a brief session?' she asked.

'Err, no, thank you, Prime Commander,' Ege replied far too quickly it seemed. 'Anyway, none of us have our own Grem's with us,' he then said in what sounded akin to relief.

'Oh, but I can have some Grem's brought quickly enough, High Commander Ege.'

'You idiot!' hissed one of the others to him. 'All you had to do was say nothing after you said *no*.'

'She caught me out, damn her!' he hissed back. Before then saying in a louder voice for her to hear, which also now sounded more like a despairing sigh, 'If that is your wish, Prime Commander. Then of course we would be more than happy to help you out.'

'Excellent!' she said, not then hearing the other curses being piled upon the offending Ege's head. As she by using her implant, quickly asked for nine extra Grem's to be brought to her personal training area outside command.

∞

The men and women who brought out the extra weapons did not return back into the building again though. As a chance to bear witness, and to see their new Prime Commander in action was an unmissable event. One which they could regale their friend and families with for a long time to come.

'What setting would you prefer?' asked Raxx after they were each handed them.

'One?' was said quickly by a hopeful Ege.

'Oh, come now, High Commander. Setting one is only at a child's level. High Commander Menos?'

'Three, Prime Commander?' at which they heard her emit a deep and sad sigh.

'For fully trained warriors upto level ten, you are certainly being very wary? So, how about a nice gentle ten setting, eh?'

She could almost hear the breath being caught in each of their throats at that number.

'May I offer the suggestion of a mid-setting of five, Prime Commander? Only as it is supposed to only be a practise battle.' asked Rist.

'Oh, very well, Octavus. And how do you wish it to work?'

'Once touched you are out of the battle. Just as any enemy likely would be - if that suits you, Prime Commander.'

'Fine,' was all she said.

'And what should the attack be?' he then asked of her.

'Well, all of you against me at the same time, of course!'

'That cannot be fair to you, Prime Commander,' Menos stated quickly at that option.

'My dear, Girik,' she said to Menos. 'I am only trying to remember my former late skills. So of course it is possible that I will lose against you.'

'The first time that Raxx loses will *indeed* be her first ever time!' muttered one of the Grem bringers to another. Which was heard by many of the audience.

Shrum, already astounded at what they were about to see, glanced up at them. 'Are you saying that even against nine of them she'll win?'

The speaker snorted derisively, 'Nine . . . up until she was about two hundred and fifty life cycles. She used to train herself against twenty full warriors even then!'

Shrum and the others in the crowd were even more alert now as to what would be taking place.

∞

As they waited almost nervously. A quite palpable tension went through all those who were watching on the sidelines. One against nine . . . Or as they thought - one young *woman* against nine well-muscled older *men*. Even though they had seen her amazing personal display just a short while ago. The main thought now was, of how could one woman ever hope to beat the nine men.

It was then that the ominous buzzing started as each Grem was given its five setting. Many there in the crowd had never heard such a thing as that before. Only Shrum and a few others who had been out with Rist. And Gremplar, when he had been approached by his captors in his citadel, who had heard them while set on ten.

'Are you all ready?' asked Raxx.

'Not really,' answered Ege. Though there was no hope for any of them *but* to train with her now.

'You may begin your attack whenever you are then,' she told them. As she then twirled the Grem behind her to cover her back while it was set on shield.

The nine men then began to creep forwards and outwards in a surrounding way. The Grem's before them were now slowly spinning. So it caused them to emit quite an ominous oscillating tone, like that of a swarm of enraged insects.

Menos, who was now positioned towards her back where she couldn't see him. Decided there and then to get it over and done with - so he made a sudden rush towards her then lunged at her.

Raxx heard his feet, spun, ducked extremely low and stabbed out with her own Grem.

'Shit!' Menos shouted as the end hit his stomach and a large flash took place from it.

Yet even before he had voiced his chosen vulgarity. Raxx continued with her turn as two others tried to take advantage of his initial attack.

With it having been so long now since anyone had been able to train with a young Raxx. None of them here having even been born the last time. They had all forgotten that her own Grem was actually very different. Which had been specialised in its manufacture to any of theirs just for her. There were not ten button settings for attack and one for shield on her weapon. There were only four, and all were close to each other. But more importantly, all could be operated by a single hand. No power. Level five, level ten, and shield were the only available options to her on hers. Her own also had another personal variation added to it, too, which was a rotator grip. This exceptional addition to her weapon, simply meant that she could spin it without needing to use her other hand to do this. She only had to spin it, then it would move freely until she grasped it again to halt it. And the required three main buttons were all there by her waiting fingers.

She was instantly back to shield which deflected their two incoming hits. And even before they could hit their own switches so as to go defensive. Raxx had already changed hers into attack and thrust it out at one of them. The one she was attacking jumped back in an attempt to prevent being hit, but Raxx's attack was still too fast for him. So another high energy burst made a flash upon bare skin.

The man hit walked away muttering who knows what at being caught by it while rubbing at the tender area.

Raxx was back into a low crouch already, the shield already back on and again covering her back. 'And then there were seven!' she said just loud enough so that everyone near enough could hear her.

The always moving group of High Commanders began to look at each other, almost in stares and eye movements. It was if they were trying to tell each other what to do next by way of telepathy. Then at a nod given by Ege who was out of her sight, they all rushed her this time.

Sadly some things are doomed to fail, and this was another of them.

Raxx again somehow sensed the impending attack coming. And while still keeping the shield on and whirling it around her as she kept low to the ground. Stuck an outstretched foot out and spun herself. Rist and another of them were whipped off their feet to thud down upon the ground. From there she leaped upwards into the air. And as she turned, caught one on his arm with a thrust; as he'd came far too near while trying to sneak up. She then rushed over to where the two men were just regaining their feet and prodded them both.

'Yo-ho-ho, only four more to go!' she said wickedly.

Another three left the battle arena with their raw burn marks on view. And then to the four remaining High Commanders' shock who stood together in front of her. She now went for them. Her shield work was just a blur, even as each of their attacks were deployed. Again and again, they desperately sought any opening, but she was just too quick at whipping it around and their hits were deflected. Her own Grem flicked out, another one gone. Three to go . . .

The strain of the last three was plain to see as they not only had to try and attack her. But also to either parry or dodge any of her own rapid attacks. Her already beaten partners who were now standing and watching outside the arena. Were not only grinning, but laughing at the way their compatriots urged themselves to survive. More than once one of them was rolling away from her upon the ground itself. While the other two on their feet tried to prevent her from reaching him.

'It's lucky this is only a fun session for her - or we'd all have been dead by now!' Menos laughed loudly as Ege's own Grem was then knocked out of his hand and he rushed to get it back again.

'Fun? This is what you call fun!' said an incredulous Borth as he looked at each of their raw burn marks.

'But of course. If our Prime Commander was fighting for real we'd all have been dead in about two or three minutes. She is just testing herself against us at the moment.'

Borth looked at Shrum who could only shrug his heavy shoulders in return. Borth could still feel the place where Rist had tapped him in with the weapon a good while ago now. As even the severe bruising he received from it had not yet completely disappeared. Yet those five were just standing there with their own livid bright red burns as if it was not even troubling to any of them.

With doing that, Borth heard, but only saw the flash from the corner of his eye. He swung his head back to the fight quickly. Only to see another of the men rolling away. Then his fist beating against the ground.

Rist was laughing mightily. 'Ege thought he had her easy there, didn't he!'

'Not for long he didn't!' added one of the others with a chortle as the same man made his way over to them.

'Back so soon, Ege?' asked Menos of the arriving man.

'I lasted longer than any of you five!' he said in answer.

Two against one should have been easy for her attackers. But then again, nine against one should have been an even easier overwhelming victory. Yet things were never as they seemed.

The two who remained were by now panting heavily. Even more so after losing another of their number to her varied methods.

Raxx then made another flurry of barely seen moves as another flash took place. The eighth man walked over to them while shaking his head from side to side, leaving only the one in place to face her now. The end was definitely nigh now ...

Raxx smiled across at the remaining man. 'You have done well to last so long, High Commander Curz.'

He eyed her through the sweat which ran down over his face. Which then dropped from his chin and continued down on to his chest like a small stream. 'Done well ... I'm supposed to be on a three day rest, Prime Commander. I wouldn't call this resting in any way!'

She gave a chuckle, and then a salute. Then her shield was on and she was advancing towards him. Curz gulped, and instinctively hit his shield button. And off they went again - Attack, defend, attack defend.

'She's taking it easy on him, he must really be feeling the pace now,' said Menos.

None of the watchers could tell that there was any drop in her speed at the way she fought. But those who had been out there with her already could easily do so.

'Well I'm still feeling exhausted from it,' said Ege. 'And as Curz's still out there, it'll just be twice as hard for him to battle her on his own now.'

It was during a quite hectic flurry of moves taking place between them that Raxx stopped dead still and placed her free hand up to her ear.

'Say that again, Morg?'

By her doing so it left the merest gap, and Curz went for it. He thought she'd made a slight mistake and took the offering. Only realising too late that she was speaking to someone via her implant as his Grem arced down towards her. And then it landed on her, even as he tried to halt its downward swing. The flash when it came was right on her left breast.

After emitting a low gasp, which was then followed by a deep hiss of breath being inhaled, she answered, 'Message received, Morg.'

Curz lowered his head abjectly. 'My deepest apologies, Prime Commander. I did not see that you were responding to an incoming message until too late.'

'Not to worry my dear friend,' she said, then poked her own Grem against him for it.

It was now his turn to suck in his breath and look back up at her smiling face.

'You *should* have been able to prevent it from making contact though! So I would suggest a few extra days of Grem training so as to get you to your peak again.'

'Yes, Prime Commander . . .'

She was still thinking of the message Morg had just given to her. Egral, she knew was the only inhabited planet in the Colus system. Her mind then thought of their star charts - that system was also a good four days travel from Haff. What kind of attack were they under? How large a force was it? Was it only ships, troops, or both? If Morg had the information she needed he would have told her. Seeing as he had not, Raxx imagined the worst scenario possible and made a swift plan.

She looked over at the group of commanders, and called out with authority, 'High Commander, Menos!'

He was instantly at attention due the vibrant tone she used and he was already saluting. 'Yes, Prime Commander.'

'We have just received a message that Egral in the Colus system is under attack. Assemble Legion Fourteen, full strength, and let me know the moment when you are ready to leave! If they have need of us, then we will come at their call.'

'Yes, Prime Commander, instantly!' Menos saluted again, before passing the Grem he had still been holding to Rist beside him, and he then began to run.

She looked at the remaining eight. Five of them had been at Gelten, so she couldn't use them. As she would never go back on her word about them resting. Ege himself had only recently returned from the Styros 5 trade meeting. So half of that legion although available, was also resting from the trip home. Ojork's legion was covering their planetary defences. Which left Curz.

'High Commander Curz!'

'Yes, Prime Commander?'

'Your Legion Seven is now to be on instant readiness depending upon what Girik learns when he gets there. I'll also let you notify High Commander Mak yourself. Her Legion Twenty-Nine is to be the same as yours, on instant readiness from now on, too.'

'Prime Commander,' he said with a salute as his fist thudded against his deep chest. Although unlike Menos, he did not run anywhere. His order had been for readiness and not assembling. Even he knew how long it would take to reach there, so there was no actual rush at the moment.

'I'm heading to Command to see if I can learn more.'

14

It was not an unusual sight on Haff to see a full legion of troops and their ships taking off a day later. So there was little to worry the populace about it. They, just as Raxx herself so far, only knew that one of their protected planets was under attack. And so as was usual, a force was being sent out to it. Right after her orders were given at the arena, a sweaty Raxx soon reached her office. Where she had called Morg into it.

'Any further news from Egral?'

'No, Prime Commander, nothing. Only the one signal on the emergency burst. We have not even had a reply from them to any of our own sent messages requesting an update either.'

She gave a thoughtful expression. 'Launch an android scout ship to reconnoitre the planet from orbit and to report back. It can get there a lot faster than our main fleet will. Also send two of our cruisers from the defence fleet after it. They'll be a bit slower, but at least it will be some kind of back-up for the scout ship if it is needed until our main fleet gets there.'

'As you command!' said Morg and left her.

∞

Life continued on Haff as usual for another two days. The Haffian's young or adult populace trained as they usually did. The retired troop members did whatever they could find to do so as to fill their own spare time. All the new nursing mothers looked after their new or growing families. And the prisoners, as ever, just wandered aimlessly about the city, or sat outside their building as per usual. For them, life was interminable as every day was very much the same.

While at the same time, two full legions were busy readying themselves in preparation for if they might be needed.

'I wonder where they've gone to?' asked Borth of his commander after they had watched an entire legion lifting into the sky.'

'A planet called Egral in the Colus system is all that I can tell you, Borth. But it must be a long journey if it will even take their troop carriers a full four days to reach it.'

'I wonder what they'll find there?'

'I have no idea. But I expect that with one hundred million troops and all of those impressive ships to use. Whoever is attacking this planet may not be there for long!'

'I would have to agree with you on that, General!'

∞

'Anything from our scout ship yet? Raxx asked Morg again for what must have been the tenth time that morning a further two days since it had left.

'Nothing Prime Commander. We did receive the signal from it that it was just about to come out of jump near the planet. But since then there has been no response.'

'I don't like it!' she said to him. 'I don't like it at all! Send a message out to the following cruisers. Advise them that we haven't heard from our scout ship, and for them to be on high alert upon reaching Egral.'

'As you command!'

As Morg walked off to do that. Raxx sat behind her desk with her fingers slowly tapping a beat out upon it in front of her.

'I really don't like the feel of this one little bit right now. Something feels different!' she said to herself. In effect right now she was just like Gremplar had been when they had dropped out of Briath's sky. Who are these attackers? Where have they come from? How many of them are there attacking? What was their military capability?

Raxx did not like unknowns. It was one of the reasons why scouts were always used initially. No actual life would be in danger at that moment. Yet if this was an attack. It had to have been planned by someone . . . or some *thing*. Or was it perhaps just a random attack by a race from somewhere that was out seeking new territory for itself? She hated not knowing what was out there waiting to meet her fleet. As she always held herself personally responsible for any fleet and its troops which she sent out.

She always required detailed information with which to begin to calculate any of her plans. But her main worry as always; was how many were in the force attacking or defending. And exactly what were *their* capabilities . . .

Was her own one legion strong force more than enough to cope with it. Or, worriedly, was it even far too small to combat this new attacker. She certainly had no idea if any other race they did not know about right now, had as many trained warriors as Haff. They had not found any so far - but that in itself did not mean very much at all.

Space itself was a vast area, comprising of millions upon millions, if not in fact billions of galaxies and their own planetary systems. So it was possible that out there, somewhere. At least one or more inhabited planets could be larger than Haff. And so could have an army that equalled, or even surpassed their own. Of this, she could only make the barest of assumptions, as at this time, she just did not know exactly who they were facing.

Their android scouts were forever out searching through the universe; and not all of them always came back. So thoughts of even higher intelligences, or just violent races. One which was particularly war-like, always dominated her thoughts on a daily basis.

Haff itself, she knew, was there mainly as a protector of planets . . . but what if a huge new force suddenly appeared from out of nowhere? That Haff itself because of this became stretched much to thinly. A large army was only seen as a large army to those who had it, and those who knew of it. It was always the many unknowns out there which caused her mind so many problems.

∞

The scout ship which had been sent out by her had been handled as skilfully as always by its android pilot. The only thing which was in their favour. As they were used to being sent out on long search trips to gather information. Was that with boredom being an unknown thing to them, its alertness was total. Having plugged itself into the ship prior to takeoff as usual. Its own source of energy never faltered. Which then meant that there was no requirement for it to shutdown to go into a typical charging mode. So it was aware all the time, and ready to react to anything instantly.

The fact that loneliness, fear, even the chance of death was not an input which had been programmed into them. Simply meant that they were ideal for this type of task. And why they were also used for them.

Android 84690012 as it was numbered did not have a normal name as others did. This was only as it was rarely expected to interact with humans much at all. They were basically just sent out to search . . . and upon its return offered their new information to those waiting to collect it, and were then given a full check over before going out again.

Android 84690012 sent a simple signal burst to Haff from the ship that it was about to come out of jump at Egral. And almost as soon as it did, the scout ship was no more. Many arcs of fire were shooting at it just as it popped out of its jump hole and it had exploded within sy-seconds.

As at Egral, there was not only as invasion taking place on its surface - but a defensive fleet was in its orbit too.

∞

Less than a day later, the two cruisers having been sent a warning to them by Raxx. Came out of their jumps early, where its pilots held a very short strategy talk over their com systems. One would go in as would be expected of it. While the other ship had its course re-programmed slightly to appear on the other side of the planet. At which point they resumed their jumps again.

From already knowing that the scout ship had not reported in, the pilots knew that were going in to what could be a hot zone. With shields on maximum and their weapons fully charged and armed, they both came out of their jumps at the same time..

The one ship which had followed the scouts path was immediately under heavy fire, and being hit with a barrage of weaponry. The second came out above the planet with nothing in sight. Though they could see the immediate danger their opposite number was in.

Through the explosions they could hear battering at their ship. The pilots of the second one heard, 'Don't bother coming to help us, Dysus!' said the pilot of the under fire cruiser. 'Head for the planet itself and find out what you can down there and then report. The Prime Commander will need to know as much as she can about them for the fleet that's following us. So we'll try and keep them busy for as long as we can so you can do that.'

'Right,' said the man who had been named in the message. And tipped the nose of the ship down to get there as quickly as possible. 'We'll do a run and scan over it, report, and then come back up to help you as soon as we can!'

'I doubt we'll still be here when you do, Dysus. Our shields are already buckling . . . but we can tell that we are at least damaging some of theirs which are bigger than we are. There are around twenty ships that are firing at us here. If we don't survive this, report, then get back out and jump to meet the fleet!'

'Confirmed.'

The ship in a full dive was much like that of a comet streaking. With fire trails behind it from the heat build up on its shields as it headed towards the ground. Scarcely five hundred feet from the ground, it pulled up until it was going horizontally. It's scanners and recorder cams working flat out as it assessed the swathe of dangers beneath it.

They soon began taking hits on their shields, but not too badly. As what they were seeing down there on the ground were a kind of mechanized robot like force blasting away at everything around it.

Targeting with their computers, all of their own weapons as the flew over began blasting away at the remorseless moving machines below. They saw much smaller running figures flying through the air as one of these things fired shot after shot at them and the ground erupting with towers of dark earth.

While from many sets of large speakers on the lower hull of the ship. A message was being relayed to those on the ground if any of them could hear it.

They were certainly taking out a lot of the machines as they flew over them. Even while their own shields were constantly under fire. But from these much smaller arms, the damage was still minimal.

'Dysus?'

'Go ahead, Jeros . . . '

'We're about lost here, so send your report and then get out while you can - Life and Death! For Haff!' they then heard he and his co-pilot shout; after that, all that could be heard was the buzz of static. The curses from the two remaining pilots were vulgar and ribald, knowing their two friends were gone. Yet also because of who they were, they were also proud that they had died in battle.

∞

The first ship with Jeros at the controls came out of their jump into the waiting heavy fire. The co-pilot Merk quickly had their own weapons firing back in return. One or two - perhaps even five they may have battled well against. But against close to twenty, they quickly knew from the striking firepower and dropping shield level on their own ship that they could not survive all of this for very long.

'Scan and prepare to send, Merk. We'll not make it, but at least Raxx and our fleet will see what they'll be up against here!' Jeros called out above the explosions as their own ship vibrated and rocked from taking hits.

'Already on it,' he replied just a calmly. 'I'll send it off just before we're finished, as that way it will be as up to date as it can be for her!'

'Good man!'

A huge hit now shook both them and their ship. 'It won't be for long either!' said Jeros as he glanced at the fifty percent level left on their own shields. 'How are we doing though?'

'We're hitting them quite well. They have some type of shield in place just as we have. But by using continuous bursts at the exact same place on one of them. I can tell that some are getting right though to their hulls now,' he said as he fired another full burst at one of them.

'Nice work.'

After a heavy flurry of shots pounded against their own hull in reply. Jeros saw that their shields had suddenly dropped below the twenty-five percent mark.

It was then that he used his com to tell Dysus to report and get away. Just as another vicious pounding hammered at the hull. Ten percent.

'What say you, Merk?'

'What else, my friend . . . For Haff, of course!' he said with a wide smile.

Jeros twisted the controls to swing their own cruiser right at the one Merk had been constantly hitting.

'Send it now!'

'Sent!'

'LIFE AND DEATH! FOR HAFF!' they both shouted as loudly as they could. Before their own dying cruiser plunged straight into that of their enemy. The explosion was sudden and brief. Space had no oxygen with which to offer support to any fire. Only that which remained in and around the two ships allowed fires, until it was all used and snuffed out.

'Cherek?' asked Dysus.

'Report sent . . . ' then he looked across at his lifelong friend. One he had known since they were both five cycles of age, as they had Jeros and Merk also. He grinned with his teeth showing at him. 'We've always said that we wanted a beautiful death, didn't we?'

'Indeed we did!' answered Dysus, now grinning back at him himself as he pulled the control column right back to his stomach. The ship changed in flight from its former horizontal level to a vertical one in an instant. And then full power was used to send it soaring upwards.

Neither ship's pilots had even thought about retreating away from a battle when it was joined. They had already known they could not win this battle due to the loss of their friends already. This time it was the other way around; too many enemy, and too few of them. Their being asked to surrender was an impossible hope if that was what the enemy may want so as to interrogate them. That was not the Haffian way . . . The ships which were heading towards them likely would not allow them time to jump out either. They had just left their scanners and monitors running now, to send a direct signal feed back home to Haff right up to the very end.

Their own final words they would shout would be the exact same ones as Jeros and Merk had. As they then took another of the enemy ships out by heading straight for it. They were both still smiling as the head-on collision took place. As in their own minds, there was certainly no doubt that they would soon be avenged.

15

Even though their encrypted heavy data signal feed was delayed by just over an hour due to the distance which it had had to travel. Unlike the holo-feed type. Raxx watched the entire feed at least three times in very close study before she sent for Morg.

The man had already seen the incoming feed himself. And who was still distressed at the sight of their two cruisers becoming no more.

'I want a copy of this feed sent over to our scientists immediately, Morg. I need to know if any of our scouts have ever seen any of these ships or machines before while out on their travels. If they have, then we may at least have a location and more information on them.'

He nodded. 'What about this feed, Prime Commander? Do we show it to our people on Haff?'

She looked up at him. 'Why not? As you know, I have never lied to them at any time. At any battle, such feeds are allowed to be watched back here on Haff by any who wish to. They were also able to watch the invasion which transpired of the Gelter system; as well as any others we've had if they wanted.'

'Only because they died, Prime Commander . . . and two ships were lost with them.'

'Morg . . . in any fight numerous troops and ships can be lost. The live feeds from Briath and Goll showed some of our own troops there losing their lives - just as it showed those they faced dying. Anyway, losing their ships or not, they all died with honour as they fought right to the very end and were not taken prisoner. I can ask no more of them than I could ever ask of myself.'

∞

155

After Morg had gone out to do the task which she had set him. Raxx paused for thought before making one of her decisions.

'Link me to High Commander Girik Menos on board the flagship of Legion Fourteen, please.'

Raxx stood and waited until the link was made and Menos appeared seated at his battle console.

'I am here, Prime Commander.'

'How far are you away from Egral now, High Commander?' Menos turned his head and swiftly questioned someone who was out of the viewers focal range.

'Thirteen more hours, Prime Commander. We are still moving at full speed as per your request when we left Haff.'

'I am going to send you a signal for all of you to watch, Girik.'

'What will it be about, Prime Commander, if I may be so bold as to ask?'

She gave a nod to him. 'As you will know, I sent both a scout ship ahead of you - as well as two of our defence cruisers, Yes?'

His own head bobbed. 'Yes, Prime Commander. I remember you telling me that at the briefing before we left. You were hoping that that would grant you extra information about who these attackers of Egral were; as well as to give us any forewarning.'

'You are quite right, Girik. However, I have to inform you that the scout ship must have been instantly destroyed as soon as it came out of its jump. As we heard nothing more from it.'

'Are the two cruisers there yet? If so they must be warned, Prime Commander.'

'They were warned with just enough time in hand, Girik. They came out of jump at my signalling of this to them. From that, they decided to approach the planet from two sides instead of just coming out at one.'

'And?' he said as he leaned forwards in his seat.

'One of our ships came out of their jump right into the sights of the enemies waiting fleet, Girik. They then began to take all their fire, while our other cruiser came out of its jump unchallenged and headed for the planet surface.'

'From this signal, you will see what this cruiser sent back to us to view. A kind of mechanized ground army, which might possibly consist of a robotic army. Sadly due to all the firepower it was coming under, our first cruiser was almost out of shield energy. They then decided between themselves to ram one of their ships.'

'For Haff,' said Menos.

'Indeed it was, Girik. And also just as bravely done as I would have expected of them as well!'

'And our second cruiser? Is that on its way home now - or waiting for us to join it away from the planet?'

'Again, I'm afraid I can only say that they are not, Girik. They sent their report back to me to show what it was like on the surface of Egral.' She lowered her head. 'The people were being chased and slaughtered down there, Girik!'

Menos jumped to his feet angrily. 'The bastards! Don't they know the planet and its population are unarmed?' Many who were inside the control room were watching Raxx back on Haff, although she could not see them. As the focus was on the one she'd named for her com link.

Menos calmed himself with an effort. 'What do you want us to do when we get there, Prime Commander? Whatever you direct us to do, we will follow - as always!' he stated to her.

'I cannot ask it of any of you, Girik There are too many in each of our ships to lose in a space battle. I am thinking of asking you all to return home.'

Girik himself only gasped. A retreat That was simply unheard of . . . He could even hear the growls of discontent from those near to him. He stepped even closer, right up to the image of Raxx's lowered head.

'No! Prime Commander. That we will *not* do!

'You would *disobey* me, Girik?' her voice now barely a whisper.

'Yes and no, Prime Commander.'

'Explain, please.'

'It is our own saying, Prime Commander. We are Haff, and Haff is us. We simply cannot betray who we are. Even if our entire legion dies from our going there. It is not only what and who we are, but what we are there to do also. We protect if called upon to do so, and fight if we must. We will not run away from a fight even if it means certain death for all of us - you especially should know this!'

'I do know it, Girik . . . of course I do. But at this time, I also do not fully know what you will find when you get there. I simply do not have enough information here yet. About their ships or machines in order for me to lay out a well ordered plan of battle for you. I can only make a few assumptions as to what you *should* do . . . which if wrong could then prove to be fatal for all of you!'

'Prime Commander,' he said softly to her, at which she raised her head to see him. 'I can speak for every single one of us here in our fleet. When I say that even without a plan of battle from you. We would *still* accept the fight ahead. You have told us many times that our own planets *honour* is at stake if we do not fulfil our obligations to others; which means to *any* of those who we are now allied to as their protectors.'

She unexpectedly then smiled at him. 'I was hoping you'd say that, Girik . . . and for that, I thank you all for it.'

He was left almost speechless. 'You knew that I would object?'

Her head tilted over to the left. 'Let me just say that I hoped you would, my friend. I hoped.'

'Well . . . I mean . . .' He then gave a sigh, 'Sometimes you do things in such a strange way that it leaves me quite lost for words, Prime Commander.'

'I know, and for that I am sorry sometimes, Girik. But you should know me well by now too. The unexpected - I do like doing things that may actually look oddly strange, random or quite uncoordinated in some way.'

He could do little but smile. 'That is I expect why you are our Prime Commander . . .'

157

'Very well then. Your own offer to go ahead has already now lifted a huge weight of burden from me, Girik. I can only hope that what I tell you now - works as well as it can once you get there.'

He walked back to his console and pressed a button that offered fleet wide communication. 'We are *all* listening to you now, Prime Commander! So go ahead and tell us what you *think* is best that we should do.'

∞

Not long after this, the two further legions which had been on instant readiness were heading upwards into the sky. They would certainly not be in time to aid Menos's legion if her own quickly formulated plan for them failed. As their four day journey meant that they would more than likely arrive far too late anyway. Along with them though, she did send many additional empty ships. The only good things about it, was that it was double the size of the first fleet. So there were a lot more troops, and far more ships too.

These troops had already viewed the data before they left. But just like Menos had done, they offered their own eager legions for her to use no matter what may happen. Although if Menos succeeded, they may have to turn around. If not, then there would still be a battle ahead for them all. This of course meant little to them. As they had since they were very young children, been trained for battle.

Many on the ground could only wonder as this new and even larger fleet took off, heading upwards; and as to where they were all going.

∞

On Haff, an alert went out for the entire planet. To inform their population that within the next few hours. A battle broadcast which had been received from their two defence cruisers at Egral would be screened for them.

There were two types of people on Haff. Some preferred to watch such things in the comfort of their own homes, or with friends. While others would make their way to wherever the ideal place would be to view such things even better on many of the enormous screens which would appear upon their tall buildings.

Gremplar and his men had no such private viewing possibilities available inside the building in which they were being housed. So they had all made their way outside. Shrum and others remembering where Raxx's earlier transmission had appeared after she had been given her memories.

So they stood or sat around, just as most Haffian's who were waiting to see it outside also did. As was usually the case, very few of them wore anything at all just like their prisoners. While to a lesser amount, others had on varied coloured items of brief clothing. None of which unless being very dark in hue, hid anything anyway.

A second alert then went out to the planet. To inform them that the broadcast would begin in thirty minutes. This would hopefully give everyone enough time to choose where they would like to watch it from - if they did. Most of them would of course, as it was a broadcast from a battle feed.

Thirty minutes later as they all waited, the screens all came on at the same time to show Raxx sitting behind the desk in her office.

'Greetings to you all, my fellow Haffian's. And also to those within our protectorate,' she began. 'As you may know or have heard by now, we received a distress call from Egral in the Colus system almost five days ago. Upon no response from our own messages to them, I assembled a fleet. Legion Fourteen with High Commander Girik Menos in command.

'However, already knowing that it would take our fleet close to four days in order to reach it. I also dispatched an android scout ship to get there first. Along with two cruisers from our planetary defence fleet since they were already stationed in orbit above us.

'After two days, our scout ship advised us that it was about to come out of its jump. We heard nothing from it after that - so I could only assume it had been quickly destroyed by whatever force was there. Knowing this, I sent out an urgent warning to the pilots of our two cruisers, who were following in its path. Who were themselves due to arrive at Egral a day later. With a different option of arrival then being decided upon. They came out of their jumps and one of them now altered their trajectory for arrival. Then they continued onwards again.

'What you are all about to see now is the recorded data which they both sent back to us. So that we here could understand exactly what was happening on Egral at this time. I will speak to you again shortly when each of the recordings is finished. The first recording you will see is from Jeros and Merk on their cruiser. Thank you.'

The screens everywhere then saw the fading frame of Raxx's upper body turn into the recording from Jeros and Merk as they came out of their jump.

'*They* look to be the ones who are well outclassed this time!' said a smug Gremplar to Shrum.

He looked at the contempt which showed itself on Gremplar's face. Shrum guessed that his former leader was pleased to see them being the ones in trouble this time. As he probably had not got over losing his own five planet reign to them yet.

'Do not be too sure, Sir. As I do know what these people are like when it comes to fighting!' he replied as they all watched the huge screen.

They saw the firepower which was being concentrated upon the single Haffian cruiser - just as they heard the pilots of it talking to each other all the time. Even while also talking to their other ship which was somewhere else. Yet even then, they still appeared to remain calm with no hint of panic. Even while being under such concentrated fire.

'By Aldur! They are insane!' gasped Gremplar only a few minutes later as they heard their shouted battle cry along with their fateful collision at the end. Shrum knew he had been right.

Then Raxx was back on their screens again

'As you could all clearly see from this first recording. Whoever this enemy is, they had a fleet orbiting around Egral. And from this record, I had no idea if this type of ship of theirs could actually land on the planet.

'From the second recording which I am now about to show you from our second cruiser; piloted by Dysus and Cherek. They have been able to show us exactly what *has* been happening at this time on the surface of Egral.'

Once again the face and body of Raxx herself began to fade from their view. To where they were now riding with the second cruiser of Dysus and Cherek as it came out of its own jump.

It was almost like being on one of the latest computer generated films made on Spirit which they so often enjoyed. Except here, as they had already seen, instead of following a plot - what they were all watching was quite real.

Along with the two pilots inside the cockpit they themselves were now diving down to the planets surface. Looking through the fiery glow against their shielding. While also able to hear the distinct com chatter taking place between each of their ships. Even the voluble cursing from them had not been extracted from this recording as the demise of the first cruiser took place.

They could then see smaller landing ships on the ground as the pilots flew over them while firing. A little further, and they were now firing at some strange looking mechanical things which were firing at something ahead of them. Until they watched the small bodies flying through the air after each explosion. Then they all knew what those same machines were firing at!

This lasted for a while as they flew along with them while dodging enemy fire as well as firing back. Some of those who were watching it. Were actually leaning this way or that way as the cruiser rolled and banked while evading being hit as if they were on it.

While in the brief moments between it being hit and firing at targets on the ground. All watching could hear a message being played over and over again to those still alive below. 'Haff is coming - stay hidden and stay safe! Haff is coming - stay hidden and stay safe . . . !'

After that came the talk between the two pilots of the cruiser. Again, they were with them as the nose of the cruiser suddenly tilted straight up. Though for those who were only viewers of this recording, they could not feel the sudden kick in their spines as its full power was brought online. Though many could remember it more personally.

And then they were back in space with them, and heading for the nearest enemy ship to them. They watched as continuous fire poured out from their own cruiser towards the nose of the other ship. Just as all the other enemy ships fire was converging like bright streams upon theirs. The nearer they flew, the larger the other ship grew in size to them, and higher damage was taking place. All watching on Haff knew that the enemy were bigger than their own cruiser - but quite small when compared to their main ships.

With eyes barely allowed to blink. They all watched almost transfixed as their own battle cry was screamed out and then the screen before them died to only blackness.

Then Raxx was back again.

'From what you have just seen on your screens before you. You will have all have noted that not only as our scout must have been, but also that our first cruiser was fired upon without any form of communication from the enemy.

'To this end, and after seeing these recordings for myself. I spoke with High Commander Menos and his fleet at once. My orders to him were: to evacuate any surviving inhabitants of Egral. And to defend them while doing so - lastly, to eradicate all enemies!'

They saw her glance to one side and then back to face the holo-cams again. 'Our main battle fleet will arrive there in less than twelve hours since all of this first became known to us. I have also sent two additional legions to Egral just in case. Only because at this moment, we do not know if this unknown enemy has requested help from any further forces it may have at its disposal, or not. What with them having now lost two of their own orbiting ships.

'When I next hear from High Commander Menos. It will be when he and the fleet are just about to come out of their jump upon reaching Egral. I will send an alert out so that you will have time to get to your nearest screen so as to follow for yourselves whatever will happen there next. Until then, my fellow Haffian's, I will bid you good day.'

The screens went dark and then appeared to disappear just as they had shown up on the various buildings Only then did those who had watched begin to talk about what they had seen.

'They're mad!' muttered Gremplar. 'Crashing into an enemy and killing yourself. Never mind losing an entire ship instead of trying to escape!'

'They do not retreat, Sir, unless it is for a strategic and preset purpose. As I told you before, they are very unlike we are in our ways. They would prefer to die in one way or another, rather than surrender or choose to retreat. In another way, just as I also told you, they do not fear death as we all do. Perhaps this is their biggest asset!'

'Killing yourself is not an asset, Shrum.'

'It must be to them, Sir. If you look at it carefully. You will understand that only for the loss of four men and their two smaller cruisers. They have just taken out two much larger enemy ships - carrying who knows what was on board them. Troops, or maybe more of those machines we just saw . . . Or if they were waiting to pick up those who were on the ground. If that is so, then whoever these enemies are, they are now two ships short to do this. To Raxx, I am sure that their sacrifice would seem justified. And do not forget that their own fleet is almost there too.'

'You think they can beat them?'

'I have no doubt in my mind that they will beat them, Sir. The only thing I am not certain about is just how many ships or troops they may lose in doing so.'

16

While those of Haff waited in eager anticipation for what seemed to be a long time for their fleet to arrive. Every other world which they protected, had also been allowed access to those same recordings along with Raxx's own earlier speeches with them. So by the time that the fleet was about due to come out of its jump. Their seventeen protected worlds, including the troops that were still positioned on the five planets of the Gelten system were all waiting too.

Although on the Gelten planets. Only the local inhabitants who could get near enough to see the screens the troops left behind were now using could do so. As the troops on those had been told by Raxx that as they had just been lifted out of tyranny. A little friendliness, cooperation and possible integration would not go amiss. Only as she was trying to show them how the freedom which they had not enjoyed for so long could be used.

She knew that the inhabitants of them had, after their fears had slowly died down. If having found that there had been no threatening demands or behaviour towards them. That they may slowly come out of their cautious shells and begin talking to the new army personnel there. Mainly asking about what they as victors might want from them now - only to learn that these invaders actually wanted nothing. But that they may be able to offer something to them instead.

The alert then went out, the one which everyone on Haff and on each of the other planets had all been waiting for; dependant upon any possible time delay of course. That the time was now coming . . .

The building which had housed Shrum and all his people was quickly emptied. As they were soon all outside as if awaiting the next episode of a series to start. Wondering whether it would it be a victory they would all see, or a huge loss for these people gathered in their multitude all around them?

The screens then came on everywhere, with only a large 5 showing on it. Then it was a 4, then a 3, then a 2 . . .

Shrum could almost feel both the nervous tension as well as the growing excitement which began to ripple through everyone. Including those of his own men as the numbers slowly counted down. As it reached 1 there was an ominous silence around them as they all stared upwards.

It was lucky that the screens themselves were actually so huge. As it was not only one picture that suddenly sprang to life on the screen - but more like a patchwork of various cam angles from many different ships in their fleet.

The legions fleet itself consisted of one hundred ships. Half were for their full strength of troops. Thirty of them were vehicle carriers. Either to use for attack or defence. The final twenty were actual ship carriers, and so these were the largest Haff ships of all . . .

∞

Many planetary populations watched as their own known protectors went to battle for those just like themselves. As did those who were in the two fleets still heading to Egral. As the fleet began to come out their jumps and were under fire immediately just as the cruiser had been.

The enemy it seemed, must also have been reinforced since their cruisers were there earlier. As there must have been at least fifty positioned in front of the bluish-green orb behind them; which was planet Egral on the screen now. The enemy had not seen *this* size of ship before though. As the most recent ones they fought with were a lot smaller.

As their own ships emerged, they could all see that it was not in a line abreast formation as it normally would be. But more like that of an spearhead. Menos was following Raxx's initial plan. Even if she had not fully known what might happen when they came out. She had just expected that their new enemy would have sent for more help. And so had devised a strategy which could help them to break through to the planet easier.

If their troop or cargo carrying ships were large in size. Then it was nothing compared to the twenty leviathans which were well guarded right in the middle of the fleet. Which as they came out of their jumps, opened up their own drop doors beneath. And from those doors, each of these colossal monsters dropped ten cruisers. After they had emptied their own bays and closed these doors, they were now just huge weapon platforms.

Shrum and his men were enraptured at such a sight taking place before them. Since even *they* had not seen such carrier ships as those before while on Haff. This was only because they were so large, that they could not land within a city as the others had done. Their own underground bases were in quite desolate parts of Haff where they had more room to land or take-off.

They watched as the fleet did not make any expected manoeuvres to turn, or even to weave. But headed inexorably towards their foe. One of the enemy ships exploded to a cheer from the crowd. The front leading ship of their own fleet was taking a heavy pounding. Then it began to slow and another one went ahead of it to take up the same leading role. The first one dropped near to the tail of their fleet as it now began to carry out any repairs.

Again and again as they got closer they would watch as their lead ship would break off and slow, and another would place itself right at the very front to face the fire. Only known to Raxx and those in her fleet . . . was that her vehicle carriers were those which were always taking up the lead. The troop carriers were safely behind all of those.

While this was happening of course, the ships of their own fleet were all firing at those of the enemy. One after another to yet more cheers, it was the turn of *the* enemy ships to suffer and explode under such a massive fire rate. The tables had well and truly been turned.

The two hundred cruisers after they were released, arced away from the battle first of all. They had been ordered by Raxx to leave those in orbit to their own ships. While their task was to head for the surface as quickly as they could. Where one unit of twenty would take out their landing craft. The rest were to begin to search out any of those machines which were attacking the planets population, and then destroy them.

The eyes of those watching were constantly moving, flicking from one view to another on the screens. The troop and machines carriers and small cruisers fired core-flux cannons. While the huge cruiser transporters fired even heavier pulse-wave cannons. These were much harder hitting, but also a lot slower to re-energise and fire again.

Some of their own ships were dropping further behind that of the main fleet. Mainly those who had led and then fallen away. Who from these front positions were suffering from various types of damage. Perhaps not what could be termed as being critical in a way, but it did severely limit either their speed or weapons. And of course, their own shields had already been hit so much that they needed time to recharge too. Repairs always took time, even longer if not on the ground for easier access. So they could now only follow on as best they could.

At that same moment, and quite unexpectedly, their latest lead ship then just blew up into a variety of different sized pieces. Whether it was simply a very lucky hit, or possibly that of a failure or flaw somewhere in its shielding, they would never know. But what those watching could see, were some of their ground machines slowly or quickly spinning through space. Some were even being pushed from its initial explosion to send them hurtling towards the cams of other ships around it. Some of the people watching ducked; as if the same pieces of wreckage or weirdly rotating machines were only just going over their own heads - so real to them was it all.

Even though the shields around the other ships simply brushed them aside. As if the enemy firepower could not get through them very quickly, then there was little chance of this smaller wreckage doing anything. Yet even as this happened, another ship had quickly moved up to take its lead place. The pilots on this one hoping that their own ship would not suffer such a similar catastrophic failure as well!

Again and again, a crippled lead ship was left to follow behind. While the enemies own losses continued to mount higher and higher. As unlike the Haff fleet, theirs was spread widely apart for whatever reason they had done so.

∞

On other parts of the large screens, others watched as the large group of cruisers swept down towards the planet. The leading group of these broke away from their formation and proceeded to fire upon the enemies landing ships they could see settled on the ground. One blowing up into a huge mushrooming fireball even as it attempted take-off.

The rest of the cruisers were in line abreast and scouring the ground from a low level of barely one hundred feet. Racing over the ground so as to find targets. Just as they fired at anything remotely mechanical, so similar fire from the ground rushed back up at them. One cruiser trailed fire and smoke from a weapon battery of some type, until a few of them all fired at it to destroy it. Just too late for the smoke and flame stricken cruiser though; as it slowly dropped from the sky to hit the ground and cartwheel. Throwing up clouds of dust and large chunks of earth as it did so when it struck.

The pilots were a little luckier though, having been able to jettison their cockpit only moments before. Leaving it far too late many had thought though. As at such a low altitude, it had very little time to come online to land them safely. It was actually jettisoned so low, that they could see it actually rolling and spinning along the ground. Leaving its own trail of dust and earth behind it. Sometimes even going end over end as it finally slowed until it came to a violent stop against a wall in a large cloud of dust and masonry.

A cheer went up as they heard the pilots reporting that they were uninjured. Their own onboard I.I.S.S had kept them safe throughout.

The other cruisers carried on with their set task. Some veering off into the towns and various cities of Egral. Flashing through some streets which were barely wide enough to take them at heights as low as fifty feet. Their weapons still shooting at anything which looked at all like an enemy machine.

There was an unexpected sight for those who could only watch on the screens. Due to so much happening, not all were able to see what else was taking place now though. As from various places, small crowds, or even in lesser numbers most times. The inhabitants of Egral who still remained, even after the many days of violent attacks upon them. And who due to this had been forced to hide somewhere in some way or another. In order to save their lives from the sudden invasion of their planet. Were now mostly coming out to watch what happened. Haff was finally here, and they cheered again and again as the cruisers took out one machine after another as they passed low overhead and darted through the rubble strewn streets.

∞

High Commander Menos had been very impressed with Raxx's own forethought. Less than an hour it had taken to destroy the orbiting fleet. And especially with her not even knowing what may have lay ahead of them. Her suggested spearhead tactic had worked superbly well

As the last enemy ship in orbit was finally destroyed. Menos quickly gave his next orders. The troop carriers and the remaining unused and still unharmed machine carriers quickly headed for the planets surface to land. While the gigantic cruiser carriers themselves now took up defensive stations in orbit around it. The ships that were lagging behind the fleet would soon join them there if they still had any engine difficulties. While those that were able to land would still do so as and when they reached Egral.

From that time on, wherever there was a major city or large sized inhabited area. The troop carriers began to land nearby, and were quickly disembarking and then being formed up into their own smaller sections. This would be the hardest time, as Raxx had told them. As she had no idea exactly what their weapons might be like power wise against their lighter Grem shields. They could only keep them at the highest setting possible and hope it would be enough to protect them while they carried out their search for survivors.

On hearing that their own troops were now on the ground. The cruisers split up into much smaller units and headed off so they could offer these same ground troops air support. Other troops had to wait for their machine carriers to land before they could get to some of their armoured ground support vehicles. When they did though, they were quickly speeding past the troops so they could go in ahead of them.

∞

While all of this was on the screen however, Raxx herself was in her office enjoying her first sexual contact after her incarnation. Even if the new Derus's body did not know what was happening to it from the start of the ship fight. The older memories of her former self certainly did. As Raxx's mind and body, for some reason or another, always became quite excited and highly aroused whenever it saw or engaged in fighting.

Nor did it take her long to find a willing partner from outside her office to help her either. The old Raxx could well have struggled due to her age and looks. And also because she had been celibate for well over a hundred years. But the new Raxx with all the advantages of youth and beauty which were now on her side had no similar problem.

And so while she watched as their fleet took incoming fire and fired back. Then the cruisers headed down to the planet and fought. Raxx was stood behind her desk. Her hands spread wide upon its surface, her feet slightly apart as her partner Ferus behind her. Offered her what she really needed at that moment in time. Which was to offer succour to her own odd coital stimulus at times like these. Even as Ferus gently thrust himself back and forth, his hands were around her front to massage her firm breasts.

Her own eyes though remained transfixed to the various incoming images of battles and deaths. No matter what he himself was doing to her - as the actual act itself really meant little to her. It was the fighting, which she already knew was her own personal stimulation. What he gave to her was simply a way for her to release her own growing urges.

For the past hour, three times Ferus had flagged, and then recovered himself enough to continue. While Raxx herself had barely showed any hint of release or fervour; or had even moved once from her position. To Ferus, it felt like he was having sex with an inanimate statue almost. There were no gasps or moans coming from her . . . none of the more usual actions or sounds he might have expected from any woman. For Raxx, it was all about the sight of the enemy ships blowing up. Or from seeing the cruisers blasting away at various things on the ground. Even to watching the troops in battle which caused her own feelings and sensations to rise heatedly within her.

The things which brought her own urges, wants, needs, lusts and predilections to the fore. Were just as she herself was - which was made for battle. Even while she was only sparring with the nine High Commanders outside a few days ago. She could feel the onset of many pleasurable orgasms rising from deep within her body. Only for them to recede again just as quickly as they came to her each time. People differed in many ways as to what type of thing or personal thrall heightened their own levels of stimuli. Raxx of course with being who she was, her own desires were purely and simply, the excitement of fighting!

Just as the troop ships began to land, she thanked an exhausted Ferus for his help. But even then she knew that her own body was still not as yet satisfied. So she brought Gorek back into her office with her. Yet another who could not refuse such a tempting and inviting offer from her either. Even after having seen the state in which Ferus was in when he left.

∞

Her own inner turmoil and stresses began to slip away only when she knew that the fleet were soon gaining a steady advantage over them. Her own instinctive and hopeful planning was working to good effect there right now.

Although what she and all the others were actually watching. Had taken place just over an hour ago now due to the time delay on the feedback . . . The battle which took place both above and on Egral itself could either be over and won by this time - or lost already!

The floating holo-cams followed the formed up troops who were walking rapidly. Then a line of shots suddenly came from somewhere far ahead of one section on the planet. Many in their front line were being thrown backwards off their feet by the unexpected force of these hitting their shields. To then lie scattered around like skittles which had been knocked over.

Following lines of troops quickly moved ahead to remake a new energy barrier, just as the lead ships above the planet had earlier. Again and again, one line after another formed at the front, doing their best to protect those who had been hit already. Even as more of those in the next formed up line were hit as well. The android medics behind were already heading to those who were constantly being swept aside. They had to keep this up continually until their ground vehicles eventually found the source of the fire and prevented it from firing.

From watching this, Raxx herself was almost heading for sexual rapture!

She saw from the cams, that the men and women upon the ground were not dead as she'd first thought. Few even had any signs of blood on them. It had been the shockwave of the shots hitting their energy shields which had tossed them around and had basically stunned them.

As the medics tended, some began to recover and rose to their feet and followed after the troops who were already trotting away from them. A few with one arm dangling uselessly when it had been broken looked disgusted with not being able to continue. Those with either both arms in a similar condition, or a grotesquely angled leg or two simply could not carry on. They could neither follow their friends, nor take further part in any future fighting to come now until their disabling injuries had been seen to. It was hard to be a warrior if you could not hold a weapon!

These injured were already being whisked away on the inevitable hover stretchers that followed behind the medics. Taking them off to the waiting medical teams waiting on board the ships.

The same fight was also over much too quickly for Raxx to gain her own much needed release. So it once again declined and died off inside her. Which also did not help the already tiring Gorek who was just about shattered. She thanked him for his aid, but as always, he simply had to give up in the end. Which left a still very much unsatisfied Raxx behind.

That was when she opened one of her desk drawers and took out a small box with wired sensor stimulators. Its attached nodes she placed upon her stomach and groin. These were just like smaller versions of the muscle tensors used in the cryo-cell. Which sent small bursts of electrical impulses through to her inner muscles. Her older memories told her that its setting of two was only to get things moving. And only whenever something highly stimulating appeared on the screen before her. Would she then turn it right up to its maximum setting of five.

∞

But wherever she looked on the patchwork screen before her, there was actually very little action taking place now. She only hoped that she was not going to remain unfulfilled!

Thankfully for her, if not for some of her troops who were cautiously entering a city on one of the screens. A similar kind of battle began to take place. The enemies shots were again scattering them around, while their ground machines hunted them down one by one.

Raxx had quickly maxed it, and all those who were not too far away from the doors to her office. Then heard her loud moans as the tremors and waves of pleasure intensified within her body. Her stomach muscles were contracting and releasing just so quickly now, that the end was inevitable. Not even able to watch the screen, her eyes began to roll before they closed tightly. Her body shook and her stomach quivered repeatedly. Until she finally succumbed to her long wait; with many deep and sudden loud moans from her multiple orgasms. She had at last received her much awaited release . . .

After that, she sat on her chair feeling a little light-headed and exhilarated. A little later after uncoupling the nodes and dropping the box back into her drawer, she then requested a cleaner to tidy things up.

17

Menos was literally amazed. They had lost more dead on all of their ships above than on the ground by the time the battle had finally ended four hours later. Only two of their troops on the ground had actually been lost, and that in itself had been unbelievable. Although many thousands of their troops had had one or more of their limbs broken or dislocated by the forces taken against their shields; but they would be safe.

He also knew that Raxx not only wanted some of these mechanical things transported back for their scientists to study in depth. But also parts of the ships they had destroyed in orbit. The cruiser carriers would be used for that task, seeing as three of them had lost one each. Possible new metals, weaponry, circuits and systems. All of these might be found after their scientists had had a chance to take them apart at home and on Spirit.

Their losses in battle had initially it had been an unarmed android scout ship. Then the four pilots of the two defence cruisers which had been sent out to follow it. Then when the fleet came, one machine carrier ship with ten on board; and then another four from the two cruisers which were lost while attacking on the planet. The two whose cockpit had been ejected had survived and had since been picked up.

So nineteen from their ships and two from their troops. Twenty-one human lives and one android had been lost in their successful battle for Egral. Not that high of a figure for what had recently been accomplished he knew. But as it also included the total obliteration of an enemy invasion fleet upon one of their protectorates. He for one could never have imagined their losses being as low as this before they arrived.

Menos's final recording that everyone watched, was of the ongoing evacuation of the people of Egral if that was what they wished. Raxx's offer was in case the same enemy returned later after them for having lost their own fleet there. None of its inhabitants left of course, as they preferred to stay and begin to rebuild their lives again.

Once again, Haff had been called upon when they were needed. And they had responded just as they had been told they would, so as to save any of their planets and lives. In essence, it was all that most on Egral had asked for, or had wanted. Now it was up to them again to try and return things there once more back to normality.

∞

'Well, Sir?' asked Shrum after the screens had finally turned off. And they began to walk back inside their building as night, along with their curfew time had came in.

'They were certainly lucky!' he responded.

'It was not luck, Sir. More like tactical awareness!' argued Shrum.

'I wouldn't say so. Did you not see the heavy hits those lead ships of theirs were taking all the time?'

'Of course I did . . . but then, if *you* noticed, they kept changing over at the front so as not to allow one to get too damaged.'

'One of them blew up!' he stated as a matter of fact.

'Unexpectedly, I think. They must have had a failure somewhere. I say that only as it had barely reached the front for very long when it was destroyed. While all of the others lasted quite a long time before switching. And *while* their enemy were concentrating on that one lead ship. Their own ships were destroying the enemies ships one at a time in response. And as for those even larger ships of theirs that carried their smaller fighters . . . I have *never* seen ships as large as those before!'

'They were not fighters, they were cruisers, Shrum . . .' muttered Gremplar.

'What?'

'I heard one of their people call the things which dropped from them cruisers. They were the same type of ships as those two which crashed into the enemy at that earlier screening we saw from that planet. I thought you would have recognised that yourself?'

'If that is the case, then even their cruisers are almost as large as our own ships which we sent here to take these planets!' replied Shrum as they entered within the building behind the long stream of their own men. All of who were as yet still discussing what they had just watched outside.

Gremplar chuckled softly. 'Those lance weapons things of theirs weren't much good on the planet surface as they were on ours, were they?'

'Perhaps not this time,' Shrum said with a shrug. 'But, also due to those same energy shields, there were not many deaths even if they did get thrown all over. And did you see just how quickly those who were behind ran in front to cover them from further fire?'

'Only to get shot at and then be thrown themselves from that same incoming fire!' Gremplar grinned.

'True. But as we saw, there were just so many of them that their front line just kept on being reformed over and over again. Until whatever it was which *had* been shooting at them was disabled or destroyed.'

Gremplar gave a long look at his general. 'You appear to be becoming quite taken with these people, Shrum. Do not forget about your own people who are now prisoners here at the same time!'

'I will not forget that, Sir. Yet by any way you wish to look at it, we have all been treated more than generously by them. And as for the people themselves, I have nothing against them . . . '

'Nothing against them!' Gremplar said furiously. 'Do you not remember just how many of our men they slaughtered!'

'Of course I do, Sir. It would be hard for me *not* to do so! But as an enemy of ours, which they were at the time of our own invasion. I was surprised that they had allowed all the rest of us to live so long.'

'What are you getting at?'

'By all rights, they could just as easily have killed all of us on every planet which we invaded, Sir. Yet they did not. Only those who fought against them suffered the consequences of their actions. Not only those here but also back in our own system, too, suffered for it - when we *all* could have been killed for it!'

Gremplar nodded and smiled a grim smile. 'That is only because they are a weak people. I myself would not have hesitated to have done the opposite to them!'

On that point Shrum disagreed and held a laugh back at his former leaders tone. Threatening as to what you *would* have done if the tables were turned, was now little more than an utter waste of breath and only a dream he thought. Shrum began to wonder if Gremplar thought he was going to return to his former home of Briath to take up where he had left off. If that was the way of his thinking, then it was a very unlikely scenario indeed. He had been the only one to cause their invasion of this system. It had been his decision to attempt to takeover all of these planets for himself.

As they now parted company. With Shrum heading towards his usual place with his men, and Gremplar to his family. He wondered if Gremplar had any idea exactly what repercussions Raxx could impose upon all of them if she so wished to. The worst one ultimately, of course, being all their deaths. He only hoped that he'd got to know her well enough by now, that such a fate was unlikely for them. Maybe the longer they were held and capitulated to any demands placed upon them. Then Raxx might just decide to offer them their freedom to return home. Even if as a former army, they may well be finished now

But yes, no matter what Gremplar himself might think about these people. Shrum was mostly in awe of them. He had now seen how they were all trained on this planet. They had not been allowed to watch the fight and occupation of his home world up on the screen by order of Raxx. His own correct assessment of that, was because it may have been too distressing for them to watch. Although they had all been allowed to watch their latest battle.

That his own men would fight, if ordered to, he knew. Though unlike those here, he also knew that they would not be as willing to sacrifice their own lives for someone else if that time ever came. That was the difference as yet which Gremplar, with all of his so-called wisdom, didn't seem to be able to understand yet.

That to fight an enemy as a soldier in an army under orders was always easy enough to do . . . However, to fight an enemy who wasn't afraid to die - and also one who was more than, of not very willing to lay down their own life for another. That was another thing entirely. One which he now knew separated their own two military groups by a very wide margin.

∞

Over the next few days everything appeared quite calm on Haff. The two legions which had been sent to help Menos had been ordered to halt in their jumps when thirty minutes from Egral. So now, they did not actually drift in space, but held their positions. Raxx wanted them close, but not at the planet itself in case a further attack was tried. And if that happened again, they would be there quickly to counter it, and also more ready to prevent it next time.

She would not leave them there though. She told the two High Commanders that seven days would be their own placement. after that, they could return back to Haff and another two legions would replace them for the same duration. This preparedness would continue for a short time. As well as advising them upon what tactics they should use if they were sent in.

Menos's fleet had by then left the planet and were on their way home. She wanted the things they'd picked up at her request back as soon as possible for them to be looked over. Just as many of the ground vehicles that were lost when the ship had exploded had been picked up. As not only did all troops have implants, but ships and ground machines had tracking devices too. Only the machines which had been too badly damaged would not be returning.

Shrum and his men continued to watch Raxx do her training on the arena. However, there was no further sign of any of her military commanders being around to offer her further practice. They knew best when to keep out of sight of her at such times now. So she was on her own when doing her various moves, jumps, spins and alternative changes.

Rist and the others had also returned to duty from their short rest periods by this time. So Shrum was again able to speak with him about many matters. His talks, offered him even more understanding of the people upon this planet. As well as just how beneficial being allied to them could be for their own system. Although it would mean that Gremplar's former rule over them would certainly stay quashed. His reign over the five planets in Gelten was over now; and for good. Rist as yet also had no idea what Raxx's purpose for them all was. But he did expect that it was unlikely that Gremplar would be free to do whatever he wanted after this.

Only when the fleet returned from the skies to land and be safely contained underground again. Did Shrum find himself being summoned to Raxx's office, although it was by her own decision this time. For Shrum, all he could think was that she had finally made her decision about what to do with them all. So he was a little worried about what he would hear when he was shown into her office,

'Good morning, Akras, please be seated.' she informed him with a gesture.

At least that was a better start than even he had expected he thought to himself, as he took the offered seat. 'Good morning, Prime Commander,' he returned.

As she looked closely at him, she saw the worry lines etched upon his high forehead. 'What's wrong?'

His large shoulders gave a heavy shrug. 'I thought you were bringing me here to tell us what is about to happen to all of us, Prime Commander.'

'And what are you expecting? I am only asking from the expression I saw on your face.'

'Execution maybe.'

Raxx gave a bubbling laugh to that.

'Akras . . . We on Haff are not a violent race, no matter what you all may think. Warriors who live only for battle - Yes.'

'But you are also a military race, Prime Commander!' he butted in before she could carry on.

'So? Not all military races are simply just that, Akras! Yes, we are indeed born to train, and to fight whenever it may be necessary. But our own lives consist of far more than just that alone you know! We also enjoy having fun, pleasure, eating, drinking, and playing games. We also enjoy watching and hearing the films and songs made on Spirit, too. Just because we *are* a military planet does not simply mean that *that* is all we are as a people! Death is a constant thing for all of us, Akras. So when we are not fighting and dying, we must also enjoy our lives to their very utmost in the meantime.'

'We are not going to die then?' he reiterated.

Her bubbling laugh was emitted yet again.

'If you were all going to die. That would have been ordered within the first few days after you arrived here, Akras!' Her laughter trilled out once again.

It was one of the sweetest sounds Shrum thought he'd ever hard. Especially as it had now confirmed not only his own, but also Rist's thoughts on the matter as well. The heavy weight of relief he now felt showed on his face to her.

'I asked you come and see me for one reason, Akras.' At which words she gained his full attention now.

'I am sending a delegation to your system shortly. To speak to the peoples on your planets about what may be best for their own future now.'

'An alliance with you, you mean?'

'Not to me personally - or our planet even. Some or all of those within our system and others if they wish. That trade option will be available to them if they, as well as those who we know wish to have it. But as you know, and as I have also told you before. We do not force any planet or system to accept. They can always refuse to do so if that is the most popular wish.'

'I'm sure they would wish to join, Prime Commander. As I feel they would certainly need all the help they could get now with Gremplar gone. They may even already be feeling quite lost as to what they should be doing now without any of the usual orders being given to them.'

Raxx nodded. 'As I said, I will be sending a delegation to visit each of your planets, Akras. Some of the Mayors from some of our planets here have agreed to go first already. Although it will also decide upon what yours may have to trade with. I will also go, since I am what is known as the head of this one. However, I also want you and a few of your aides to come to.'

'Why us?' he gasped.

'Well, you *were* living there were you not? So surely the people there will also know you better than they do any of us. All we can do is to make offers to them - which they may decide to accept or reject. You yourself however, have been on a tour of the Barathon system with Octavus. So your own experience from this, and perhaps any advice which you can offer to them may help them make better choices.'

'Well I'd be happy to go, Prime Commander . . . although, not if I have to look like this in front of them!' he said with a gesture towards his own naked self. 'Only the Great Aldur knows what our people are making of your troops right now who are there with them. They, just as we here, were certainly not used to the sight of so many naked people on our planets.'

Raxx smiled widely at him. 'I'll see what I can do for you, Akras. Of course your military uniform would be out of the question now though. Since at this time there are none of your military remaining on them. To us now they are seen as being free planets. If they themselves, as I'm hoping some will become their own planets leaders, just as they do here. Then it will be for them to decide if they wish to have any kind of military forces created again.'

Shrum was suddenly worried. 'Most of us have been in the military under Gremplar since young boys, Prime Commander. So we really know nothing else now. So what else would we possibly be able to do back there if we are allowed to go back to our homes again?'

Raxx pondered on that herself for a minute or two. 'From what I seem to know of you, and of the things which we have spoken about since you came here, Akras. I would personally judge you to be quite intelligent. So, I see no reason why you should not put yourself forward to become a hopeful candidate to lead one of your planets, if not that of your own?'

'Me!' he croaked. 'I know nothing of what any of you do here on your planets. I was simply used to being given orders and following them. I would have no idea at all about what could be needed to be in charge of an entire *planet*, Prime Commander.'

Her mouth held the hint of a smile at his possible predicament. 'I am not saying to you that should try and run it all on your own, Akras ... '

'You're not?' he said breathing easier.

'Of course not. As you yourself just stated, you have been a military man for far too long. However, something like that should mean that you were good at organising. Yes? Troop deployments, as well as supplies for these troops, and such like. Yes?'

'Well sometimes, Prime Commander. Though there were others in charge who handled things like supplies.'

'Indeed. And so, just as on most planets in our system, a vote could be taken to place a group of you in power for a certain length of time. If you do the job particularly well, then at the next election - if your people are happy about what you have done for them. Then they will vote for you all again to continue in the way that you have been doing it.

'All you have to remember, is to try and get people around you who know about many different things. The more areas or backgrounds that they come from, then the better you will begin to understand your planets problems and issues.

'What I am saying to you is this. If your planet grows anything, then someone from that background. No matter if they were once considered as being of a lower class than you. They will definitely know more about that than any of you do. The same goes for your transportation, any building or construction, solving your clean water distribution. As well as actually having someone who you think would be able to handle trade deals between your planet and others. Each of your cities could have someone in charge, under whoever has been placed in complete charge and who would be held responsible for all these matters.'

'I do not know if any of our planets could manage to do something like that, Prime Commander. We have lived for far too long under the Gremplar's reign. He made all of those decisions for us.'

'Perhaps you can, perhaps you can't, Akras. But until you all *try*. Then you will never know what having the yoke of tyranny being lifted from you can truly mean. Right now, since our invasion of your system, there now is no single ruler of the Gelten system. So this is your own peoples chance to take charge of their own lives and affairs again. And begin to build your civilizations in the way that you yourselves may *want* them to grow. Which means instead of only one major family telling you what *they* want you all to do. It would now be up to *all* of you to decide the best way forward for all of you instead!'

Shrum's cheeks puffed out as he took all of this in. As he for one had no idea if there was *anyone* on their planets who was actually able or capable enough to do any of this.

'Don't look so worried, Akras. It is only my suggestion of a new life for you and others anyway. The Mayors who are going there with us will be able to explain to them in far better detail than I ever could. Of what forming a free government would allow them to do for their futures.'

When Shrum left, his head was still buzzing with everything that she had tried to explain to him. Behind him, remained an even wider smiling Raxx. She herself had high hopes for Shrum. He wasn't stupid.

That much had shown when he surrendered instead of fighting on Jitrus. Nor was he as ignorant as some were - particularly Gremplar!

He also appeared to have enjoyed seeing many new things which could benefit his system. Or so Octavus had told her after their journey together. It was why she thought of him as being a good candidate to help his people out at first by setting up a government. All he needed, it seemed, was a little help for him to understand what doing such a thing would actually entail . . .

18

As the scientists began to not only dwell upon, but delve over the alien wreckage which was brought back for them. Quite excitedly almost, seeing as it was also something entirely new for them to work on. Raxx as she usually did, granted High Commander Menos and Legion Fourteen their own three full days of rest this time.

While this took place, Raxx herself took control of one of their own extremely fast but small fifty-seater ships, along with the requested cargo she asked to be loaded upon it. Then with Shrum, Borth, and a further three of his men. Along with Octavus, two of her own maids, and another of their female High Commanders by the name of Lemane Der. They then proceeded to pick up the nine Mayors who had said that they were willing to help her out.

She had decided to head to Briath first, what with it having been seen as the main planet for so long in that system. With all the required spatial data then being input into the flight controls. Not only as to where they were going to for the jump itself. But also to set the ship at its highest rate of speed possible. The I.I.S.S. came on as they took their jump.

The time stated by the flight system was of twenty-three point sixteen hours. Or twenty-three hours and sixteen minutes as they thought of time in the Barathon system. Far quicker than had been the case of their invasion fleet when it went to the Gelten system. Though those were far larger ships with a much higher mass compared to this mainly unarmed and lightly armoured smaller speeder. It did have its own bio-shielding of course, just as all their ships did which were able to jump space. As protection during any jump was necessary. The shield was always there just in case it ran into anything unexpectedly during one. Most things would easily bounce off their shields and cause no damage at all. However, if a large asteroid managed to turn up in their direct line of flight. Then it was quite possible that the ship and all those in it would be vaporised instantly!

As they travelled on their journey, all but the maids would sleep. Sitting beside each other while also being plugged into energy sockets, Mi and Dorro passed the time in low voices and in various ways. They had no need to power down to recharge because of this, so were also the only ones awake for the entire trip. Raxx had also brought them along because they were programmed as pilots too. And being plugged in as they were, if any sign of danger appeared they could hopefully take evasive action.

Raxx, true to her word, even if not what Shrum and the men accompanying him expected. Were given clothing for their trip to wear, which was black. Yet even if what she saw as being appropriate clothing, it felt to these five men more of a loose term though. These so-called clothes had no sleeves or legs. It was simply an over the head fabric which hung to just above their knees, a bit like a sack really. They would certainly not be trend setters in any fashion stakes that was for sure. Yet they did the job and would hide what had worried Shrum most.

The Mayors were of course bedecked in far more decorous clothing due to where they came from - and because that was what they typically wore. To help, Raxx had even suggested to Octavus and Lemane to wear something as well. Just as she herself, and her two maid would.

Of course, what the Mayors and now Shrum and his men wore. Were quite different to what any Haffian actually would consider being discreet. Raxx, her maids, and her two High Commanders probably should not have even bothered really. As their clothing was *somewhat* similar to Shrum's, but that's where it ended. Yes, it certainly went over their heads. Although lengthwise, it just barely covered their groins. Basically like most Haffian clothing that was worn, it was more akin to that of an off the shoulder, or open at the centre toga. Which did little to hide what was hidden behind or beneath them. Shrum decided when he saw them, that any length they would have been would not have mattered anyway. As just like all the others he had seen being worn around on Haff. The fabric was of such light pale colours and so thin so as to be transparent and hid nothing from anyone else's view as usual.

∞

Waking twenty minutes out from the Gelten system with no warnings or urgent alterations taken by her maids. In fact they were waking for the second and last time, as they had all woken up once to eat and drink something when the I.I.S.S. was briefly switched-off so that they could move. Then they talked for a while when it was on again before sleeping once more.

The reason as to *why* they mostly slept all the way, was simple. Unable to move as they were, they could do little else but talk then. And even doing that would become boring after a while. While sleep offered them both rest and relaxation, as the ship took you to where you were going without having to actually pilot it all the time.

Raxx announced her imminent arrival to the stationed troops who were still on Briath. The rest of that time she was sending messages back to Haff. Of which any replies she would receive whenever answers to them were known.

Her last act before coming in to land at its capital, was to make an all round low fly over the planets landscape for herself. When she banked the ship, they could spot some of the left behind cruisers and land vehicles after the brief battle. Just outside where any of its larger populations on the planet could be found.

When Shrum had questioned her as to their presence there. She had told him that it was simply to offer security to everyone after their troops had been destroyed. She did not want any looting or possible rioting taking place after their main fleet had left the planet to return to Haff.

Shrum had also asked her something else as well. As to whether it would be possible for he and his men to go to their homes to change into something that was a little more familiar to them to use. She agreed to that without much thought, knowing just how sensitive they would be upon seeing their own people again. Although she did state that nothing with any military adornments could be worn. Nor if they also looked like their former military clothing. To which they all happily agreed, only so as to wear anything that appeared decent on them again.

After their low yet quite rapid fly over, Raxx judged Briath to be a bit like old Earth. When it appeared to her that there was no separation between their mining, agriculture, and manufacturing facilities. As she had seen the grassy lowlands with what may well be animals moving around. Then the quarries were beside the mountains and hills were they must mine their minerals. Some large buildings which she saw, she deduced were likely to be their own factories; although compared to the ones in their own system they were quite miniscule by comparison. While the majority of their populations also lived in or very near to the cities on it.

∞

Just as soon as they had landed, Shrum and his men were quickly off at a run to change. They wanted as few to see them in this lack of clothing as was possible. Raxx herself quickly called in all their small transporters. Where as they arrived, her two maids shared out a fifth of her cargo between them all. These were actually box upon box of smaller sized holo-cam screens, each box containing many hundreds of them. The reason for only a fifth being given out, was because she still had four other planets in this system to visit yet.

She also created a message for these same transporters to play repeatedly to them as they flew low overhead in their own language as they dropped each holo-cam down onto the ground. By the time Shrum and his four men had returned back to her, these were already on their way.

'What now? he asked of her, while she just grinned at the sight of all of their entire bodies now being fully covered.

'We have to wait for about one hour, until all the deliveries have been made across your planet.'

'What deliveries are these, Prime Commander?'

'Some of our small holo-cam screens. I have sent our small transporters out to have them placed in the best areas where your own people can gather to view them. From your small villages or towns, as well as to your other cities.'

'For what reason?'

'The reason itself is quite simple really, Akras. If you wish to speak to a population, you want as many of them to not only see you, but also to hear you when you do this. We use the same method on all of our own planets. You yourself will have already seen some of them on Haff by now.'

'The ones on your buildings were huge!'

'True, But as you do not have many such buildings to use the type we have on Haff. I brought the smallest ones that we have instead. The transporters are also relaying messages to your population as they

179

deliver them. For them to be near one of these screens within an hour so as to hear a planetary announcement.'

'Will you be taking them away with you again when you leave?'

'No. These ones will be left for those who are chosen by your planet to use as information carriers. Any of the larger ones can be traded for whenever you may start to build some larger structures.'

∞

At the appointed time set by her, Raxx had them all switched on at the same time. On their own screen which the troops had erected after being left. A similar patchwork of new screens appeared and disappeared as various ones came on in all of these places. Some had quite large crowds looking back at them, while others in more rural areas may have had as few as twenty showing.

'People of the planet, Briath,' she began, speaking in their own tongue, of course. 'Your former Tyrant, Bork Gremplar, is no longer in control of any of the planets in your system of Gelten.

'I am Prime Commander Raxx, of Haff. The one who sent our troops here in retaliation due to what Gremplar tried to do in my own system. I must tell you that, although Haff is a planet of warriors, we are not a war-like race - unless *we are forced to be*. Gremplar's own decision to invade our system of Barathon forced us to act the way we have. You may have noticed that when we attacked, we did not harm those of you who were without weapons. That is *our* way . . . we do not attack the defenceless; we do our best to protect them.'

She heard a low voiced mutter come from one the cams, and answered. 'The troops which were left here was done only for you own safety. As with your army defeated, we did not want any acts taking place which would cause any unrest with your own population problems. So, I left them here as security to prevent this from happening.'

'You actually heard me?' queried the same voice.

'These are what we call holo-cams, which are used on our own system of planets. They offer both vision and audio both ways. They can also be used as a means of spreading or exchanging information over long distances upon any planet. I brought them here with me today, so that this actual meeting between us all could be accomplished. You, as well as the other four planets in your system are now all *free* planets . . .'

At this, there was a general large buzz of conversation taking place on all of the screens now. It was a good ten minutes before it began to die down. That was until another voice shouted out.

'What do *you* want from us instead of him then?'

'For myself, I want nothing from you. Yet much can actually be offered . . .'

'I don't believe that you want nothing! All armies are the same!' argued the same female sounding voice.

'I can assure you that *we* are not the same! Anyway, it's difficult for me to tell who I am speaking to right now. You are only seeing one view of me, while my screen is switching continually between thousands of them. So please wave your hand so that I can hold an image.'

Parri pointed out the waving hand to her. Which she was then able to control.

'I am Prime Commander Raxx, what is your name?'

'I am Gek.'

'Thank you, Gek. As to your last question. Neither I nor my planet require anything from any of your planets, simply because you do not have a trade deal with any of ours. As I said before, we ourselves on Haff are a warrior race planet. So all that we can offer to others is a military force by way of trade. However, also here with me are nine people from fourteen of the planets which we have in our system. They are who are at the moment are in charge of their planets. And they, by the way, use trade with us as a means for their own protection.

'When Gremplar sent his troops against their planets to take them over - who by the way have no armies or defences of their own. All they did was to send us a message, and we immediately came to their aid.

'These people you see here have been placed in their high positions by the majority of people upon their own planets as temporary leaders. But I will allow any of you to speak with them now so that you can learn much more.'

Over the next two hours, the nine Mayors and Mayoress's were asked a wide variety of things by someone from one of the live feeds. And just as Raxx had, they were able to make an answer to whoever did so.

'So what you are telling us now. Is that even with Gremplar gone, we *still* need someone in charge of us!'

'Any planet is only as good as its chosen government,' explained Inas Rouf. 'We nine here were picked from a handful of options available by our populations. By them each using their votes on our planet every five years. As they choose their leader, then it is up to all of us select the people who we think can carry out decisions in many different areas. One area could be looking after our roads and transportation. Another might be the selected trade delegate for us in such matters. While yet another may be seeing to our own planets infrastructure. And there is always someone who must look after the taxes all of us pay so as to do all of these things.'

'So we're still going to have to pay taxes? Even if Gremplar is no longer here to take them?' said a voice.

'Do you wish your planet to flourish independently now - or to simply die due to your own personal greed?' asked Palacas Grinjor, the Mayor of Hende to the speaker.

'On my own planet of Hende, where we are makers of various transportation devices. We do not grow food, nor do we have much of a sea so as to fish. We also do not mine for minerals.'

'So how can your planet possibly survive then!' queried a rather loud voice.

'It's quite simple really. As I said, we make or build transportation devices. We trade these to the other planets for what we need. From Inas's planet of Jitrus, along with others is where we get our food crops.

We trade both people and food carriers for them to use. From Mena's planet of Aqua, which is mostly a planet of water. We gain our fish supplements from making them water based craft.' He was gesturing to each of them as he spoke their names.

From Urse of Marmm, they offer us building supplies, while we give them load and people carriers. It is the same with mineral planets, and so on. As for Haff, we give them a few types of transportation vehicles in return for always having their protection. In essence, we all have something that another planet may wish to use. That is how we all trade with each other.'

'So what do we have that you may want to trade?'

'As of now, we do not know what you can offer,' Inas Rouf came back in to the discussion. 'You may have different metals being mined to what we have at home. You may have meat that tastes a lot different to our own, or even what you drink. The same goes with what you can farm and grow. Or breed and sell. What I am saying to you all, is that every planet has *something* which another one does not have. And so will be willing to trade for.

'But, this will only work as long as you don't become too greedy at what you charge for it, or then you may end up not trading these things at all. You have to be fair so as to give each side a good deal from it. It is only when something is either very hard to get, or to make, is when the price could be higher. But then those who want it already know how hard these are to get so will offer more for them.

'The meats and fish *we* see as being quite ordinary to eat at home. To you here might taste even more delicious. Just as the same might apply to some of yours to us . . .

'A few planets who are already in our trade alliance prize many of our things, so they are priced higher to them as these are our own basic needs leaving us. Other things we have may not be as highly prized to them, and perhaps us too. Their prices will then be lower just to sell them. As we have all said during our talk with you. It all depends on what you have - and what others might want.'

∞

There was then a further hour or so of discussions taking place as Shrum and his men now took over the debate. They were from their planet and as for Shrum himself, he had seen all of theirs and what they had to offer. So he was of course the best informed of them about any of it.

He told them of their bubble-pods which could not only travel fast over the ground. But which could also fly at low level to take you somewhere even quicker. He talked of the foods which they had had to eat while being held captive on Haff. What they had all been eating were from something called insti-packs. Also know by their name as rations. Which were actual packs of various sizes and foods which self heated before you opened and then ate it. The larger packs of course held the large meals, while others contained things they called soups or desserts.

Shrum and his men had already found many of these rather particularly palatable and enjoyable to their own tastes.

Then he also told them about their huge ships and other ways of transportation. Of the planets which built these structures and machines. Of the non-alive androids they had and used. He presented her two maids to the holo-cams for them to be able to see these unusual beings.

On and on it went as he not only talked of what he had seen, but because he was also being questioned by so many of them about so much of it.

Finally, when the screens were all turned off, they left the people to decide what they wanted out of their new freedom. She only hoped that her own personal suggestion to them earlier. Which was that only those who may be wise in many things. Would now decide to offer themselves up as possible leaders for a new government for the people of Briath to vote for and finally elect.

Again, she allowed Shrum and his men to leave them, so that they could go and sleep in their own homes. Making sure that they knew it would be an early start for hading to the next planet on their agenda.

Raxx and those with her were quite happy to sleep onboard ship. As the seating inside it had also been designed to cope with long periods of travel. So they all knew that they were also very comfortable to do that on.

From Briath, the next two days were spent on Goll and Chell. Where they all did the exact same thing with their populations.

They were now on their way to Pelus on the fourth day when Raxx had a call which all those on board could hear.

'Prime Commander . . . it's Morg here?'

'Go ahead Morg, I can hear you well.'

'I am using the military channel so as to speak to you in real-time. We have had some good, and also some bad news back from the scientists.'

'I'm listening, Morg.'

'According to them - after they had ran some tests. Our armour is slightly weaker than the alien fleets was. While our weapons are superior.'

'That's good to hear. So what do they suggest to alter this problem?'

'They said that we would need a far higher refined type of zerium to upgrade any of our ship's armour.'

Raxx gave a deep sigh. 'Have you contacted Trade Minister Terrus on Zerros to see about this yet, Morg?'

'Yes, Prime Commander. And as he told me, any higher concentration of zerium needing to be made will definitely not come cheap. Especially if you are talking about upgrading our entire fleet! As even they would need to begin building new equipment just to be able to make it for us.'

'I don't really want to ask this, Morg. But I also know that I sadly must. And what *would* the price for this new zerium be, does he think, and can we possibly afford it?'

'His price for an entire fleets supply of the new zerium was quite agreeable, Prime Commander. However, only you can agree to it if you really want it that badly?'

His words made Raxx wonder what he had asked for. 'Well, we will need it if it's better than what we are using right now, Morg. And . . . what exactly *is* the cost?' she asked, almost wincing as she waited for him to reply.

'They saw the battle of Egral on their own screens, Prime Commander.'

'So?'

'Well, Terrus, reporting from those who are on their planetary seat, said that we would have to station one of our full legions at Zerros for at least six months. I think this was just in case that same race came to attack them as well.'

'Impossible! How can he ask such a thing of us? Doesn't he know that we cannot station an entire fleet of one legion in their orbit for that long! Our people cannot just sit in one place like that without regular incoming supplies. Nor would I allow one of our legions to be left there for so long either!'

'I already knew you would say that, and told Terrus what your answer to it would be, Prime Commander.'

'So, I guess we won't get that new zerium then!'

'I thought so too, until he offered us a compromise.'

'I am still listening, Morg?'

'Terrus told me that those on their planetary seat had envisaged such a possibility eventually happening ever since they became allied to us. So, he then informed me that it could actually be stationed *on* their planet.'

'Even that is still impossible. As since we cannot breathe their atmosphere, our people would have to stay on all of their ships all the time. So that could not work either . . .'

'They have also been a little sneaky too though.'

'Sneaky? How so, Morg?'

'Well. From what he said, they have been converting all of their older unused mines into underground hangars.'

'So *that's* why they wanted to trade with us for so much of our construction material!' muttered Urse.

'It's still the wrong atmosphere for our people though, Morg.'

'*Sealed* hanger chambers, Prime Commander,' Morg then added so she would understand. 'Along with the generators to provide the correct levels that we would need to offer natural breathing outside of our ships.'

Raxx chuckled. 'You were right. Those Zerrosians are very sneaky indeed! Very well then, Morg. If that is what they need in order to supply all of that to us. Then what I'll need you do to is to check back with Terrus. Make sure that what they do have already *can* handle an entire legion. Both ships *and* that many troops. And if they *can* do everything that they say they can to manage that, then a deal has been struck between us.

'If that is then all agreed. Have the next legion for duty assembled as well as its fleet and send them on their way to Zerros. Advise its High Commander that their duration there will be for a thirty days - before another legion will take over from them there, and so on until the trade period is up, or re-contracted if we still require more of the new zerium.'

'You do remember that Zerros is a ten day jump, Prime Commander? So will their duty time have the leaving and returning included in their duty time?'

'No, I'm afraid not, Morg. Otherwise they would only spend ten days out of a full months duty there - with twenty of them being used on travelling. As would the next one and the next . . . In which case, each legion would be spending more time in their jumps out and back than they would actually being on duty on Zerros. You *can* add though, that a weekly supply run will be made to them.'

'Very well, Prime Commander.'

'Anything else, Morg? I remember you saying to me that there was both good *and* bad news. I'm not sure which news that was now, so what news is left?'

'Bad!'

'Oh! Well in that case, Morg, don't keep me in suspense any longer.

'While some of our scientists were going through some of the ship wreckage here on Haff. A light appeared on a small part of it and began to flash on and off . . .'

'A system working again, but on only a part of it you mean? That does sound a little strange I must say!'

'Our scientists think it may be a beacon of some kind, Prime Commander.'

'I see. So the exact location of our planet may have been compromised - is that what they are thinking now?'

'Yes, Prime Commander. And as they could not turn it off to be able to study it more, I'm afraid they had to destroy it instead.'

'Hmmmm,' she hummed to herself as she thought over that. It certainly wasn't good news, that much was for sure! 'So, if it is some kind of an homing beacon. At the moment, we have no idea if it could actually reach to wherever they are. And if it does, how long it could take for them to reach us if they wished to retaliate against us and attack.'

'Exactly.'

'Very well. Have all of Haff placed on Alert Stage 2 just in case they might. Also alert all planets within our system just so that they know as well. As for us here, we'll be finished our tour of this system in two days and should be back home almost in three. If you need to speak to me urgently at any time before then, you already know what to do, Morg.'

'Indeed, Prime Commander!'

As the com call ended, it left some of them in grave concern. While all were wondering if there would be a battle taking place on Haff itself soon.

What they all did note though. Was that whatever Raxx may have been thinking about it herself. Nothing showed on her own face if she felt any worries about it at all. Nor did it affect her flying skills either as they came in to land smoothly on Pelus.

19

They began their return journey after their five day tour of the Gelten system with hope, yet still unsure of any outcome. Each planet had been able to question the various people from onboard the ship if they wished to. Which caused further time being used in offering explanations.

Now they had left to return to their homes Except in the case for Shrum and his men, who were still heading back to Haff. Raxx had already made her own decision about the captives though - she just had not told them yet. A decision which meant that all but Gremplar and his family would be released to return home.

Gremplar would either remain on Haff under planetary arrest. Or if another planet was willing, then they would be transferred there. But in no way would she allow them to return back to Briath again. The people there were now free to decide what they wanted to do after having been a long time under his family's rule. So allowing them to return to where they may try to do it all over again was out of the question!

∞

Even with Haff being on Stage Two Alert for a good few days. The people on Haff certainly breathed far easier when she had returned to them.

Back once more inside her office, decisions and orders had to be taken over many things which she knew now needed doing. Of which many went out quite rapidly upon her return. She ordered that all of their scanners looking out into space were to be extended to their maximum range at once. Just as she doubled their defence fleet around it. As if an enemy *was* indeed coming to attack Haff. Then she wanted to know about it as soon as possible!

She knew that a ship already positioned in orbit, was faster to use than one which also needed to be crewed and still had to take-off from the ground. No matter how quickly it could get up there! Even if with so many now in orbit, further ships would be able to get there without being fired upon. At least that was her hope.

She had no idea when the first shipment of the new higher grade zerium would turn up. Which was why she also had to plan on using her fleets with their older armour.

The uncertainties to any possible planning was still an enormous, yet uncomfortable hurdle that she faced. Her information and knowledge of what *could* become their new enemy was still as limited as it had been earlier. And due to their own fleets recent utter destruction, it was also just as possible that they were also upgrading those which might be coming to Haff!

The same problem which always existed had still not changed her thoughts though. Which were always: Who were they? Where did they come from? And what exactly did they want? Did they have one or more planets of their own out there somewhere to use as permanent bases, or were they only a race moving around in space? Or were their attacks on planets simply for raw materials, or to take such things away with them to use? Maybe they just attacked planets to kill, so as to eradicate all life upon them. Just so that they could then use anything that was on them for themselves.

She pondered for many a long hour over these issues, but for her it always ended the same way. Without any knowledge of them yet, they were still an unknown quantity to her. Even any of their own known scout reports had shown up nothing similar to any race which they'd met, or to what they had used.

∞

Raxx had also used one of their empty carriers with which to send all of Gremplar's troops home. Because if a battle *was* coming, she just did not want them in the way now.

She also arranged for a meeting to take place at their unusually small convention house as it was called. Typically this building was only used when any grave matters arose which concerned Haff itself. Those invited to this were the usual figures. The Royals, every Lord and Lady, as well as any available High Commander not away on a particular duty. Raxx did not do everything as to her own thoughts. Not when something as far reaching as this was to be talked about. She called such meetings as these to hear the opinions and thoughts of others.

That same meeting was already ongoing . . .

'So, if we had not defended Egral, Haff may not have been in danger?' Lord Arne spoke out forcefully.

'You as well as I know that Haff had no choice *but* to defend them, Lord Arne!' King Jaaf responded. 'They have an agreement with us just like many other planets do. Derus could not just sit back and allow them all to die because of this. We are seen as protectors, and you should already know this well!'

'Perhaps . . . but from what was only a small battle - we could now be facing a full scale war!' Arne said bitterly.

'Because of who we are, Lord Arne. We should almost expect to have enemies - or be at war with *someone* at one time or another,' Queen Lerus said softly.

'That was not my point,' he argued.

'Then perhaps it should have been, Lord Arne. You must remember that without our planet trading protection to others for what we receive from them in return. Even Haff would not be able to survive on its own.'

'Of course we could!' was the answer he put forward.

Raxx smiled at him. 'I know your thinking, Lord Arne. You only want us to be overlords. Yes? Not offering help for what we receive, but simply *taking* what we need from any of them.'

'That is what superior armies have always done for eons!' he almost shouted at her.

At such an attack on her, Raxx's eyes narrowed. 'Lord Arne . . . ' she said so quietly, that those in the room became subdued, barely even breathing. 'If Haff cannot win this battle which may be coming. Then as actual protectors we are also useless to others. As a military planet - and that is all that we are. It is our responsibility to take upon us such things on behalf of all those who are allied to us in this way - and who *expect* us to do so for them.'

'I could not have said it better myself, Derus!' stated the king. 'As a nation of warriors, we live or die by what we do. And with Raxx leading us, we have always had far more hope of winning than we otherwise would have had.'

The arguments continued for a while longer, until in a way, they finally began to understand why she had convened it in the first place.

'Not only a battle in orbit, but possibly even one here on our own dear Haff, too, Derus?' queried, Lady Winsher, 'is that what you are trying to tell us?'

She gave a small nod. 'Egral as you all know had no military of its own. So that was why this enemy was able to land so easily. Here on Haff it will be quite a different matter for them to do so though. You should all be able to recognise this fact for yourselves.

'As we not only have our defence platforms, but also our defence fleet - which I have doubled since hearing of this possible beacon. However, if they somehow still *do* manage to get some of their landing ships down on to Haff. If the cruisers and smaller fighters we have on this planet cannot beat them. That only leaves our troops.

'So, if our defence grid fails, our defence ships fail, our planet bound ships fail, as well as all of our troops. As a planet containing only warriors we will *all* have failed! Not only ourselves, but each and every planet in our system and others which count on us. As this enemy will show then no mercy whatsoever. And as we saw on Egral, all of them will soon end up in the same way! Personally speaking, I do not want to let them down - never mind ourselves! In a way, we may have to do *whatever* it takes so as to protect Haff.'

'Which means what exactly?' asked Lord Budle.

'Remember our first two cruisers that reached Egral?'

'Suicide attacks!' gasped, Lady Yu.

'I would only ask that as a last gasp stop measure, Lady Yu. One cruiser of ours for one of their larger ships would still be a good result for us. And we do have over two thousand cruisers! Yet what we must do first and foremost is to prevent any of them from being able to land here on our planet. I am hoping that our perimeter defences along with our now doubled defence fleet themselves may be able to handle that. But, as I already told you earlier. At this moment, we do not truly know who they are or where they come from. Nor do we, as yet, know what their own possible force may actually contain.

'You all know that without such data, I can only surmise our best tactics until any battle is joined. Just as my idea for our fleet at Egral was instigated at seeing how our two cruisers had attacked them. That way worked out for us very well indeed, as we all saw. What we do not yet know though, is if they will change their tactics to counter what we did there. If they don't, then we have a very good chance of doing the same to them again. If they do change . . . then I will have to respond to their new tactics as quickly as I can.'

More talking ensued as was normal at such a meeting. Until finally they reached an impasse. As nothing was certain until they came . . . if they even did. The king, being as usual placed as the chairman of the meeting. Then asked if anything further was to be discussed between them.

'I have only one further concern of my own to offer to those of you who are here . . .'

'Go ahead, Derus, we are all ears!' Smiled the king.

Raxx looked at Arne and gave him a brief smile. 'All that I would like to know, is why our Lord's of Haff here want me dead!'

The clamour which erupted at her own bald statement left few of them able to hear much apart from those shouts of "Traitors" or "Treason".

'Who ever said that of me lies!' Lord Dacras of Erin almost screeched in panic.

King Jaaf was then quite busy slapping his hand against the table in front of him, until the uproar her announcement caused had died away.

'That is a very serious statement to make here in this building, Derus . . . Have you any proof of this treachery?'

'It is the sole reason why I awaited such a convening to be held, your Majesty. So that we were all here together.'

She then rose to her feet and stood looking over to the five lords where they all sat together. 'Do any of you wish to deny what I have just said here?'

All eyes turned to them, some quickly noting the sudden appearance of perspiration on some of their brows.

'You had better have certain proof of what you have just stated against us, Derus!' said an unusually calm Arne; unlike so many of the others.

'I have. Although I will only use it if necessary, *and* if none of you are prepared to admit to it.'

'We will admit to nothing of the kind . . . Such a thing as what you have just implied is unheard of here on Haff!' he said in reply, and rather admirably it must be said.

'Very well then, if that is the answer you are all going to take.' Using her implant, she said, 'Leenis, please come in now if you would.'

The door opened as her maid entered inside and it closed itself behind her as usual. She had been waiting outside for this call all the time, if it was given.

'Still no change, my Lord's?'

'Without some kind of evidential proof to be made as fact. You have nothing with which to raise such disparaging statements against any of us, Derus.'

Raxx gave a low sigh. 'As you wish, Lord Arne. I only hoped that you may have all been honest enough men to have admitted to what you had been planning for so long to my own face all this time - or even here and now! But perhaps I am expecting far too much of any of you!

'Leenis, play the first memory record in your new file for me if you would now, please.'

Her maids eyes closed as she did so, and began to speak. Only she wasn't speaking in her own usual voice, but that of one of the lords present. Then another, and another.

Four of these same lords shrunk into their seats as what they had said was now being heard by all. While only Arne looked back at her with something more akin to an malignant look. The rest of those in the meeting were stunned. Mouths were open, gasps were heard, even some fists were tightly clenched at their hearing such damning words. And all in the five lord's own voices.

'That could easily have been fabricated against us!' claimed Lord Arne.

Raxx just gave him a very chilling look. 'That was their very first monthly meeting which they held to discuss my demise,' said Raxx as she looked at them. 'Ten years ago at the palace of Lord Dacras of Erin. Leenis here holds all the file records dating from back then, right to their meeting last month at Lord Dacras's palace again. Please play the last record on file for me now if you would, Leenis.'

Leenis did so, and the result listened to was even more damning than from most of the other meetings which they had had. As this time it also had a certain finality for the Royal Family as well.

As it ended and her maids eyes reopened. Only silence ensued. To all but five of them, the recording which they had just heard had sealed their fate totally. Lord Wynoc had his head in his hands. Lord Budle sat there with tears streaming down his face. The Lord's Dacras and Flent's bodies were shaking uncontrollably as if they were suffering from a fever. Only the stoic Arne appeared unmoved.

'So what now then, bitch? As I suppose you've just escaped your own death sentence!' he laughed harshly at her. But it was the king himself who spoke.

'I simply do not know what to think of the five of you! You not only planned the death of our revered Prime Commander---'

'The one and only never dying bitch of Haff!' interjected Arne with a sadistic grin.

As if he had not heard the vulgarity, King Jaffe continued, '----Even to planning to kill all of us if you had to also. I'm only really surprised you left the three good *Ladies* here out of any of your plans.'

Arne only laughed again, albeit in a quite mocking and bitter tone this time. 'By three good Ladies, do you mean *those three*! Why should we have bothered with them? Winsher's so old that she's about ready to die. While Mell's always too busy just looking for men to have sex with her. And then there's virgin Yu . . . so stupidly naive in everything that it always made us all laugh at her!

'What she really needs is something good and stiff placed inside her just to wake her up! Maybe Mell should introduce her to some of the men who she already knows so well, eh? That would soon have her sorted out.' Arne again laughed at how he had described them, and at seeing each of their faces when he did so.

The king looked at Raxx. 'We've never had anything like this happen before on Haff, Derus. What do we do about it?'

'Treason has never been a good word, your Majesty. Yet that's what this is. You all heard the recordings, so also know that what I stated to you is as fact now. From what my own memories tell me about the legalities of such a thing, there are really very few options available. They also employ very old terms for dealing with it, hence the strange words. Exile. Banishment. And Execution . . .

'However, as we heard in the last recording, I will not allow any judgement made here on them to affect their own family members. As none of them were apparently aware or a party to what they were planning.'

Lord Flent was actually amazed at Raxx's own personally offered leniency to the rest of his family. Even though he still had to ask, 'But how did you ever find out about it?'

It was Raxx's turn to laugh at Arne. 'And you called our dear young Lady Yu here stupidly naive, Lord Arne! When the five of you are seemingly no better yourselves!'

'Well then?' he said scathingly.

'The androids we use may be machines but they are *not* deaf you fools! No matter if they are not in a room with you, they are still there to serve you! In which case if not in a room with you, then they have to be even more alert for any call that you might make for them to return.

'One of Lord Wynoc's servants began my search. As when it was called in for its scheduled maintenance work. The android operator tasked with this work noticed a recording blip in its held files. Androids as you know cannot harm anyone, but that does not mean it will ignore something which is like a threat either. That is the same reason why that recording in its own memory file storage was never erased like so many others had been.

'That file was sent to me simply as it had my name attached to it so often. After I had seen that, I then requested that all the androids which serviced your palaces to then be called in for a similar maintenance check. I must however offer my apologies to you, my Ladies, and also to you your Majesties. For I had to be sure that none of you were involved in this nefarious act too.'

'Quite understandable, my dear, Derus,' said the queen. 'I would also have wanted to know that myself.'

Raxx gave a small bow. 'And so, one by one as they each came in to be checked. I made sure the same android was the one who checked them all. And who had strict orders from me to only to send anything like that if found to me alone. When all that was completed, I deleted that order from its memory, along with any file appertaining to it. In that way, it was now hidden from anyone else finding out about this.'

'So what happens now then?' asked a still smarting Lady Yu.

'Usually a court of peers would be brought in to judge them. And then they would be sentenced to one of the earlier verdicts which I told you of. Which were exile, banishment, or death.'

'Are you saying that we will now have to judge them ourselves, and then decide which fitting punishment of the three it should be?' asked the king.

'Yes . . . Unless of course you would be happy just to leave any final decision to me?'

King Jaaf looked around the table. And from all those who he looked to gave a nod. 'We agree to leave it completely in your hands, Derus. I can understand why though. Simply because the actual threat of this was aimed at you most of all. But can you tell us what your choice will be?'

'If I was the person whom they seem to think I am, your Majesty. I would have had them executed right away!' The five faces which paled considerably at her words, told her that that was exactly what they thought she would do.

'But, no matter what I may personally think about what they attempted to do to me. I am also not such a person to wish for them to being publicly executed in front of our people and their own families. Especially for my own vindication! Their families who would then perhaps have to live with that shame of dishonour being placed upon them for many centuries to come. So instead of any of those three options, I choose another option entirely . . . Oblivion!'

Everyone now looked at her, as not one of them quite knew what she meant by it.

'Oblivion . . . ' she said again. 'I will arrange for a small ship to be made ready for all of you with one month of food supplies for each of you. I will even allow you to tell your families some lie created between you. A lie which when told to them will allow the next in your line to take over your family mantle. You must also tell them that you will never be returning to Haff. So just make sure you all come up with a truly amazing tale to tell them together.

'When that has been done, you will then all board your ship and go. Holo-cam images of your faces will be sent to any world with which we are allied to. So do not go to any of these. For if you do so, you will be held by them and brought back here to face an immediate death sentence instead. I am not doing this for any of you due to what you were wanting to do to me - but more for your own families future peace of mind. So do not make the opposite happen.'

'But we will just die out there,' exclaimed Flent.

'*That* is up to you! You may find a world which we have   no knowledge of and be allowed to live out the rest of your days there. I have now given you a way out that will certainly save not only your families heritage, but also their honour will remain intact, too. However, if you choose to reject this, then watching you die through execution is what they may have to witness instead. Choose . . . '

Arne looked at them. Seeing the absolute fear and foreboding etched upon each of their faces. Even he understood what Raxx was doing to avoid such an event as their public execution taking place. Yes, they may well end up just dying out there in space. But if there was at least a chance they could find somewhere as she had said . . . ?

Arne rose to his feet and gave her both a salute and a bow which the other four copied. 'We accept your magnanimous offer of a ship, Raxx. We will also do our very best to make our leaving Haff to be as uncomplicated as we possibly can for our families.'

She bowed back to them. 'In that case, my Lords, and your Majesty - this meeting can finally now be brought to an end.'

20

Raxx was in a contemplative mood, as one area of concern had been dealt with now. She had heard of the title bequeathing in their families. Although their actual inaugurations would not be held for quite a while yet. There had of course been a great deal of wondering about why the five lords of Haff had decided to make such a strange journey as this together. Only those at the meeting really knew the whole truth; but a vow along with a veil of secrecy had been cast over it all by Raxx's order.

She had watched from her office balcony, even waving to them as their small ship rose into the sky until it vanished from her sight. They were alone now, but being alone was far better than what would have awaited them here. She herself was not a callous person, unless it was merited, of course. Which was why she was so pleased they had chosen to leave. Her own ancient memories of their family line had been one of utmost respect up to that time.

Now though, with them breaking that respect as well as leaving. She only hoped that as their line continued. So she could put that behind her and offer the same respect to the younger people who were now being entrusted with these same duties.

∞

Forty-three days later, some of the promised newly refined zerium had already been delivered. On each delivery, one or perhaps two ships would be quickly refitted with it, and it then returned back into orbit. Hopefully much stronger now, and in place if need be.

It was only seventy-three days after the lords had left. When their own furthest reaching scanners spotted a large blip and it was reported to her. One that was also heading their way. At its calculated speed, only thirteen days before it would arrive. Raxx could only begin to wonder all over again to herself. How many? How powerful? Can we stop them . . . Can we win?

Was the battle for Haff itself just about to begin . . .

The End

I hope that you have enjoyed reading this novel which I entitled,
The Lords of Haff?

If you have, and enough of you actually do so in order to make a sequel to it viable for me to write, then please watch out for:

Haff at War
(Preliminary title of the sequel at the moment)

I will also be waiting, just to see what you may say about it in any of your reviews too . . .

N.B. If you may have been wondering throughout this novel why the names you have seen appear to be so different from those which we know so well right now. I can only tell you that in the end, the final blame for this will lie with all parents.

As ever since the twentieth century, very ordinary and well known names of children began having one or more extra letters being placed or added to their birth names. Only so as to make them look different to everyone else. Or, that a typically used letter was suddenly exchanged for a far less common one.

In effect, their birth names were becoming dissimilar to the norm. What had once been the name Kim could now become Kym or Kymm. Sonia may change to Sonya or Soniya. Geoffrey altered to Geofrey, Geofree, even Jeffrey or Jefree.

By the end of the twenty-sixth century, it was extremely hard, or perhaps even just rare to find any of the former original Earth names being given to children which had once been so commonplace. As by now, they had been bastardized just so much that they had become quite unrecognisable as actual names. Even if that is what they were. Until here where we are in the fortieth century. Where new parents of course just carried on doing the very same thing as time went by. Simply because they wanted *their* children's names to stand out from their contemporaries more and more. And so, the much older versions of such once well known names from way back in the past; apart from the few rare ones, finally just died out altogether . . .

A Note from the Author

I thank you for purchasing/borrowing my Science-Fiction novel entitled, *The Lords of Haff,* and I do hope that you have enjoyed reading it? There may be one or more sequels to it coming through if the reader/fan demand is high enough.

I am sorry if any of my books in paperback appear to be a little expensive for you. But sadly without any Agent or Publisher showing any interest in any of my novels over two decades - it left me with only one possible way in which to bring them out into publication for those of you who prefer actual printed books. Although in same cases, you can always ask at your local library if they could order it in for you . . .

As both a writer of various genre stories, and as a reader of them myself. I do enjoy stories that appear to flow naturally without having any great difficulties in following the plot, or story line in them. I call these *"immersive"* books. In a way, I like to feel as if I am there seeing it happen in front of me as I read. This is also the way I try and write my own books for others to enjoy in the same way too.

To me, personally, you should be able to just pick up a book and read it from start to finish. Without being caught in a maze of words you cannot even begin to try and understand, or need a dictionary at hand in order to work any of them out. I like them, as I like my own, to be plain and simple, and easy to read.

Perhaps my own may not be not as technical as some you may have already read. Or as filled with an array of characters who are detailed to their utmost, offering a complete warts and all biography of literally everyone and anyone who plays each part in them. That is just my style of writing, and I concentrate more on the main principal characters involved, and on the general flow of the story itself, rather than on too many character descriptions when I don't think they are needed.

I do have a Facebook, Twitter, and Goodreads page if you would enjoy joining any of those to keep up to date with any messages or news, or to perhaps just to say Hello - or even have a chat. You are more than welcome to join. Just as I also now have an Author page on Amazon to show what books are listed there and now available to be purchased.

www.facebook.com/Author.Keith.Gardner/
http://www.amazon.co.uk/Keith-Gardner
I'm also on Twitter As: @AuthorKeithG

The only thing I would like to ask you to do after you have read any book however, would be to leave your comment and a star rating for what you thought of it afterwards from wherever you purchased it. As I really do appreciate any responses such as these from readers, as your own thoughts and insights on them will tell me how you personally viewed any book.

Other Books by the same Author:

Spirit of a Dragon

Spirit of a Dragon is an Adult Crime Thriller

Actions which have taken place, will bring together the North-East and the Far-East together in this raw and uncompromising erotic crime thriller.

Detective Inspector Douglas Hyde is given the task of apprehending a serial killer.

While from Japan, Kumiko Hirano arrives in order to also seek out the same killer of her sister, and one of their own ninja clan. Although her own task, is to offer a very different kind of ending when the person concerned is found . . .

Little Haven

Little Haven is a fictional story of the Wild West.

Julian Armitage, an Englishman who had once served in the army, and by no means any slouch with a gun himself. Against all odds decided to settle in Indian Territory alongside the Cherokee in 1775.

A lonely life was not for him though, so he slowly began to build his own town from the ground up.

From wagon trains and those who were simply passing through, he soon had a small nucleus of inhabitants living within his town. It was actually a peaceful place, which is also why he had given it such an unusual name.

That only lasted until the Hill's arrived. A Father and two sons whose robbing, plundering, and murdering were almost legend at the time. And who were not averse to seeking an opportunity anywhere, and from anyone if it could be had.

They were only looking for a hideout over the winter, after they had recently committed a number of deadly robberies. And Little Haven when they decided to stop there, so they thought, appeared to be just the place for them to take over with their brutal regime. Little did they know what would happen when they tried . . .

Honour The Star

Honour The Star is a fictional story of the Wild West.

Daniel Goest was a well travelled man. Over the years his name became spoken of in the West, especially when a town needed Law & Order brought to it.

Now, much time had passed, and he wasn't getting any younger. So his thoughts of being a lawman had changed to that of retiring.

His arrival in the small town of Windy sparked little interest, at first. As not everyone noticed the two tied-down guns he wore, which appeared to blend into his clothing.

It wouldn't be long before those who were there, would soon see exactly what they could be used for when a call to action was required.

This novel was originally planned as the finale story of his life - but there could yet be a further one after it to end it in the way that I really want.

N.B.

The 1st prequel of this actual story series - "Goest Goes West - The Early Years, Part 1" is already on with being written right now (July 2016 and is almost ready).

Which will both detail and chronicle the time and events in his life from when he first left home at the age of sixteen - to finally lead up to his becoming the man and legend which you will you have read about in the actual novel above.

A Silent Land

A Silent Land is a fictional Western Adventure Novel

Is suitable for both Men and Women, who enjoy Westerns, Action, Adventure, Romance, and Drama.

The story is set in the 1700's and being told through that of a young poacher by the name of Sam Hope. A young boy from the North-East of England, who aged sixteen found himself press-ganged on to a visiting naval ship.

Torn away from his former life and family, as so many others were in the day and age of wooden sailing ships, simply to serve the needs of the fleet and its large navy. He soon found out that despite having far worse food to eat, as well as fewer options allowed. His new life aboard was also showing him a lot more than he could ever have once imagined. Far away from the local forests, where he had once both roamed and hunted.

Finally, upon being left marooned upon the almost unknown coast of America by the jealous captain of a pirate ship. Older he may have been, perhaps even by now a little wiser than when young also; but he was also about to find himself beginning yet another new way of life. Although this time, one where he knew very little at all about anything to do with the peoples and country which would lie all around him. Would he even be able to survive in this harsh wilderness . . .

N.B.

There is also a planned follow up sequel to this book - if not more than one on this particular story as time unfolds with it.

The Magical World of Cassie Carey

The Magical World of Cassie Carey is Fantasy/Science-Fiction.

Do you believe in Witches and Wizards?

Elves and Fairies?

Dragons and Goblins?

Troll's and Ogre's?

That Animals are able to talk?

No, did I hear you say?

Well neither did Cassandra Carey, until she reached her thirteenth birthday. As on that very same day, everything that she had known or thought possible before soon changed for her as well.

An Unexpected Christmas

An Unexpected Christmas is a fictional Christmas story for all the family.

With the mixture of Santa Claus stories and others, like that of A Christmas Carol - it should offer readers a pleasing book to enjoy over holiday periods for many years to come.

It is only a few days before Christmas and Santa has become ill. His Elf Doctor, and his Head Elf, Gabriel, had already told him that there was no way it will have cleared up in time for him to be able to do his present deliveries this year.

A rapid, but thorough search of the Claus archive records dating back to when the role of Santa first began. Only showed up one distant relation in them so far, who had already had suffered from the same illness - and who may be the only one possible to be able to assume the role.

Leonard Claus, a wealthy Banker in the financial capital of London was his name. However, his own lifestyle and personal thoughts and ideals on what Christmas had since become from his own youth, were far different to that of a budding Santa Claus. The only thing he did have going for him at the time, was the inherited Claus laugh.

Would he be able to assume this highly regarded role, and carry out the task required of him? Or will his own background simply turn Christmas into a complete mess and leave a disaster behind him!

Once in a Lifetime

Once In A Lifetime is a Romantic Drama . . .

True Love . . . Does it really exist, and does it actually happen?

Well, Roger and Suzette were sure that it had for them. From their first ever meeting at school in this heart-warming story when they were both only ten years of age.

They would soon become inseparable, beginning as childhood sweethearts, which would then lead up to much more as the following years unfolded.

Life as we know it though, is never always a bed of roses. There are highs, just as there are lows. There can be happiness, just as there can also be sadness.

You can follow their story, seen from various viewpoints. Will it be a very happy one, or one tinged with sorrow. What you will read, could make you smile, bring you to tears, even just to laugh, or offer a huge sigh. A lump in the throat perhaps, or the simple sensation of complete enjoyment.

How you will see this story for yourself is what will matter the most.

The Brotherhood

The Brotherhood is an Adult Erotic Supernatural Crime Thriller

(It can be seen as both raw and brutal to some readers - so please note that you have been warned in advance!)

In the fight against an occult group which practices the purest form of Occult Black Magic, one man alone, Tom Jones, stands between all that is good and evil.

Magic against magic is needed when it comes to such fierce battles as these will be.

But can one man endure in this fight against, The Brotherhood . . .?

Keith Gardner